Black Diamond

ALSO BY JOHN F. DOBBYN
Neon Dragon
Frame-Up

BLACK DIAMOND

A Novel

John F. Dobbyn

Longboat Key, Florida

ISBN: 978-1-60809-022-8

Published in the United States of America by Oceanview Publishing, Longboat Key, Florida
www.oceanviewpub.com

10 9 8 7 6 5 4 3 2 1

PRINTED IN THE UNITED STATES OF AMERICA

There is just one reason that this novel is seeing the light of day—and that reason is the inspiration, the constant devotion, and the endless love that makes every day of my life a celebration–all of which flow from the one I love more than I dreamed one person could love another—my bride, partner in everything, and my very best friend—Lois.

Black Diamond

CHAPTER ONE

A track-wise old denizen of the backstretch at Boston's Suffolk Downs once shared with me his conclusion that there are dozens of ways a horse can lose a race, and only one way to win. It sounds poetic, but it's basically bunk. There are as many ways to make a horse win a race as there are devious twists in the minds of those who stand to make a buck.

That thought cruised through my mind the afternoon of the Massachusetts Handicap, the granddaddy of New England stakes races. I was in the grandstand at Suffolk Downs early in the afternoon to watch Danny Ryan, a buddy from my youthful days when we were both stable hands for my adoptive father and patron saint, Miles O'Connor. Danny was riding a two-year-old colt, Black Diamond, in one of the earlier races. The Diamond went to the post as a twenty-to-one long shot.

I had a few bucks on him, but that aside, when he entered the starting gate, my heart was pounding for the sake of Danny. He had run a painful gauntlet with some unhealthy substances, but now he was clean. This was the start of a major comeback.

Rick McDonough, the trainer of Black Diamond, had gone out on a limb to give Danny the mount. According to track scuttlebutt, Rick's stable needed this win to keep the thread it was hanging by from snapping. In the salad days, when Danny was the leading rider at Suffolk Downs, he'd brought in winners for Rick's stable more often than not by putting his body at risk with moves that would give most jockeys the shivers. His wins bought a lot of hay and oats, and Rick never forgot.

The race was five furlongs, a little over half a mile. Black Diamond broke well from the third post, and Danny settled him nicely into a comfortable fourth position on the rail. They just cruised in that position until they hit the far turn, and my heart went into a slow seizure. Danny was completely boxed in by the three front-runners. He had no choice but to stay in the box, hard on the driving heels of the horse ahead of him, catching clods of dirt with every stride, until they hit the top of the homestretch.

In one magic moment, the horse on the rail ahead of Danny veered to the right just enough to open a bit of daylight. Black Diamond blew through the opening and went for the lead. Over the crowd, I could barely hear the track announcer booming, "Here comes Black Diamond, and the Diamond is flying!"

And flying he was. Hector Vasquez, the jockey on the leader, Sundowner, went to the right-handed whip. His horse veered left, and pressed Black Diamond nearly to the rail, but the Diamond never slackened. They were noses apart, swapping the lead with every stride. Danny was hand riding him. He never went to the whip, but by the eighth pole, it was becoming clear that Black Diamond was seizing the lead for good.

A sixteenth of a mile to go, and I was yelling my lungs out, though in that din, I wasn't sure I was making a sound. Black Diamond's lead of a nose grew to half a head and kept growing. I was picking my route to get down to the winner's circle to congratulate Danny.

This is where it gets fuzzy. I've tried a thousand times to put together what I saw next. Some of it doesn't scan, and I'm never sure what my imagination is adding or subtracting.

In a fraction of a second, Danny went from the rhythmic crouch of a jockey aboard the front-runner to a splaying spasm of arms and legs that had him hurtling over the rail into an unnatural twist of body and limbs on the inside turf.

Black Diamond went on to cross the finish line riderless and therefore disqualified, but every eye in that suddenly hushed crowd was on the still figure of the jockey. For seconds, I was too stunned to move. I just stared with everyone else, trying to will movement into Danny's distorted body.

The ambulance came flying down the track behind the final finishers. The first EMTs who reached Danny immediately signaled for the brace that would hold his head and neck in line with his spine. The rest was blotted out by people and horses in the way of my view. In a matter of minutes, all I could see was the track dust behind the wailing ambulance. I prayed to God that they were taking my buddy to the hospital and not the morgue.

CHAPTER TWO

There was no word from the hospital that afternoon or evening. Danny was in what seemed like interminable surgery. A few predawn calls the next morning zeroed me in on the intensive care unit at the Mass. General Hospital. I arrived there before the night shift changed. Experience taught me that it's easier to get past the nurses' station at the end of a long night shift than to avoid the attention of the alert, more populated day crew.

Danny had just been moved to a private room, but he was still under guard against visitors. I approached the two-hundred-pound Cerberus in a nurse's pantsuit and asked her for a quick minute with "my brother." I figured that small deviation from the truth would obviate the usual, "Are you a member of the family?"

Nurse Ratched compared my six foot one to Danny's five foot three and gave me a look of squinting disbelief. I gave her an understanding nod and my most ingratiating smile.

"He's the runt of the litter. I'm abnormally tall."

She relented an inch.

"Give me one reason why I should bend the rules, 'Brother.'"

"We've been estranged for years. I just realized how much he means to me. Before anything happens—"

"Let's play it again, 'Brother,' this time without the bullshit. You're working on your third strike."

When all else fails, try the truth.

"It's like this. Based on what got him here, he could need my help in ways you couldn't even imagine. I need to talk to him as soon as possible."

She gave me another squint, but she had a nose for the truth.

"You get one minute, 'Brother.' That's sixty seconds, not sixty-one. And—"

"Thank you."

"You didn't let me finish. If after those sixty seconds, his pulse is two clicks higher than it is right now, you're going to be wearing this bedpan in a funny place at an unusual angle. Are we clear with one another?"

"I take your meaning."

"Good. He's in there. That's one second—two seconds—"

In spite of what I expected, I was stunned. Whatever parts of Danny were not encased in elevated casts were receptacles for tubes or wires. He looked like a string puppet in the hands of a mad puppeteer.

I sensed the time bomb ticking in the hall and got down to business.

"Danny, can you hear me?"

I saw one finger slowly flicker at the side of the bed. A gurgling voice that seemed to come from deep in his chest rasped something like, "Could only be Mike. How'd you get in?"

"You're my brother. Mom says 'Hi.'"

"Nice. Yours or mine?"

"Let's not blow my cover. What happened, Danny?"

There was silence that could have been pain, weakness, drugs, whatever. Then he gurgled again.

"Mike . . . leave it alone."

"Danny, I've only got a minute. I think you need help on the outside. But I have to know what's going on. What happened? Who should I be looking for?"

"Mike, back off. This is not yours."

"Danny, would you back off if it were me?"

He opened his eyes a crack for the first time and looked in my general direction.

"Don't make me come over there and slap you around, Mike. I want your word you'll stay out—"

He went back to wherever the drugs were mercifully taking him. I gave it a few seconds, and touched him as softly as I could.

"I'll be back, Danny."

When I got to the door, I barely heard a thin voice. "I'll be here, brother."

It was about three o'clock that afternoon when I got back from court to the offices at 77 Franklin Street in the center of Boston, which had, for the last eight months, housed the law firm of Devlin & Knight, of which I was the junior partner. My senior partner, Mr. Alexis (Lex) Devlin, was, to be poetic but truthful, the Paul Bunyan of the criminal defense bar, aging a bit to be sure, but on any given trial date, the source of everything from butterflies to ulcers for any unfortunate prosecutor.

I spent the rest of the afternoon trying to be absorbed in returning clients' phone calls, drafting motions, whatever might distract my preoccupation with Danny. The visions of him, both splayed on the track and trussed up in the hospital, dominated my thoughts.

We had a strange tie, Danny and I. After my father's death when I was an early teen, my mother moved us from the WASPish neighborhood of Winchester outside of Boston, the ancestral home of my father, to the then heavily Puerto Rican barrio of Jamaica Plain, my mother being full-blooded from that sunny isle.

She meant well, but without knowing it, she plunked me smack on the turf border between two of the diciest teen gangs then in existence. Not to join one or the other would have been like being a mouse between an alley cat and a coyote. For arbitrary reasons, I cast my lot with the coyotes.

As an initiation, I was sent out to hot-wire—as any thirteen-year-old in my neighborhood could in those days—a classic Cadillac. I was caught, tried, and in short order convicted, in spite of the nervous efforts of my court-appointed lawyer, on whose law school diploma you could still smell wet ink. To be fair, it was no miscarriage of justice; I was the dictionary picture for the word "guilty."

I was about to be sentenced by a crusading judge to the Lord only knows what graduate school of criminality, when the owner of the Cadillac asked to approach the bench. Miles O'Connor was defense counsel to some of the top white-collar heavies of Boston's political and financial communities. I sweated bullets while they bargained in whispered tones over my future—if any.

When the tête-à-tête broke, the judge rapped the gavel, and I followed the summoning finger of my new guardian, Mr. Miles O'Connor. That path brought me into a life of rigid demands, no such thing as rest, and the eventual opportunity to walk through any door in life that could be opened by hard work on my part and unlimited financial and spiritual backing on his part. God love him, he's passed on now, but there never lived a man on earth for whom I would more gladly walk off a cliff.

My current life really began at the age of thirteen as stall mucker and horse waterer in the Beverly Thoroughbred horse stables of Miles O'Connor. My partner in grime, in those days, was another O'Connor rescue, a diminutive Irish kid from the streets of South Boston by the name of Danny Ryan.

The two of us spent the first three weeks at the stables covering for each other, trying to find shortcuts and cover-ups to hide a job half done. We finally realized that Miles O'Connor's time was never so taken with momentous cases as to distract him from checking every minute detail of our menial labors. Within a year, Danny and I absorbed the O'Connor principle: perfection is the barely passing standard. That scale has driven the lives of both of us to this day.

Danny and I took different directions when we left the O'Connor nest. I went through Harvard and Harvard Law School, did a stint as prosecutor with the Boston U.S. Attorney's office, and then went into a criminal defense practice that ultimately paired me with the only man on earth who could stand on the same pedestal with Miles O'Connor, my senior partner, Lex Devlin.

Danny, on the other hand, had two natural attributes, an abiding love and understanding of horses, and a body that could sustain a weight of just under a hundred pounds. He rode his apprentice year as a jockey at Suffolk Downs the year I entered Harvard College. He went on from there to become the leading rider at Suffolk and held that distinction for five years running.

Then Danny made the acquaintance of demon rum and a few other things that knocked him off that elite roster. It took a few rough years, but he finally managed to climb out of the pit. On the day of the accident, he was back in riding condition.

However separated we were by the demands of dissimilar careers and circumstances, I don't think in all those years, two consecutive days went by that we didn't contact each other, at least by phone. I guess what I'm saying is that, blood aside, what I told that nurse about being his brother was as close to the truth as a lie could come.

I heard the elevator door open onto our suite of offices about four o'clock. I thought it was Mr. Devlin coming back from court, but my secretary, Julie, buzzed my line with word that a gentleman wanted to see me. My curiosity was up, because I had no appointments, and we hardly ever get walk-in clients. Curiosity won out over the urge to have him wait while I checked with the hospital on Danny. I asked Julie to send him in.

I was just standing up to shake hands with whomever it was, when I had one of those moments that hangs your jaw at half-mast. I'd have sooner bet on Elvis coming through that door than Hector Vasquez, the jockey who was crowding Danny toward the rail when he fell.

I automatically held out my hand to shake hands, but the usual words of greeting just wouldn't come out.

"I'm sorry, Mr. Knight. I didn't give my name to your secretary. I didn't think you'd see me."

I recovered enough to follow through on the handshake, and motioned toward the chair across from me. He sat on the edge of the seat as if he were riding it in a race. I'd felt perspiration in the handshake. I was glad it was his.

He read the look of complete bafflement on my face and didn't play around with niceties.

"I want to hire you to represent me, Mr. Knight."

The bafflement deepened, and he must have noticed.

"It's a criminal case. I was indicted this afternoon."

That pushed it to another level. I went with a noncommittal question.

"Indicted for what, Hector?"

He wiped his large jockey's hand across the tiny beads forming on his forehead and edged even closer to the front of the seat. He looked like a jack-in-the-box on a hairspring.

"I know you've got reasons not to, but—"

"Hector, indicted for what?"

"Murder. I want you to know, Mr. Knight, I'm innocent. I wouldn't be here—"

I held up a hand.

"Hector, go slow. Murder of whom?"

He took a breath.

"Danny Ryan."

The only response I could muster was disbelief.

"Wait a minute. You mean criminal assault. I saw Danny this morning."

He pulled back and winced.

"Damn. I'm sorry. I thought you knew. Danny died this morning."

Everything shut off. It was like a blow that doesn't let you feel pain, just numbness, knowing the pain will follow. I couldn't hear what Hector was saying, so I held up a hand to stop the flow while

I just walked to the window. The first thought to pound its way through the log jam was that when I call Danny tomorrow, and the next day, and the next, there'll be no Danny there. I was losing count of the ways the world without Danny in it would seem more bleak.

I forced myself back to where Hector sat waiting and tried to pull it together. I had at least eighteen questions, but I had to start somewhere.

"Why murder? What makes them think it's murder?"

"It's not, Mr. Knight. I swear it. They say I jammed him in the ribs with my whip."

I was still off balance. The main obstacle was suppressing judgment of this jockey that I saw crowding Danny dangerously close to the rail when he fell.

"They must have a reason. What do the pictures show, the stewards' videos of the race?"

"We were tight together just after the eighth pole. Danny was inside on the rail. My horse bore in. I switched the whip to my left hand, the hand between us. I wanted to haze my horse toward the outside away from Danny without breaking stride. That was when Danny tumbled. I never touched him. The films don't show I did. But they don't show I didn't either. They just show the whip in my left hand."

I had to sit down to get some order to the thoughts that were flowing too fast to process.

Danny is gone. That's number one. Hard on that one, I had to decide if I could possibly find the commitment to represent the man who was charged with killing him.

A far third were all the more mundane points screaming for attention, like how did Danny's death that morning result in an indictment so fast? And why was the grand jury interested anyway? Rough riding, even an occasional assault between jockeys, is handled by the track stewards, or the racing commission in an extreme case.

And constantly hovering over my private mental din was the picture of Danny, with his wife, Colleen, just three years married, and the two-year-old bright light of his life, Erin, who would also have to endure that stinging absence for the rest of their lives.

I became aware that Hector was speaking, and I had to reach a decision.

"—because I can give you $10,000 right now."

He laid an envelope on my desk. I was focused on other things.

"I was at the track yesterday, Hector. I saw Danny fall. It was—unnatural. Like he just lost control of his arms and legs. I'm giving you the benefit of the doubt for the moment. Assuming it wasn't contact with you, what else could have caused it?"

Hector sat back in the chair, still rigid, but his silence and body language spoke of stalling.

"That's a question, Hector. I haven't taken your case yet. I want an answer. You were the closest to it. What's your explanation?"

"I don't want to say anything about Danny. This shouldn't come from me."

"Really. Then who else? I'll be straight with you, Hector. You know Danny and I were close. Like brothers. I need a reason to take this case. It's only fair to you too. What caused Danny to lose control in the middle of a race?"

I could sense that I was going to get minimal information from this source. Hector's stalling was tipping the balance to the side of all those nerve fibers that were screaming, "Stay the hell away from this."

He finally broke the silence.

"There was some talk around the jockeys' room, Mr. Knight. Like maybe Danny was back into some heavy stuff before the race."

"What stuff? You mean drugs?"

Hector held up his hands.

"It was probably just talk, Mr. Knight. I didn't know Danny that well. The Latinos tend to hang together. Mind our own business.

But there was a buzz around the other part of the jockeys' room yesterday about Danny. I could just pick up traces. It was a big race for him. Coming back. You know. He seemed—"

"What?"

"Jumpy. Maybe he took something that caused a seizure. I only know it had nothing to do with me."

"Did you ever see him take anything?"

"I didn't pay that much attention. Like I said, the Latinos were at one end of the jockeys' room. He was at the other."

This was getting complicated. If we took the case, we might have to bring out ugly things about Danny to save a client. On the other hand, I brought my own answer to that question right out of my gut. Danny had cleaned up his act. He would not have taken even a diet pill before that race. My certainty was so deep that it pushed me into half a commitment.

"Here's where we stand, Hector, so you know. I don't buy that drug theory. That said, I'll go this far with you. I'll do the investigation and the pretrial work. I'm doing this partly for Danny anyway. If I find you're clean, I'll go all the way with you."

He bounced up like a spring toy with his hand out to seal the deal. I stayed where I was.

"Understand the other half. If I find you had a hand in Danny's death, even remotely, you'll be looking for another attorney. Do we understand each other?"

"We do."

The hand was still out there. On those terms, I shook it.

CHAPTER THREE

The lines on Mr. Devlin's Mount Rushmore features deepened the further I got into explaining the circumstances of our new maybe-client. A day of combat in the criminal session of the Suffolk Superior Court left him more depleted of energy than I liked to see. I knew it was not the best moment to broach a subject that left even me with second, third, and fourth thoughts, but the timing couldn't be helped.

"You've thought about this, Michael."

It was a question.

"Not for any— No. There was no time. That's why I left the escape hatch open. If our investigation shows that he's guilty, we withdraw."

He leaned back, folded his arms, and gave me that look.

"You have trouble with that, Mr. D.?"

"I'm sitting here praying to God that my junior partner has an equal amount of trouble with it."

The eyebrows went up, and he waited.

"I know. You've always told me that you can't base a defense on the belief that your client is innocent."

"And the reason?"

I'd often thought he was a frustrated law professor.

"They lie. Then you find yourself up the creek and paddling backward, to quote your words. I'm still not totally convinced of that theory."

An argument always brought him up with his elbows on the desk.

"Then let's play it your way, Michael. What possible evidence, other than his word, do you have of this jockey's innocence?"

"That's why I left the escape hatch."

That had him up and pacing.

"Let me set the scene. We take this case on. Judge whoever-it-is sets a trial date, which rapidly approaches. You turn up something down the road that suggests perhaps that our client is not altogether innocent. You make a motion to withdraw from the case."

"I see where this is going."

"I'm just getting warmed up. The judge asks, 'On what grounds, Mr. Knight?' You say, 'I want out because my client is guilty.' Ninety percent of the defendants the judge tries are guilty. The judge says, 'If I let lawyers out on those grounds, this court would look like musical chairs. Denied.'"

"That's not exactly—"

"Oh, that's right. There's another ground. 'Your Honor, the victim was my good friend.' 'Oh,' says the judge. 'That's different. I'll disrupt my trial schedule. We'll put off giving this defendant a speedy trial under the constitution while another lawyer gets up to speed. We wouldn't want you to have conflicted feelings, Mr. Knight.'"

His pacing had brought him next to me. I felt his hand on my shoulder. He said one word that carried with it a paragraph.

"Michael."

"Doesn't play, does it?"

"Not in this lifetime. You have my sympathy, but you've got to fish or cut bait. We're in or we're out. You make the call. Either way, I'm with you. But there's no halfway."

I knew he was right before he even started. On the other hand, Hector Vasquez didn't. And yet he accepted my representation with a trapdoor that would throw his case into turmoil if it were ever sprung. That was some indication that he was innocent and he knew I'd never have cause to use it.

Mr. D. was still waiting. On the basis of little more than instinct, I said two words.

"We're in."

Mr. D. nodded, and we were committed to a road we could both have lived a happy lifetime without traveling.

"Where is he now?"

"I told him to wait in my office."

"Good. If he was indicted this afternoon, there's a bench warrant out for his arrest. We'll arrange to have him turn himself in. That'll give us bargaining chips with the D.A.'s office. Which raises the question, how did he learn about the indictment in time to come to you before he was arrested?"

"That'll be my first question. My second is how did this journeyman jockey put together ten thousand dollars in cash for our retainer on short notice."

Mr. D.'s eyebrows lifted. "The cards are not all on the table, are they, Michael?"

"Are they ever?"

He ignored this self-serving observation on his way back to a seat and a sturdy grip on the telephone. I marveled at how the challenge of a new legal set-to could start the juices flowing through a body that had been running on low fuel.

I filled him in on what little I knew about the case. When I finished, he punched in the numbers of the Suffolk County District Attorney's office and put it on speakerphone. The receptionist recognized his courtroom baritone as soon as she heard it. I could hear the smile in her voice. I always had the feeling that she favored Mr. Devlin in his verbal jousts with her employer, District Attorney Angela Lamb.

"Good morning, Susan. Let me speak to the brains of that shop of yours."

"You want the district attorney, Mr. Devlin?"

"Susan, don't be political. I said the brains of the outfit."

Since apparently no one was within earshot, Susan had no need to be coy about transferring the call directly to Billy Coyne. Billy was one of the extremely rare career veterans of the office. As deputy district attorney, he was the constant rock that kept the office functioning at a professional level through the ins and outs of the political climbers who passed through the top title of district attorney. As two old war horses who had tested each other in a hundred courtroom joustings, Billy and Mr. Devlin had developed a rare mutual respect, trust, and, truth be known, affection for each other.

"Good morning, Lex. And to what do I owe this profound honor?"

"It's your lucky day, Billy. I have something you want and I'm offering it to you on a silver platter."

"And that crock of Irish bull feces means I have something you want, and I'm about to get the horse trading of the week. What've you got, Lex?"

"I have your newest indictee, Hector Vasquez. He'll turn himself in. Michael will personally walk him right into your office."

I could hear Billy's low whistle of surprise.

"That little son of a gun moved fast. The ink is still wet on the indictment. And here he is on your doorstep already."

"The same thought occurred to us, Billy. Who do you suppose tipped him off to the indictment before the arrest warrant was executed? Sounds like there's a hole in your little boat over there."

"It sounds to me like maybe he's connected to people you don't generally get into bed with, Lex."

That idea was nudging me too when I thought of that envelope with $10,000 on my desk. Someone wanted Hector to be well represented in this case for reasons that might go beyond Hector's personal welfare.

"Not to change the subject, Billy, but in gratitude for our putting Hector on your doorstep, I thought you might like to share a little information."

"Here it comes. Just remember, I'm as Irish as you are. What do you want, Lex?"

"A modest request. What have you got on Hector?"

I could see Billy rock back with a laugh you could hear in Charlestown.

"Why don't you just come over so I can give you the key to our files?"

"Now, now, Billy. You'll have to disclose most of it eventually. Let's just make it a fair fight."

"We have the race films. They show Vasquez riding next to Danny Ryan on the right. He has his whip in his left hand. Ryan's horse is taking the lead. All of a sudden, Ryan shoots out of the saddle and tumbles over the rail. Ryan winds up dead."

"I see. And the film clearly shows beyond a reasonable doubt that Vasquez poked Ryan out of the saddle with his whip."

Mr. D. winked at me. I had mouthed to him what Hector had said about the films.

"No, Lex."

"Oh, that's unfortunate, Billy."

"Nor does it show that he didn't."

"Then what does it show that you're going to build a case on, my optimistic friend?"

"The opportunity."

"And exactly how are you going to spin that into a conviction?"

"Did you ever hear of the old Latin concept *res ipsa loquitur*? The thing speaks for itself."

"They mentioned it in law school. They also said it only applies in civil cases."

"It has a counterpart in criminal cases. It's called circumstantial evidence. Works all the time."

Mr. D. rocked back in his chair, and the little smile was gone. "Uh-huh. Now let's get to the heart of it, Billy. You've got a case that's as weak as dishwater. You rush to a criminal indictment in what has to be record time in a situation that would be handled in every other case by the track stewards, the racing commission at the most. What the hell's going on?"

There was a moment's pause that was significant enough to set both of our spines on edge.

"A jockey died. That's more than the stewards' office can handle."

"And you think Hector deliberately murdered him. Billy, have you lost the few marbles you have left? It was a freak accident. Jockeys have survived spills twice that bad. There are more certain ways of doing him in if that was the plan."

"It's felony murder, Lex. Someone died during the commission of a felony."

"And the felony is?"

"The race was fixed."

"You don't mean it. A race fixed at Suffolk Downs? Please say it isn't so."

I could almost feel the sarcasm wash over my shoes.

"Billy, do you remember when we were kids, the ninth race at Suffolk was called 'the jockeys' race'? The jockey's would pick a long shot, bet on it, and then make it happen. You and I used to stay for the ninth just to guess which long shot it was."

"And may I remind you, that it's been a few years since we were kids. Times change."

It was Mr. D's turn to pause.

"You don't want Vasquez. Fixed race or not, he's like swatting a mosquito. This sounds like the machinations of our eminent district attorney. Angela Lamb wants to nail Hector to get him to flip. On whom, Billy? She must smell some headlines. Who's she after?"

"You're fishing, Lex."

"Am I? You got that indictment before the sun went down on Danny Ryan's body. That means you had a grand jury in session investigating something that ties into that race. And it's one hell of a lot bigger than little Hector Vasquez."

"You have a fertile imagination. You'll want copies of the race films and the autopsy report on Ryan. I'll send them over. That's the best I can do for you."

"And for that you expect me to deliver Vasquez like a Thanks-giving turkey?"

"No. You'll deliver Vasquez to avoid a charge of harboring a fugitive."

"And that's all I get after a lifetime of personal favors to you, Mr. Coyne?"

"That would be correct. When can we expect Vasquez?"

They arranged for me to bring Hector directly to Billy Coyne's office. At least we'd have the arguing point before the jury that Hector voluntarily surrendered to the D.A. A bit disturbing was the fact that Billy told us to use the rear entrance with an elevator directly to the district attorney's offices. The reason for that bit of added security escaped us at the time, but it set off alarms in the central nervous system.

Before Hector and I left our offices, the three of us had a chat about the race the previous day. He denied knowing anything about a fixed race then or ever at Suffolk Downs. Mr. D. and I exchanged looks that said we had a client who was selective about his moments of truth telling.

We also quizzed him about who tipped him off to the indictment before they could serve an arrest warrant. That was a dead end too. He mentioned an anonymous caller that afternoon and stuck to his story. His answer to our questions about the source of the $10,000 was simply his savings account.

I came to the uncomfortable conclusion that the only word out of Hector's mouth since I met him that came within a mile of the truth was that he did not cause Danny's death. And that was a leap of faith.

CHAPTER FOUR

I explained the situation to Hector and escorted him to the district attorney's office as promised. Billy met us and took Hector into custody. The arraignment was scheduled for the following morning. There was no rush, since Hector already had counsel, and any bail that he could post was not an option in a felony murder case.

That done, I turned to something I had been anxious to do, and yet dreading all afternoon. I drove to Danny's home in Beverly.

Danny's success as a jockey took him all over the East Coast, from Saratoga Springs in New York to Gulfstream in Florida, but his heart always remained on the north shore of Boston, where he and I had spent the better part of our teen years with our foster-father, Miles O'Connor.

Miles had a daughter, Colleen. He raised her from the day his wife died in childbirth. If she'd been raised in a convent, she'd have had a more liberated upbringing. At the top of the list of negative worldly influences to be kept as far outside of her world as humanly possible were Miles's live-in rescues, Danny Ryan and myself. We barely knew she existed until she was in her teens. But the day that the gate that separated the stables from the wing of the mansion that was her castle was accidentally left ajar, Danny and Colleen caught a glimpse of each other face-to-face. It was actually little more than a glimpse, but it was as if Danny's heart and mind were locked tight, and only one soul on earth had the password.

I won't say Danny never dated during the years I was in college and law school and he was working his way up the list of leading jockeys, but we kept in close contact, and I could sense that something kept him from getting serious with any of the girls he dated.

It's strange, or perhaps fatalistic, that it was Miles who ultimately brought them together. After a lifetime of vacuum sealing Colleen in schools for young ladies, Miles died of the trial lawyers' curse, a heart attack, and Danny and Colleen saw each other for the second time at Miles's funeral. Maybe it was the common bond of a love for Miles that united them instantly, but my money is on that glimpse of each other that had occurred eight years earlier.

Whatever the cause, Danny and Colleen were like the negatively and positively charged particles of an atom from that moment on. The obvious love between them was so tangible that it seemed to put smiles on the faces of anyone who came into their presence. The only thing on earth that could have deepened that love was the birth of their daughter, Erin.

All of this ran through my mind on the drive to their home in Beverly. I was just barely holding it together when I thought of the hole Danny left in my life. But when I thought of the enormity of Colleen's loss, I had no idea how I'd be able to pass on the strength I wanted to give to her.

It took three of my ritual knocks before the door slowly opened a crack. There were none of Colleen's familiar rapid, almost dancing footsteps and welcoming flinging of the door wide open. There was no hug and kiss on the cheek and smile that could inspire yet another Irish song. In fact, I hardly heard her come to the door, and it opened just enough to identify the visitor. The drawn, pale, expressionless face that acknowledged my presence was hardly recognizable as Colleen.

I wasn't sure she was going to open it the rest of the way until I spoke. She just retreated inside, and I pushed it myself.

Whatever empty, idiotic, useless words I said accomplished nothing to break down the wall created by her blank expression. I don't know what I expected. Maybe a consoling hug and the release of a flood of tears. It didn't happen.

I made a perfunctory offer of help, but since I was incapable of bringing Danny back, anything else fell short of rousing the least spark of interest.

I gave it a full ten minutes before getting a grip on the obvious. For whatever reason, Colleen had locked herself away from the intrusion of well-intended consolation—at least mine. I decided to favor her with that which she seemed to want or need the most, my absence.

The hollowness that I'd felt since hearing of Danny's death seemed at least doubled when I turned to leave with nothing but frost in place of the mutual consolation I'd imagined. I reached the door alone, when I realized that something else was missing. The iciness of Colleen had blocked out my expectation of two tiny feet running like trip hammers and two tiny arms that leaped toward my neck in the constant faith that I'd catch her and lift her the rest of the way. The smushy feeling of that angelic face rubbed into my nose and cheek was as much of a ritual as my signature knock on the door.

"Colleen, where's Erin? Does she know?"

The question seemed to jar her out of the deep freeze. There was a hesitation, but at least she spoke a full sentence.

"She's at the neighbor's."

"Have you told her?"

Again the pause. "No."

"Colleen, I know it's hard, but—"

"I can't. Let it go at that!"

It came out sharper than I think she intended. I couldn't block the stunned look. I think it was that look that first registered whom she was with. She took a hanky out of her pocket and let the tears flow into it. I came back to her, and she let herself sob on my shoulder for what seemed like several minutes.

I thought it had washed away the wall of ice, but when the flow stopped, it was back. I wondered if she had heard that I was representing the man charged with Danny's murder, but that seemed unlikely.

We walked to the door. This time she opened it. I stepped outside and turned back.

"Colleen, I guess you know that if there's anything I can do—"

The only response was a nod with her head down. I hated to leave that way. I felt as if I were failing Danny. On the basis of what the hell, I reached out and grabbed her shoulders. The shock of it brought her head up, and for the first time she looked me in the eye.

"Colleen, this is not some stupid, half-wit mumbling of the right thing to say. I'm really here to help you. If only for the sake of Erin, can you get a grip?"

She pushed away and went inside the door. I thought she'd slam it, but she turned back from the darkness inside and said in the coldest tones I'd ever heard, "I've got a grip. I've got a grip on the fact that everything is gone. Can you hear that?"

I had no answer. I was completely empty. I started to leave, when Colleen's voice caught me. It was just as cold, but there was more steel in it. "Can you hear that, Michael? There's nothing left."

She closed the door. I stood there for a moment without a rational thought in my mind. I walked to my car in a state of numbing shock. The end of the visit had been even more bizarre than the beginning. The person I had just left was as complete a stranger as if I'd knocked on the wrong door.

The drive back to Boston was on instinct while I tried to make sense of that whole conversation. I don't even remember the first ten miles. Nothing about the previous twenty minutes rang true to the Colleen who was like the closest family to me.

I think I was passing through Lynn when ideas started dropping into my consciousness like pieces of the sky falling, and each connection multiplied the panic brewing in the pit of my stomach. I reached into my pocket for my cell phone to call Colleen. I found the handkerchief she had been using. There was something hard and round rolled in it. I pulled over and unraveled it slowly to postpone what I sensed was coming, but there was no preparing for it. My chest seized and I could barely breathe when I saw in the folds of the handkerchief a tiny gold ring with a ruby birthstone. I had given it to Erin for her second birthday. Danny had told me she loved wearing it.

I wanted to run back into the house to ask Colleen directly, but I knew she couldn't talk. She had made that plain to anyone who wasn't so shocked by rejection that he couldn't read the signs.

I took a minute to put together the barest bones of a plan and drove at nearly twice the speed limit to the Walmart in Lynn and then a florist friend in Winthrop. That done, I took the Sumner Tunnel back to Boston and the office.

Before entering the tunnel, I used my cell phone to reach Mr. Devlin. Thank God he had not left the office.

"Michael, you sound breathless. What happened?"

"I just saw Colleen, Danny's wife."

"How's she doing?"

"About as badly as possible. She's in pieces. I don't think it's completely Danny's death. She seemed almost afraid to talk to me. But she gave me a message. She slipped a little ring I gave Erin into my pocket so I'd find it after I left. She said she's lost everything, emphasis on everything. She said it twice. I think she's saying Erin's been taken."

"Damn it, Michael!" I could feel the pain in his voice.

"She's also saying she can't talk in the house. I think she's afraid it's bugged."

"How can I help? I have contacts with the Boston office of the FBI."

"That's good, but not yet. We need to get more information. I have an idea. If it works, Colleen will be leaving her house in Beverly. We need to know if anyone follows her, and whom they report to. Will you call Tom Burns and have him put his best man on it? That would be Tom himself."

I gave Mr. D. the address in Beverly to pass on to Tom Burns. Tom had been our dependable go-to detective agency for as long as we'd been a firm. He charged rates that would make a neurosurgeon blush, but expensive though he was, I'd never consider him overpriced.

I was in the office in fifteen minutes flat. When I passed my secretary, Julie, on the way to Mr. Devlin's office, I told her to hold any call that wasn't a notice of fire in the building or a call from Colleen Ryan. She put that bit of dramatics together with what must have been the look on my face, and her natural empathy went into overdrive. That meant a flow of questions that I put off with a promise of full disclosure before the sun set.

I had just time to explain to Mr. D. that when I left Colleen, I had picked up a prepaid disposable cell phone at Walmart that couldn't be tapped or traced. I programmed our office number into the phone and put it into the bouquet of cut flowers I had my florist friend, Max, deliver to Colleen. A floral delivery would seem natural to anyone watching the house.

The note I enclosed with the flowers told Colleen to drive to Revere Beach Boulevard and park on the ocean side close to Kelly's Roast Beef sandwich stand. It told her to buy a Coke, and drink it on the public benches by the ocean across the street. The traffic around Kelly's Roast Beef is always brisk. It would give Tom Burns a chance to get a lock on whoever might be following her without blowing cover. My note said to then walk into the public women's restroom down the shore to the left and call our office using the phone she'd find in the flowers. The assumption was that anyone following her would likely be a man, so she'd have about four safe minutes in the ladies' room.

The briefing of Mr. D. was quick. The wait that followed seemed interminable, although it was only ten minutes. Julie put the call through to Mr. D.'s office, and we hovered around the speakerphone.

"Colleen, are you where I think you are?"

The response was punctuated with barely restrained sobs.

"Mike. Thank God. I'm so sorry for before. I didn't know what to do."

"I know, Colleen. It's all right. Did you go where I told you?"

"Yes. I'm here now."

"Good. Then we have just a couple of minutes. Mr. Devlin is here. Tell us everything you know about Erin."

"Dear God, Mike. Someone has her."

She got that far before sobs choked off her voice.

"Colleen, you're not alone. We're going to get her back. I promise."

It was a wild promise, but I put it in the hands of God and said it with all the assurance I could muster. Wild as it must have sounded, I could sense the tiniest bit of calming creep into her voice.

"What can I do, Mike?"

"Exactly what I tell you. First, fill us in. What happened?"

"Yesterday morning, early, Danny was going to the stables on the backstretch at Suffolk. He was riding Black Diamond in one of the early races before the MassCap. He wanted to ride him out to get the feel of him before the race. Erin liked to go with him to the morning workouts, so he took her. There was never a problem. That area of the stables is more secure for the sake of the horses than any daycare center. Dear God, Mike, if we had only known then."

"It might not have made any difference. Go on, Colleen."

"I got a call from Danny about eleven. He said—" Her voice choked off again.

"Colleen, I wish I were there to help you, but you've got to pull it together. You only have a couple more minutes to talk. Danny said what?"

"He said someone took Erin. He said I had to stay in the house, that somebody'd be watching from the outside. He said he was taking care of it, and he'd get her back."

"Did he say how?"

"No. He just said I had to stay in the house in case the phone rang. He also said I couldn't tell anyone, or Erin would—you must know how much I wanted to tell you this afternoon."

"You did tell me. That was a great trick with the ring. You're a trooper, Colleen. Think about this. How did Danny sound on the phone?"

She gave it a few seconds. "I don't know. Of course he was frightened for Erin, but he sounded stiff, like he was being told what to say."

"Okay. We have to keep this short. I want you to calm down, wash the tears off your face, and go back to your car. Drive directly home and stay there. I know it's hard, but I want you to know that people are working on this for Erin that you don't know about."

"Mike, Danny said we couldn't call the police or they'd hurt Erin."

"We won't. This is not the police. You have to trust me. No one will know. Keep that cell phone with you in case you need to reach us. I'll call you tonight. When I do, don't say anything over the phone about Erin by name. I'll get any message across somehow. Do you understand all that?"

"Yes, Mike. Thank you, thank you. Is there anything else I can do?"

"You know the answer to that one, Colleen. And we'll be praying with you."

CHAPTER FIVE

The most painful way possible for Mr. Devlin and myself to pass the next hour and a half was in enforced inaction. But given the need for secrecy and no promising leads, we had no choice. We each hunkered down behind any office work that could possibly absorb our attention while we waited for a call from Tom Burns.

I used the time to do some computer research on the race that had taken Danny's life. It was a sprint race over five furlongs, a little over half a mile, for two-year-olds, the youngest Thoroughbreds that can be raced.

I checked out Danny's mount, Black Diamond, on the *Daily Racing Form* site for any recorded workouts before that race. He had been bred in Ireland at a small Thoroughbred stable in Kildare. His bloodlines were not remarkable, and his training times even less so. He had never breezed the half mile in less than fifty-three seconds and change, which would not excite the most generous handicapper.

He had been shipped to Rick McDonough's stable at Suffolk Downs just two weeks before the race. Under Rick's hand, he still couldn't break fifty-three seconds for the half mile in a couple of morning breezes. It was no great surprise that he was a twenty-to-one long shot the day of the race.

My office clock had just struck six when Julie buzzed me with the word that Tom Burns was on the line. I had her transfer it to Mr. D.'s office and sprinted down the hall to be there when he picked up. Mr. D. did the talking, but we listened together.

"Gentlemen, your intuition was on the button."

"Meaning what, Tom?"

"There was a tail waiting to follow her when she left the house. I tailed both of them to the roast beef sandwich place on Revere Beach Boulevard. She picked up a Coke, drank it on a bench, and went into the public women's room. The tail and I both waited till she came out and we started the parade again back to her home."

I jumped in to set my mind at ease. "Tom, tell me the tail never spotted you."

"No, Mikey. I won't tell you that. Based on what you know about me, you should assume that without question."

"Assumed it is. What next?"

"The tail stayed on station a few houses down her street until a few minutes ago. A second car pulled up, apparently the relief shift. The first tail took off."

"Any idea where?"

"That's why I need your instructions. I thought you'd want to know where he went. I'm traveling three cars behind the first tail now."

"You guessed right. Stay with him. Get back to us as soon as he lights somewhere."

"Will do."

"Two more things. I need a description of the tail you're following and also the make of the car that's at Colleen's house now."

"Right, Mike. This guy is about six foot two. Looks trim, athletic. Sandy, curly hair. About thirty. Definitely Irish."

"Takes one to know one, right, Tom?"

That brought my Irish senior partner's eyebrows up a notch.

"In this case, a blind Swede could tell. Hang on a sec, gentlemen."

There was silence for about a minute and a half before Tom was back.

"The name of the tail I'm following is Vince Scully. He has a Southie address. You want it?"

"You're golden, Tom. Shoot."

"Four twelve G Street. Not a bad neighborhood. A lot of classy renovation. If the Lincoln this guy's driving is his own car, and I'm assuming it is, he makes a hefty income for someone who tails people."

"Again may I say, it takes one to know one."

"Now, now, Mikey. In case you're wondering what you're paying for, I used my personal contact to run his license plate. Try that with your average P.I."

"Point taken. What about the second tail's car?"

"It's a two thousand nine Ford Taurus. Gray, inconspicuous. Parked three houses south of her house. Too dark in the car to get a description of the driver except he's male. I was out of position to get the license number. I didn't want to lose the first tail trying."

"Good call. One last thing. Can you get a man over to Colleen's house to keep an eye on her from the outside. They could turn on her."

"Consider it done. Anything else?"

I looked at Mr. D. He nodded agreement that all the bases were covered for the moment.

Mr. D. and I left the office with the mutual agreement that whoever heard from Tom first would notify the other. I could have gone to my apartment to wait, but doing nothing was chafing my nerves to distraction.

Without giving it a lot of thought, I drove to Beverly. I cruised past the Ford Taurus parked three houses from Colleen's without slowing or looking to either side. I did, however, get the license number.

One loop around the block raised an idea that would be minimally dangerous to Erin and Colleen, and yet might get things off dead center. I pulled into the driveway of a house three down from the Taurus. There were no lights in the house at that early darkening hour. At least for the moment it was a fair guess there was no one home. The name on the mailbox was Justin Clifford.

With the help of 411, I called the Beverly police. One thing I've noticed about the police in a wealthy, secluded community is that their top priority is the peace of mind of the residents who pay their salaries.

"Beverly police. Sergeant Barnes. How can I help you?"

I slipped into my best north shore accent.

"Sergeant Barnes, Justin Clifford here. I believe we've met."

"Of course, Mr. Clifford."

I figured he'd never deny it, whether they'd met or not. I also figured that nothing would give an incentive to fulfill my request to the letter like the notion that I could hold him personally responsible.

"Small matter I'd like you to check on. There's a car parked by the curb just down the street. Not familiar. The driver seems to be just sitting there. Been there for some time. Possibly stalking. Do you suppose you might check it out?"

"Of course, Mr. Clifford. I'll have someone there immediately."

"Excellent, Sergeant Barnes. One thing. In the interest of privacy, no need to use my name."

"Absolutely not."

One minute and twenty seconds later, a police cruiser slid in behind the Ford Taurus. I saw the driver straighten out of a slumped position. It was too late for him to hit the gas.

I had a front row seat as the officer rousted the driver out of the Taurus. My heart rejoiced to see the driver take out his wallet and show identification to the officer. They chatted for a minute or two before the officer walked back to the police car. I gave him two minutes to pass information back to the station house before getting Sergeant Barnes back on the line.

"Sergeant, Justin Clifford again. Excellent response. Did your officer learn anything."

"I have him on the radio now, Mr. Clifford. The man said he'd lost his way and he was just resting. He'd fallen asleep. We could take him in and hold him for loitering."

"No, no, Sergeant. No need. I've been in that position myself. May I ask if he had identification?"

"Yes. He's not from the north shore. Sean Flannery. He's from South Boston."

I decided to push the sergeant's earnest desire to please a wealthy resident, possibly a powerful one, one more notch.

"I know South Boston well. Is there an address?"

"Yes. One eighty four B Street. Are you sure you wouldn't like us to—"

"No, Sergeant. It's probably as he says. Our roads are confusing. If there was a problem, I'm sure he's impressed with the efficiency of our Beverly police."

That encounter with the local constabulary spooked our boy off station. It was my turn to make an attempt at following him. I'm no Tom Burns, and on dark streets in a neighborhood with zero traffic at that hour, I worried about being spotted. That could tip the kidnapper to the fact that Colleen had broken silence. What that could lead to in terms of Erin I couldn't risk.

I noticed that the driver cruised south slowly while he made a cell phone call. When he closed the cell phone, he picked up speed, and still headed south toward Boston. I figured he'd been recalled by whoever was pulling his strings. That was probably the spider at the center of the web.

I decided to exploit my one advantage—knowledge of every street and alley north of the tunnel. I put my Corvette in overdrive and took streets Mr. Flannery had never heard of to beat him to the tunnel. I parked well before and to the side of the line of toll booths. When he showed up, I swung into line a couple of cars behind him. Even I could safely follow him on the heavily trafficked, well-lit streets of Boston.

We played bumper cars with the late rush hour traffic on Atlantic Avenue until he turned onto Summer Street and cruised into the bowels of South Boston. He was on his turf now. He could navigate traffic on instinct and be alert to any inexperienced tracker on his tail. My comfort level dropped a notch.

Much as I needed to know whom he was reporting to, I seriously considered pulling over, when my cell phone vibrated against my ribs. Mr. Devlin reported that Tom Burns had tailed his subject to an Irish pub called Failte on C Street in South Boston.

That made it easier. On a hopeful hunch that my subject was heading for the same spot, I took a more round-about course to the pub. I cruised slowly, and within a block of the pub, I spotted the Ford Taurus parked on C street. I pulled in and parked a few spaces behind the Taurus.

Now what? I got the shivers every time I thought of precious little Erin in the hands of these thugs. My overwhelming desire was to call a couple of off-duty Boston cops who owed me favors and blow through the doors of that pub like Wyatt, Virgil, and Morgan Earp. Simplistic and satisfying as that urge was, it was also the straightest path to harm for Erin. That chilled the desire.

I called Colleen's number to get a cautious update. She had sense enough to remain as cold and distanced as she had when I visited that morning in case anyone was tuned in.

I asked if she'd heard from her father. She translated the question into what I was really asking, since her father had passed away ten years ago.

"No."

"Okay. Let me know if he calls. I'd like to speak to him about Danny."

"All right."

"Try to get some sleep. I have to do some work on a case that came in today, but if I get time, I'll call tomorrow."

I hoped she'd caught my meaning about the "case." I'd have forfeited my bar membership to be able to give her more hope, but you can't give what you haven't got.

❧

On the notion that any action still seemed better than inaction, I made a call to a former client. Binney O'Toole was, by any measure, a piece of work. He was five foot two from his upturned shoes to the top of his cap, with a nose that glowed in the dark. If you sent to central casting for the consummate red-faced pub crawler, they'd have pulled Binney out of a bar and sent him over. He immigrated from the old sod at the age of twelve, and spent the next fifty years perfecting his Irish accent. He also had the useful credential of being the clearinghouse for South Boston gossip.

As memory served, the offer of a taste of Tullamore Dew, one of Ireland's finest distilled nectars, would open the vault to the hidden scandals of anyone who had lived in Southie since World War I. For an offer to split the entire ambrosial contents of one of those green porcelain jugs, Binney would have given condemning testimony against his grandmother. On those terms, I phoned and invited him to join me at the Failte Pub.

Binney was practically tap dancing when he came through the door. I had dipped into the jogging wardrobe I keep in the car to change from a suit coat to a bulky dark sweater with a Red Sox cap pulled down to my eyebrows. Nevertheless, Binney's instinct for "a wee drop" led him unerringly to the dark booth I had chosen at the far end of the pub.

"Michael, me lad. What a grand thing it is to see you."

His fidgety, sweaty little hand came up for a brief shake, while his watery eyes scanned the table for a glimpse of the promised Dew. I waived to the waitress who had the familiar green jug with two shot glasses ready to deliver. When she came within sight, the smile of anticipation on Binney's roundish face would rival that of any child on Christmas morning.

I pulled the corked knob and poured us each a tall shot. By the time I raised the glass to my lips for a toast to the muse of Irish whiskey makers, Binney was wiping his lips and looking expectantly at the jug for a second shot. In the words of an old Irish drinking song, I "filled him up a full glass once again."

I gave him a third to lubricate his memory and his tongue and got down to business. I leaned close to Binney's ear, and he followed suit, taking careful note that I was not tilting the jug for a fourth.

"Binney, my man, whatsay to a bit of information? Is there anyone in this kingdom of South Boston that you do not know?"

"If there is, he's a tourist." A proud and mellowed grin rested on his lips.

"Then tell me about Vince Scully."

He bounced back as if I had jabbed him in the ribs.

"Oh shite, Mikey. Not that one. You want to keep your distance from that one."

"I'm sure you're right, Binney. Why?"

"Sure I want to live to see the sun come up. I've nothin' to say on that one."

I slowly reached for the green porcelain knob with the cork and silently sealed the bottle. I had Binney's rapt attention.

"That's unfortunate. I thought we might enjoy each other's fine company down to the last drop."

Poor Binney's entire body deflated. With each squeak of the cork, his countenance bespoke the wake of his last friend on earth.

"Ah, Mikey. You've a cold, black heart, and that's the truth." His fidgety little fingers drummed on the table while his eyes never left the jug. I felt heartless myself, but one thought of Erin, and I got over it.

"I'll tell you this, Binney. You have my word. What you say stays at this table. No one knows me here, and no one can hear us. Give me a reason to pull this cork."

He put his head in his hand and wrestled with the decision. When he spoke, it was so softly I could barely hear him.

"That's himself at the bar. The tall thin one with the gray sweater."

He nodded at the bottle to urge a reopening. I took a grip of the nob to encourage his optimism.

"Who is he, Binney?"

"Ah, shite, Mikey. You'll be the death me."

I twisted the cork half off. And stopped. He was almost in tears, but he leaned so close to my ear I could smell the whiskey he'd had for breakfast.

"He works for Paddy Boyle. They say he's his number one man."

"You're getting close. Who's Paddy Boyle?"

"Oh for the love of the saints, do I have to say it? He's the king of South Boston."

"Are you talking Irish Mafia?"

"Put it as you wish. There's not a politician elected in this ward without the nod from Paddy Boyle. And I daresay, not a family in Southie whose vote Paddy can't deliver."

"Out of fear?"

"Out of love and respect. And gratitude. If there's a family in Southie he hasn't helped with a word to a judge for a kid, with a delivery of groceries when the old man drank away the paycheck, with a boost for college money when it wasn't there—"

"What is he, Saint Robin Hood?"

The eyes darted right and left like little blinking lights before he spoke.

"Well now, that's one side of it. The other side, I'm only repeatin', there are those who say there's not a criminal act in Southie that doesn't put more than a penny in Boyle's pocket. And that one. Vince Scully. He'd as soon cut your throat as look at you. You don't know what you're dealin' with here."

"I'm learning, Binney. I'm learning. How about Sean Flannery?"

The pump had been primed. "He's part of the same mob. No better than Scully. He was here a bit ago, but he left."

I thanked God that I'd asked Tom Burns to put a man outside of Colleen's house. I had one last question. "Where do I find Boyle?"

He looked at me as if I'd turned purple.

"Did you hear nothin' I've said? Have you lost the few brains God gave you?"

I finished the shot of the Dew I'd been nursing and said into his ear, "We do what we have to do. Right now, you have to say one more word, and this fine bottle is yours. You'll take it and leave. No one the wiser. Where do I find Boyle?"

He leaned close enough to kiss my ear.

"For better or worse, here it is, Mikey. You're sittin' next to it. That door to your left leads to Boyle's office, not that I've been inside of it."

When I slid the shiny green jug across the table into Binney's quivering two hand grip, he breathed a sigh of fulfillment.

"You've earned it, Binney. Thank you."

He pulled his cap down to eye level and darted glances left and right.

"And I'd say you're welcome, Mikey. But we may both regret this night till our dying day, if we should live that long."

CHAPTER SIX

I was back sitting in my car outside of the Failte Pub, stymied for a next move, when my cell phone buzzed. I could tell from the tightness in Mr. Devlin's voice that what was coming would not make my night.

"Colleen called, Michael. They called her. They've shaken her up pretty badly."

"What did they say about Erin?"

"They were pretty rough. They threatened things—"

"Dammit! That could be my fault. I should never have called the Beverly police."

"Hang on, Michael. There's good news here too. At least we know Erin's still alive."

"Did Colleen talk to her?"

"Yes. That was part of the threat. They let Colleen hear her crying."

It took every ounce of restraint I could muster to stay in that seat. It was only possible because I had no idea of what direction to go.

"What else did they say?"

"They had a demand. Ten thousand dollars."

That jarred me from several different directions.

"How do they want it delivered?"

"They said they'd call tomorrow morning at eleven thirty with instructions."

I sat there with the phone in my lap, trying to square the inconsistencies that were banging off the walls of my mind.

I put the phone back to my ear when I heard Mr. Devlin's voice.

"What are you thinking, Michael?"

"Probably the same as you. It doesn't make sense. It can't be worth the risk of kidnapping to these thugs for ten thousand dollars."

"Let's think about it, Michael. Assuming it's not for the money, why make the demand?"

"I still think it's tied to that race that killed Danny. I'm sure they didn't plan on a murder charge. They may have a tiger by the tail. They've got Erin and don't know how to end it. If they hurt her, they'll be tracked down if it takes forever. If they can make it look like a kidnapping for money, it doesn't tie it to anyone involved in the race. They can return her alive, and it all blows over."

"That was my thought. They picked an amount low enough so they'd be sure Colleen could raise it."

"Did they say anything else?"

"They repeated the warning about going to the police."

"That means they still don't know we're in the game with her."

"Probably not. Colleen called on the prepaid phone you gave her."

"That could give us a free hand for the time being."

"Stay calm, Michael. Right now there are no safe moves."

"I'm trying. All I know now is that I'll be at Colleen's house tomorrow morning. She may need help with the ten thousand."

I dropped the phone onto the seat beside me and tried to separate panic from rationality. At some point, my mind leapt ahead to a conclusion. I knew to a certainty what I was going to do, but I had to backfill with logical justification, or I knew I'd carry the boulder of guilt for Erin's harm for the rest of my days.

I built from the ground up. First, this was no gang of loose canons looking for a ten thousand dollar score. The price was not worth the risk. That meant there was more to it. Second, the coincidence of that fixed race on the same day Erin was taken was too much to ignore. Third, If Binney O'Toole was to be believed, the tie-in to Vince Scully and Sean Flannery as stakeouts laid the whole rotten business at the door of Paddy Boyle. Fourth, every minute that little girl spent in their grip could be both dangerous and damaging. They were concerned about Colleen's talking to the police. If I could convince them that my involvement would not lead to the police, maybe I could broker a deal that would cut the time in getting Erin back to her mother.

It was that last part that drove the decision. I took another minute of chilling in the car just to quell the flashes of emotion that electrified my entire nervous system when I thought of Erin crying. When I finally felt stone cold, I laid the sweater and cap on the seat, put on the suit coat and tie, and walked back into the Failte Pub.

I took as deliberate and unhurried a pace as I could manage to the middle of the bar. I stood at the bar immediately to the right of Vince Scully. He gave me a bored glance and turned back to his beer.

I summoned the bartender over close before speaking.

"I want to see Mr. Boyle."

The bartender and Scully both looked more closely at the only one in the pub in a suit and tie before the bartender spoke.

"I don't remember Mr. Boyle sayin' he wanted to see you. Who are ya?"

I took a Devlin & Knight business card out of my pocket. I wrote two words on the back of it and handed it to him. I looked him dead in the eye and lowered my voice.

"Tell him it's about ten thousand dollars that's going to walk out that door in two minutes flat."

The sardonic look on the bartender's face faded. He picked up the phone. He said a few words and looked toward the back of the pub. I could feel the cold eyes of Vince Scully taking a new interest.

The door that Binney said led to Boyle's office swung open. A fat, fiftyish, splay-footed form filled the opening. A halo of frizzy, salt-and-pepper hair framed his otherwise bald head. He was tieless in an open suit coat that probably looked better on the mannequin.

He scanned the five or six men at the bar, and locked onto me. I watched him waddle his way down the bar until he was standing behind Scully. He looked at me, but he spoke to Scully.

"Who might this be, Scully? And what makes him think I owe him ten thousand dollars?"

Scully shrugged. I kept the voice level low.

"You got the message wrong, Mr. Boyle. I'm here to give you ten thousand dollars before I leave this place."

My heart would have leapt at any glint of uptake in Boyle's face, but there was none. It apparently needed more explanation. At least I had raised his interest.

"Would you look at this, Scully? He wants to give me ten thousand dollars just like that, if you please. Let's not keep the man waiting."

He turned on his heels and marched back into his office. I took it as an invitation to follow. I could feel Scully following close behind.

Boyle planted himself in a chair behind an oversized desk in a room about fifteen feet square. He pulled open a drawer and plunked his feet on it. I stood at the front of the desk. My shadow, Scully, leaned against the wall behind me beside the door.

I led from my strongest suit. "Mr. Boyle, I have a check made out to cash for ten thousand dollars. Consider it a delivery made free and clear."

"Free and clear is it, Boyo. Do you know who I am?"

Tough question. How informed I should seem was a touchy issue. When in doubt, hedge.

"Word has it you're a man of importance, Mr. Boyle."

He looked at Scully and broke into a grin.

"A man of importance, Scully. What do you think of that?"

Scully followed suit with a grin and a nod. Neither of us knew where this little scene was going until Boyle slammed the drawer shut with a kick and stood up. The volume went up ten decibels.

"Then take your head out of your arse, you little shyster. I learned one thing on the way up. No one ever gives me a damn dime without expecting twenty cents change. The question is what do you want from me? And the first word of bullshit I hear, Mr. Scully throws you out on your arse."

One thing was clear. Boyle enjoyed his own dramatics. The test was not to flinch. I kept the tone low. He was still holding my business card in his hand. I nodded to it.

"Turn the card over, Mr. Boyle."

He did. He glanced at the two words I had written on the back—Erin Ryan.

I figured that would lead to a rush of comprehension and we'd get down to business. I could not have misfigured more completely. There was not a glimmer of recognition.

"So? Who the hell is this?"

I could feel my heart physically fall to the pit of my stomach. I had hoped as never before that I could make the deal for Erin's release on the spot. The total brick wall I ran into caused a dizziness that made it difficult to go on standing. Worse than that, this absurd scene that I had promoted could result in harm to Erin and Colleen. In my silence, Boyle turned to Scully behind me. He held up the card.

"You know who the hell this is, Scully?"

I was snapped back into the game when I put two realizations together. Scully was clearly up to his ears in the kidnapping. He had been the surveillance at Colleen's home all afternoon. Match that with the total oblivion of his boss, and you got the inkling that Mr. Scully was playing his own game behind Boyle's back.

Scully's nerves must have been a bit strung out. There was a slight hesitation before he shot back a quick shrug. "No, Mr. Boyle."

I picked up the flash of a look in Boyle's eyes before he turned back to me.

"So what the hell is this about, Knight?"

"It's about a mistaken identity. My mistake. It's a business matter. I jumped to the conclusion that you were one of the parties involved. You can consider yourself fortunate that you're not. It's about to fall apart. There'll probably be indictments for anyone connected."

Of all of the words I could have used, that one struck home. All of a sudden this lawyer and his deal that was about to bring indictments were the last things he wanted in his office. He saw what I'd hoped – that his safest move was to clean house.

"Get this bum the hell out of here, Scully. Then come back."

I took that as an exit line. I walked through the bar and out to the sidewalk. Scully was one pace behind. When I cleared the door, I felt an iron grip on the back collar of my coat. It practically lifted me off the sidewalk and slammed me into the brick wall of the building and held me fast. Scully's face was an inch from mine. He spit the words through his teeth.

"You've got a death wish, lawyer. I'm going to grant your wish."

I could hardly get the words out of my constricted throat, but I knew it might be my last chance to say them.

"It'll be the last thing you'll ever do, Scully. You screwed up, and you know it."

That bought me a couple of seconds of silence, but not a loosening of the grip.

"You saw it. You saw that look. He asked if you knew the name on the card. You denied it without even reading it. You couldn't have read it from across the room, but you knew who it was. Boyle picked it up. Good luck when you go back in there."

I heard a click down around my belt. I felt the grip tighten. Something sharp was penetrating just below my ribs. I realized that his other hand was holding a knife.

"You going to kill me here? How are you going to explain that to

Boyle? Right now you can say you saw the card when I gave it to the bartender. You kill me, and Boyle's going to want some answers."

It was my best shot. I could only hope that Scully was a reasoning animal. During the next five seconds I could feel moisture run from the point of the knife. I knew he was drawing blood. I'd given up hope, when slowly the pain of the steel point lessened.

I used the moment to try to make sense.

"There are no police involved, Scully. You or whoever you're working for can have the ten thousand. I just want to end it."

The fist that gripped my collar banged my forehead against the brick wall with a crack. His mouth was next to my ear. "Then get your nose out of places it doesn't belong."

The grip on my collar tightened again. I gagged as I felt my breath cut off at the throat. He finally used the grip to throw me to the sidewalk like a rag doll.

Scully turned and walked back to the door of the pub. Before he disappeared inside, he looked down at me and made a gun of his fingers. He cocked his thumb and fired an imaginary bullet between my eyes. Imaginary or not, I thought I heard the angel choir.

CHAPTER SEVEN

By the time I got back to my apartment, the temple bells in my head were putting on a recital. I doubled the usual recipe for Motrin and wolfed down four. Within ten minutes the constant gongs were down to an occasional ding-dong. A butterfly bandage stemmed the trickle still oozing from the puncture below the ribs. A couple of squirts of Bactine soothed concerns about where Scully's knife might have been previously.

Before calling it a day, I called Mr. Devlin. I filled him in on my tête-à-tête with Binney O'Toole. That went well. He was less tickled, as was I, with my blundering into Boyle's den half-cocked.

"What in the name of the saints did you think, Michael? That he'd give you a receipt for the ten thousand and take the girl out of the closet?"

I had to admit that that was pretty much what I'd hoped. I guess I was counting on my boyish frankness to convince Boyle that after the wished-for exchange, I could guarantee no repercussions.

I decided there was no point in mentioning my little encounter with Scully on the way out. It would be like the kid who gets reamed by the teacher and then gets it again from his father when he gets home. I was more in need of a night's sleep than another pummeling.

The morning alarm at five thirty brought back reminders from previously silent muscles that Mr. Scully had gotten the best of me in the set-to. Added to that, it was two hours earlier than my usual wake-up call.

I made a brief stop at Starbuck's for a black eye. This little known Bucky special, strong black coffee with two shots of espresso, is guaranteed to rip out the most persistent cobwebs. Combine it with a couple of Motrin and you have the true breakfast of champions, and one I hope never to have to repeat.

After the previous day, I decided to follow the physicians' oath to the letter—first do no harm. Rather than exacerbate Colleen's situation further, I focused on the case against our client Hector Vasquez.

The backstretch at Suffolk Downs, as with any horse track, is a self-contained world. Life among the trainers' barns begins sometime before dawn. Grooms, stall muckers, feeders, hot-walkers, all go into their well-practiced routines like an ant colony. The buzz and hum that thirty years ago had a southern African-American accent is now uniformly in Mexican Spanish.

Trainers move from stall to stall to check legs and ankles for heat and decide on the regimen of the day's training for each horse before the exercise riders check in for instructions.

On the drive to Suffolk Downs, I called Rick McDonough, Black Diamond's trainer, on his cell phone and asked him to leave my name with security at the gate. That greased my path directly to barn 23.

I found Rick with a cluster of riders outside the stalls where grooms were tacking up for the morning ride-outs. He was giving specific instructions to the riders for each mount when he saw me. He pointed toward the coffee shack and gestured an invitation for a cup. I nodded acceptance and went to the shack to wait.

I had two cups waiting when he ambled up with a walking gait that could only be produced by bone breaks he had suffered as a saddle bronc rider in Montana in his youth. Rick was somewhere between fifty and eighty years old. It was hard to tell, since the creased, weather-worn skin of his face and the angular mismatch of all of his limbs could have passed for ninety.

Rick had trained racehorses for my adopted father, Miles O'Connor, back when my days began with mucking out the Augean stables on Miles's estate. They made a hell of a pair. Miles was the personification of the Harvard-trained, elite Boston trial lawyer, and Rick was a horse whisperer of mythic insights who was probably still wearing the jeans and boots he had worn when I was a stableboy. What linked them was a consummate trust and belief in the depth and truth of the character of each other. I don't think Miles had a closer friend than Rick, and it was mutual.

Rick accepted the cup of strong black caffeine I offered and leaned against the counter. He looked a good deal more life-worn and tired than the last time I saw him.

His only greeting was a shake of the head. "Hell of a thing about Danny."

I knew he felt it as deeply as I did. He had trained both Danny and me to breeze horses in the morning workouts. I did it until I passed a hundred and twenty pounds. Danny was smaller, so he kept on until Rick had given him every trick and nuance of riding a jockey can use. Rick believed in Danny through all of the pitfalls of money and the fast life that Danny fell into. Rick was there with an offer of a mount on Black Diamond when Danny finally climbed out of the pit.

"A hell of a thing indeed, Rick."

He just nodded.

"I better tell you up front. Hector Vasquez is being charged with his murder. I took on his defense."

He glanced over at me with one of those looks only a face like Rick's could give.

"There's a reason, Rick. I think he's innocent. It also gives me a chance to find out what happened to Danny."

It took him a second, but he nodded again and turned back to the cup. I understood him well enough to know he was saying it was all right. He accepted my decision.

"Tell me about Black Diamond. What was going on in that race?"

He picked up his cup and turned to lean his back against the counter.

" 'Bout two months ago. I got a call. Some Irish guy. He has a breeding farm somewhere in Ireland. He was sending this horse over. Wanted me to train him."

He walked a ways away from the counter to stand beside the track rail with no one in earshot.

"I'm gonna tell you this 'cause it might help clear Danny."

"Clear him of what, Rick?"

"Just listen, Mike. Danny came by to give the Diamond a light gallop about this time the morning of the race. Danny seemed good."

"Was Erin with him?"

"Yeah. She liked to watch from the rail. All the riders spoke to her. Anyway, Danny left the track about nine thirty."

"And Erin was with him?"

"Sure. Anyway, that afternoon, I'm saddling the Diamond in the paddock for the fourth race. Danny walks up for the mount. He knows my instructions. Let the Diamond run his race. Only thing different, I told him we needed this win for the stable. Things have been a little tight."

"So?"

"He didn't say anything. That's not like Danny. He just took the reins for a leg up, like he wanted to get it over with. Just before the pony led him off to the track, he turns around and looks at me like he's gonna say something. Only he doesn't."

I could feel the tumblers click. I figured by that time Erin had been taken. But Rick didn't know about Erin, and I couldn't tell him. Rick looked over at me for an explanation. I had no words.

"Damn, Mike. I think the race was fixed and maybe Danny knew it. I think he knew someone was going to get him during the race. If he'd told me, I'd have scratched the horse on the spot."

"Not your fault. I guess Danny was right. How do you think they did it? Danny didn't just fall off that horse."

Rick rubbed the random strands of his hair and shook his head. "I've watched that damn race on the film a hundred times. Two hundred in my mind. Whatever the hell they did, I can't see it. One thing's for damn sure. You're right. Danny doesn't just fall off a horse."

He finished the coffee and tossed the paper cup in the basket to get back to work. I had one more nagging question. "You saw Black Diamond's workout times before the race. Pathetic. Where'd he get the speed he showed in that race?"

Rick wiped his leathery face with a hand that was more callous than skin. He looked back at the track. "Horses are like people. Some days they want to run. Some days they don't."

"Yeah, Rick, and pigs are like dragonflies."

I didn't actually say that. I didn't say anything, which probably meant to Rick just what I was thinking. *Bull.* I had checked the *Daily Racing Form* fractions for that race. The first three furlongs had been run in blazing speed, and Black Diamond was close to the pace. It was as if the Diamond had been reborn that day as an athlete.

About that time, the exercise riders began to ride their mounts out to the track. A fair number of the regular Suffolk Downs jockeys were there to exercise horses in the morning workouts. Some do it to make extra money, some to get the feel of a horse they're going to ride in an afternoon race, and some just to be where they'd rather be than anywhere else on earth—hanging with the real horse people.

I was there to find out who was pulling whose strings in that race that ended Danny's life. I wore jeans and boots and a denim jacket, the better to blend in like a piece of wallpaper. Given my early Puerto Rican upbringing, there were two doors open to me. I could approach the Anglo jockeys or the Latinos. I chose the latter for no better reason than that there are more of them.

By about seven thirty, a number of Latino riders had finished the first ride and were clustered with coffee by the rail. I spotted several who had ridden in Danny's race.

The trick, since I'd be walking on tender ground, was to break the seal of secrecy. I knew they'd be cordial to any stranger, friendly to anyone who spoke Spanish without an accent, and hopefully willing to open the store to one of their own who had taken on representation of a Dominican jockey as a client.

I exchanged *hola*s and got a warm reception as anticipated. We coasted harmoniously through such sensitive topics as the weather, the track condition, and whether Big Papi Ortiz of the Red Sox would break his slump. With a bit of false confidence, I decided to wade into deeper waters before they disbanded for another ride-out.

"My name's Michael Knight. I'm a lawyer. I'm defending Hector Vasquez. He's charged with the murder of Danny Ryan."

That's a translation from Spanish. Needless to say, I had their full attention. The translation continues, "I need your help. The D.A.'s going after Hector with all guns blazing. I think she's after a lot bigger fish than Hector, but she's going to use him as a weapon to get them. I think that puts Hector not only in trouble but also in danger. Do you hear me?"

I got nods all around, but also a lot of foot shuffling that I took as a desire to relocate quickly. I needed a hook.

"What I need is information. Right now, the D.A. knows a hell of a lot more about that race than I do. That could be a fatal disadvantage in defending Hector. I know that race was sour one way or another. I need you to tell me how."

I looked from face to face. All I could see was tight lips and look-away head shakes.

"Just tell me this. Did Danny Ryan and Hector ever have any problems?"

One of the riders, the youngest by appearance, started to say something about an argument. The jockey beside him gave him a jolt with his fist behind his back. It stemmed the flow of words like shutting off a valve. I lost eye contact and a wall of silence slammed into place.

"Let me lay it out for you, gentlemen. If you stick together and help, we stand a chance of pulling Hector out of the fire. If you stay in your shell, the D.A.'ll pick you off one at a time till she gets what she wants. Please tell me what you know about that race."

The glow of collegiality I rode in on had drained to the last drop. One by one they had to "see a trainer about the next ride."

The last one to walk away was Vinnie Hernandez. When he walked close to me to throw his cup in the basket, I barely heard the words, "Go down to the starting gate."

I stayed by the rail for a few minutes in the unlikely event that anyone heard what Vinnie said. Then I walked the quarter of a mile to the left down the rail to where a starting gate had been set in position across the track. A few riders were taking their mounts to the gate for training in entering one of the narrow compartments and breaking smoothly when the steel doors swung open at the start of a race.

In about ten minutes, I saw Vinnie riding a dappled gray along the rail toward the gate. I stayed about thirty yards up from the gate to be out of earshot of the assistant starters on foot who guided, cajoled, or shoved recalcitrant starters into a compartment in the gate and held their bridles to keep their heads straight for the start.

Vinnie's horse was prancing sideways with a wide eye on that green steel monster that would soon swallow him up. I could see Vinnie working his left rein and right boot to have the gray pass me as close to the rail as he could. The rapid snorting breath of the colt all but covered up the words Vinnie forced through his unmoving lips.

"Alberto Ibanez. See him alone. Tell him I said this may be the time we talked about."

I was surprised that he said it in English, but then I noticed three Latino riders twenty yards behind him. He never looked at me, but his last words were, "¿me *comprendes?*"

"Sí, Vinnie."

"*Buena suerte, amigo.*"

CHAPTER EIGHT

It was a little before eleven when I pulled into Colleen's driveway. There was no need to play hide-and-seek. Scully and anyone he reported to knew I was in the game on Colleen's side. They apparently realized that we had still not gone to the police since nothing catastrophic seemed to have occurred since the previous day.

This time when I rang the bell, Colleen took my hand and led me into the house. It was dark and silent as a tomb without Danny's laugh and the constant jabber of little Erin. The wet droplets in each of Colleen's road-mapped eyes told me how much sleep she'd had.

"Anything new?"

She just shook her head, holding back the torrent that needed to escape. I took her by the arms and put her head on my shoulder. That did it. The floodgates burst. She sobbed until her entire body shook. I could feel the moisture seep through the shoulder of my shirt. She let it pour out of her until she had no more strength to sob.

I walked her back to a chair and just let her collapse.

"Have you had anything to eat?"

She just shook her head, almost too weak to say the word, "No."

"Stay there, Colleen."

I went into the kitchen and found the makings for what a physician friend of mine would have prescribed under the circumstances. I put four pieces of bread into the large toaster and turned the knob to "dark." In a house with a child, it was no trick to find the peanut butter. Since one more cup of coffee would have eaten a hole through my stomach lining, I made each of us a cup of double strength tea, black with a splash of sugar for energy.

When I came back to the living room with a tray, she gave it a glance that was less than eager.

"You are about to be treated to my mother's recipe for what's ailing both of us. Peanut butter on toast, tea, and commiserating company to share it with."

She gave me a sidewise look.

"I know your mother, Michael. She'd serve fried tortillas and salsa."

"This is the Irish equivalent. Danny would approve of the menu. In fact he'd insist that you eat. And you know it."

I set the tray down and took the first piece of toast. Reluctantly, she followed suit.

I was glad to see her sit up straighter when she finished. It was approaching eleven thirty.

When the mantel clock struck the half hour and the phone rang, we both jumped, even though it was what we were waiting for.

"Let me take this one, Colleen."

She was on her feet beside me at the phone.

"Okay, but I want to talk to Erin."

I steadied my voice for a quick hello.

There was silence on the other end. All I could hear was slow breathing. In about four seconds I heard the sharp South Boston accent of Scully.

"I said you had a death wish, lawyer. Looks like you've got a death wish for the kid too."

I wanted to go through the phone at him, but I wanted Erin's life more. Besides, I'd clearly lost round one of physical combat with Scully. I prayed for control.

"Nothing's changed, Scully. You knew yesterday that I knew you were in on it. There are no police involved. If there's any doubt, let me say it again. There's only one thing in this world I want from you.

I want Erin back unharmed. I'll follow your demands to the letter. We both walk away, and no looking back."

Another four seconds before he spoke. I knew he was controlling an Irish temper that was aimed directly at me. He might also have realized that dealing with me was his best shot at avoiding a kidnapping charge, or God forbid, a murder charge in connection with Erin.

"Ten thousand dollars. Cash. In a briefcase. Park Street subway. Wait at the bottom of the escalator. Eleven o'clock tonight. Exactly. You got that?"

"I'll be there. I'll have it,"

"The hell you will, lawyer. You're out of it. The mother brings it. Alone. You hear me?"

Alarms were going off like fire bells. Every nerve was screaming, *Bad arrangement*.

"No. She's been through enough. I'll—"

"Watch the papers tomorrow morning, lawyer. The police will have discovered the body of a kid."

"All right. All right. Whatever you want."

"Alone. One hint that she's covered, and the deal's off. Can you guess what that means?"

"I know."

"That's it. Eleven o'clock."

"Whoa. The hell that's it. How do we get Erin back?"

"That depends on how smooth the delivery goes."

"Scully, I've got two things you'd better hear. You're on thin ice with Boyle. I think you've also screwed up with whomever you pulled this kidnapping for, because it clearly wasn't Boyle. That ten thousand dollars is bullshit. You want that little girl off your hands as badly as I do. Get this. You have my absolute silence as long as we get Erin back unharmed. One small hint that it's otherwise, and you can check the front page of the *Globe* for some publicity you can't afford. That's a promise."

"You make a lot of noise for someone who's not holding any cards, lawyer. Don't push me."

"Give back the girl, Scully, and I'll have the pleasure of having nothing to do with you for the rest of my life. You have my word on that."

Another three seconds.

"Eleven o'clock. Alone."

Click.

Colleen was beside me trying to catch the conversation on both sides. I knew she caught the gist of it.

"What about Erin? Is she all right? You didn't ask to hear her."

"I'm sure she's all right, Colleen. His life depends on it as much as hers. I don't think she was with him or he'd have let us hear her to keep us in line."

What I didn't say was that I didn't press it because I didn't want Colleen—or me—to hear her crying. It would tell us nothing about her condition. It could even have been a recording. And we needed to keep our emotions under control.

"He wants you to deliver the money. I'll put it together. Do you think you can go through with the delivery?"

"Yes. Whatever it takes. How?"

"Park Street Station tonight at eleven. I'll pick you up here at ten."

My first stop was the in-town branch of my bank to draw out ten thousand dollars in cash. I figured I could get it faster than Colleen.

I drew some comfort from the fact that Scully was clearly new to the business of kidnapping. He didn't know enough to specify small denominations, old currency, unbound, unmarked, random serial numbers, no exploding dye—any of the usual precautions to prevent tracing. I was not about to educate him. The downside was that his inexperience could lead him to panic with Erin's life if his plans went off track.

I had the afternoon and evening to ride herd on nerves that were eating little craters in my insides. The best antidote was to accomplish something positive.

I was at Suffolk Downs before post time for the third race. I checked the *Globe* and found that Alberto Ibanez, the jockey Vinnie Hernandez mentioned, was riding the favorite in that race. I watched the race from the rail as Alberto broke from the starting gate with his mount on top and went the six furlongs coast-to-coast, as they say, opening the lead steadily to win by four lengths.

While Alberto went through the winner's circle photo-taking with the trainer and the owners, I waited just beyond the weigh-in shed. I knew that as the winner, he'd be the last jockey to unsaddle. He'd also be the last to pass through the weigh-in scales to certify that the horse carried the right weight before the results of the race could be made official.

I was alone at the rail beside the path Alberto would take to change silks for the next race. When he passed, I congratulated him in Spanish. He smiled and said, "*Gracias.*"

I asked for his autograph and held out my program. Alberto was the second leading jockey at Suffolk, so the request was not unusual. He came over and signed his name with the pen I offered. I could see him reading the words I wrote over the place he signed: Vinnie Hernandez sent me. He said this could be the time you talked about. Can I see you?

He handed the signed program back to me. I thanked him for the signature. He said, "*De nada.*" And nothing more.

I watched him walk up the path, and realized that he'd be seeing Vinnie Hernandez in the jockey's room.

I was at the rail by the paddock for the saddling of the horses for the fourth race. Alberto never looked at me when he came out with the other jockeys to mount up. He just looked at the head of his horse when he rode by on the way from the paddock to the track.

I stayed by the paddock rail, puzzling over a next move, when I

saw Alberto's groom, who sets out his change of silks and helps saddle his mounts, drift my way. He waived and said hello in Spanish
like an old friend.

I asked in a low, conspiratorial tone the question that is asked of
grooms in the same tone fifty times a day by the bystanders—"Any
good tips?"

He responded in Spanish in the same tone, "Sure. Let me see
your program."

He took my pen, wrote in the program, closed it, and handed it
back. I saw what he wrote and must have reacted with a slightly
stunned look. The groom just shrugged and went back to business.

At exactly five thirty that evening, I paid the entrance fee and
climbed the marble steps to the east wing of the Boston Museum
of Fine Arts. I knew my way to the room of Dutch masters. All of the
tourists, copying artists, and class trips had abandoned the room in
search of an evening meal.

I could see the back of one man, seated on the bench in the
center of the room gazing at *Portrait of a Woman Wearing a Gold
Chain* by Rembrandt. He was alone in the room with the exception
of the guard at the door. I sat on the bench beside him, although neither of us looked at the other. The guard was probably not within
earshot, but we kept it in Spanish.

"Alberto, my name is—"

"I know, Mr. Knight. I spoke with Vinnie. You seem to have made
an impression."

"Call me Michael. I'm representing Hector Vasquez."

"I know."

"Thank you for seeing me. You like Rembrandt?"

There must have been just a taste of surprise in my voice. He
gave me a sidewise glance.

"What's not to like? Tell you the truth, I'm more into Frans Hals.
All those happy Dutch smiles." He nodded to a Hals painting to the
right. "You seem surprised."

I couldn't help an uneasy smile. It seemed an occasion requiring truthfulness, even in details.

"A little."

"Uh-huh. Jockeys are not supposed to appreciate art, right?"

"I suppose they could. Nothing personal. I notice we're not exactly surrounded by jockeys. I also suppose you picked this place because you figured it's unlikely we'll run into any other jockeys here, no?"

He smiled. "Touché. Would it be offensive to notice that we're not exactly up to our elbows in lawyers either?"

This time the smile was real. Some ice had been broken. For some reason, I felt on steady ground talking to this man.

"I wish I had longer, Alberto, but I don't. Cards on the table. Hector is being charged with murder because Danny Ryan's death occurred in the course of what the D.A. wants to call a felony. The felony is a form of racketeering. She claims the race was fixed."

"What did Hector say? I'm sure you asked him."

"Hector is scared out of his wits and protecting his hindquarters. If I asked him if he'd ever jaywalked, he'd deny it. I need the truth about the race. If I don't get it, and I walk into that courtroom without it, the D.A.'ll blindside me in ways that'll kill us with the jury."

"So you're asking me?"

"Vinnie Hernandez gave me your name. Let me tell you what I think. Whatever happened to Danny Ryan to knock him off that horse was connected to fixing the race. Hector's horse won, so I have to believe that's how it was set up. But Hector says he didn't touch Danny. For no particularly good reason, I believe him. That's why I took the case."

He said nothing, but his eyes were glued on me.

"I need to know who was behind the fix. I figure if this race was set up, it's not the first time. Quite likely, it happens on some regular basis. That would mean you jockeys, to give you the benefit of the doubt, are under the thumb of someone who can pull your strings whenever it suits him. How'm I doing, Alberto?"

He looked back at the Rembrandt in silence. I gave him the slack.

"You have a family, Mr. Knight?"

"Michael."

"I'll stick to Mr. Knight till I know you better. We're not pals yet. Same question."

"I have people I care about."

He nodded. "So do I." He stopped there.

"I think I get the picture. You jump when you're told to—which means pulling your horse—or there are threats. I assume the threats come from an organization you believe can carry them out. How do you and the others feel about that?"

He looked around and found that the guard had moved to the adjoining room. Alberto was on his feet directly in front of me.

"I hear you did some exercise riding, Mr. Knight. Ever ride in a race?"

"No."

He nodded, and turned back to the Rembrandt.

"Think about this. A Thoroughbred can hit forty miles an hour. We balance on two little strips of metal and ride so close to the cleats of the horse ahead they sometimes click hooves. When they do, one horse or the other usually goes down. That puts the jockey under the horses coming from behind. There isn't one of us that hasn't been in the hospital. Broken bones, worse. Could happen every time we take a leg up on a horse for a race."

"I know what you're saying."

"No, you don't. Hear the rest. We love racing, the sport, so much that there isn't one of us would give it up for anything in the world. We love to compete for the win seven, eight times a day, and we forget the danger."

"Alberto—"

"Just listen."

His emotion was generating a heat I could almost feel.

"How would you like to sit on a horse in the starting gate, knowing you're risking being crippled for life before that horse crosses the wire, and being told there's no point to it. You have to lose the race. You're asking me how we feel about having the thing we love enough to risk everything for turned into a damned toy for a bunch of gangsters."

I hesitated to push it, but it was all cards on the table.

"I have to ask. Do you get paid to lose? Do you take the money?"

There was a fire in his eyes when he said it. "Yes. Now ask me why?"

"Go ahead."

"Because if any of us didn't take the money, they'd think we refused the fix. We could find one of our family dead. We know that."

I got up and stood close enough to whisper.

"Alberto, you and Vinnie Hernandez talked about ending it. Suppose I could give you a way to do that. Suppose I could give you an assurance that your family would be safe."

"What kind of assurance?"

"I'm working on that. Suppose I could satisfy you. Could you get the other jockeys to band together against this?"

"You don't know what you're up against."

"So I keep hearing. I'm learning. I won't come to you until I'm sure. When I do, will you work with me?"

I could see the faintest light in his eyes, and the beginnings of a smile.

"Who the hell are you, Mr. Knight?"

"I'm someone who wants you to call him Michael"

I held out my hand. He hesitated but finally took it.

"I'll say this much. When you're ready to talk, I'll listen, Michael."

CHAPTER NINE

I was back at the office just before six that evening for a much-needed conference with my senior partner. I breezed into his office, oblivious to the head scabs I still carried from my tête-à-tête with Scully.

"What the hell, Michael?"

"Looks worse than it is. Little bar incident. Good as new."

I sat while he insisted on examining the dents. I sometimes wondered if he went to law school or medical school. When he saw fit to release me from the Devlin Clinic, I told him the whole story, beginning again with Boyle to put it in context, and ending with my quasi commitment to Alberto Ibanez. There was no point this time in not touching on the Scully run-in.

"We have to see our client, Mr. Devlin. Can you get us past Billy Coyne?"

"We'll see. What's your theory?"

"I don't have one. Yet. If Hector didn't knock Danny out of the saddle, who did? There were riders behind him, but how could they reach him?"

Mr. D. was leaning back in his desk chair in his heavy thinking position looking at Boston Harbor.

"I've seen that race film a dozen times. I can't see how it happened."

"I've seen it two dozen times. I can't either."

"Could he have been shot with something from a distance? He

fell to the left, so it had to come from the right. Someone by the rail or in the stands?"

"I thought of that. It had to hit him pretty hard to send him out of the saddle. That means it would have left a mark."

"Billy Coyne sent over the autopsy report this morning. I scanned it. No mention of a mark."

"They may not have looked for it if it wasn't fatal. Can we get our own medical examination?"

"We can and will. I filed a motion in court this morning to allow an independent examination of the body. Billy assented to it, and the judge allowed it. Dr. Gregg's doing it this afternoon."

"Good. That could help clear Hector."

"It's a dream, Michael. Don't count on it. That would have been one hell of a shot at a moving target, in public. Besides, Billy Coyne's sharp. I'm sure he had the coroner check for the same thing the first time around."

"It seemed like a good straw, and we are grasping."

"Granted."

"At least we know this much. The race was fixed for Hector's horse to win. Hector was obviously in on the fix."

"Which he denies. Will you believe me now that clients lie to us?"

The debate that started the first day I walked into Mr. D.'s office was raising its head for another round, with me on the short end.

"Not to get sidetracked, Mr. Devlin, the next question is who was behind the fix."

He grinned at my end run, knowing he had scored a few points for his side. I pressed on.

"From what Ibanez implied, I get the idea these race fixings happen with some regularity. Whoever's pulling it is connected enough to have all those jockeys scared stiff."

"Smells like organized crime. But which group?"

"That's the twist. I'm certain Erin's kidnapping is connected to that fixed race. We know Scully is up to his ears in the kidnapping.

That should lead us to Boyle. But it doesn't. As I read Boyle, he never heard of Erin Ryan."

"So what do you hope to get from our mendacious client?"

"Maybe with a little pressure he'll tell us who's behind fixing that race. Behind all the fixes. And why the dead end at Scully."

Mr. D. gave it three seconds of pondering before dialing the number of the district attorney. Another twenty seconds and he had Billy Coyne on the line.

After the usual banter, Billy arranged for an interview with our client, Hector, the following morning in police headquarters at Government Center. The unusual rigmarole to see our client was caused by the D.A.'s decision to hold him out of the general jail population in protective custody. She still chose not to disclose the reason, and Billy was bound by her orders.

It was nearly eight that evening when I left the Prudential Center Legal Seafood restaurant. With a nerve-wracking night ahead, I succumbed to the fortification of a baked stuffed lobster so sinfully good that it should have been called "Illegal Seafood." I had two hours before leaving to pick up Colleen for a meeting with the devil in the Park Street subway. It being Monday night, there was only one place on earth this creature of habit would spend it.

The little row of circular stairs that led from the darkness of Beacon Street near the golden domed State House into the deeper darkness of one of Boston's hidden jewels was for me like a passage from the helter-skelter world into semiparadise. Two feet inside of Big Daddy Hightower's jazz club, I could feel the fractiousness of the outside life ebbing and the magic of Daddy's stand-up driving bass coaxing harmony and joy back into my soul.

With the exception of a tired ten-watt bulb on the miniscule bandstand, there is scarcely a ray of illumination to be found in the club when the musicians are playing. It's deliberate on Daddy's part to keep conversation during the sets to zero.

After five years' worth of Monday nights, I can find my favorite stool at the bar by the Braille method. I've never reached a full sitting position before my favorite barkeep, Sam, has placed three fingers of that liquid gold called Famous Grouse Scotch over three ice cubes within an inch of my expectant grasp. This night was no exception.

I had used my cell phone on the way over to call Terry O'Brien, one of the three nonfamily people on earth whom I rank above my Corvette—Lex Devlin and Big Daddy being the other two. I left a voice mail asking if she'd like to meet me at Daddy's if she had the time. I knew her chores as fashion consultant for Filenes would keep her at work until sometime later.

Meanwhile, about an inch into the Grouse, I felt an enormous presence slide in next to me at the bar, and a hand that could palm a watermelon resting on my shoulder.

"Must be Monday night, Mickey. Who needs a calendar with you around?"

"Hey, Daddy. You were really cooking up there. Who was with you? That sax sounded like Sonny Ammons."

"Good ear, son. Yeah, Sonny's in from Chicago. Got a gig at Dizzy's in New York. He always passes through here."

"Who doesn't?"

"Yeah, well, only one thing missing. I want to hear that piano that reads my mind. Let's get it on before Sonny leaves."

If I had a reason to decline, it could not have withstood the giant arm that lifted me off the barstool and guided my feet to the stand. I had met Sonny on his previous swing through Boston. He, like every major league jazz musician, holds a pedestal in his mind for Big Daddy and the swath he cut in the New York scene in the days of Charlie Parker, Miles Davis, John Coltrane, and the other musical behemoths.

Daddy deposited me on the piano bench and wrapped himself around his stand-up bass. Sonny came back up, sax in hand. Daddy gave us a full ten seconds to renew acquaintances before he started a driving introduction on the bass that you could feel in your stom-ach. I recognized the tune, and the three of us launched into our own conception of Ellington's marvelous "It Don't Mean a Thing."

We found ourselves on the same wavelength and cruised through nine or ten choruses before Daddy brought us back down to earth. I had been so totally absorbed that I didn't notice an auburn-haired goddess led by Sam to a front row table. That little ten-watt bulb cast a beam that reflected off of a gleaming white smile and two lips that blew a kiss in my direction. After nearly six months of dating, the sight of Terry O'Brien was still like plugging my heart into an electric socket.

Daddy waved to her and said, "You can have him in ten minutes, Terry." She smiled and waved to Daddy, whose size could belie the romanticism in his heart. He took us so smoothly into "There Will Never Be Another You" that it would have brought tears to writer, Mack Gordon's eyes—as it did to Terry's.

We were into the final chorus, when one of the customers, a man of about Daddy's height, if not proportions, came quietly up to the stand and slipped a note with a request on the piano in front of Daddy. It happens from time to time, although deep-rooted jazz fans generally know that jazz is such a personal mode of expression that they avoid requests and leave the selections to the mood of the mu-sicians.

Daddy glanced at the note and nodded to me. I picked it up when I had a free hand. It caught my attention because it was a re-quest for a little-played but exquisite tune by Frigo, Ellis, and Carter called "Detour Ahead." It also had my name on it. When I opened the note to the inside, there was a message printed in large letters to compensate for the lack of light.

Mr. Knight. When the set ends, stay on the stand. I'll escort Ms. O'Brien out the back door. Better if you're not seen to-gether. Wait for me. Important we leave together. (TDB)

I'd have been completely flummoxed but for the "TDB," which meant he was one of Tom Burns's men. I had to assume that Tom had put him on me at the request of Mr. Devlin. Beyond that, I was in a disturbing state of ignorance.

We finished the song we were playing, and I watched as the tall man came up behind Terry. He whispered something to her that brought a look of total dismay in my direction. He overcame hesitancy on her part by lifting her out of the seat by the elbow. They walked together toward Daddy's office in the back of the club. His whispering as they walked seemed to freeze her inclination to look back at me on the stand, where I sat with a similar look of dismay.

The lights in the club came up a tiny degree between sets. A number of these cloak-and-dagger incidents involving me over the years had reduced the shock value to Daddy. He gave me a look, not of puzzlement, but simply inquiring what he could do to help save my imperiled posterior this time. I gave him a "Who knows" shrug, and sat there.

In about thirty seconds, the tall man was back, taking my arm with a rock-hard left hand to keep me close while we made our way through the tables to the front door.

I assumed we were making a straight line for the street until he suddenly veered toward the bar. He grabbed a fistful of the back of the jacket of a small red-haired man with a weasely looking face sitting at the bar. He lifted the little man bodily off the seat and scarcely let his feet touch the floor on the way up the stairs and into the chill of Beacon Street.

We turned right and marched up the sidewalk like two puppets in the hands of a puppeteer. When we reached my Corvette parked at the curb, the big man let go of his left-handed grip on me and held out his hand.

"Key!"

I obeyed the command and handed it over. The tall man hit the unlock button and pulled open the driver's side door. He shoved the little man into the seat, pushed the key in the ignition, and stood back.

The little man sat there with every drop of blood drained from his reddish complexion. Even clutching the steering wheel, his hands were shaking violently.

The tall man leaned into his face. "Start the car."

The little man was frozen.

"Start the car, you little weasel."

He gained enough control to just shake his head.

The big man reached across his chest and gripped the key. One twist would have started the engine. The little man grabbed the massive forearm with his quivering fingers and pleaded to the point of practically sobbing.

The big man grabbed a fistful of the front of his jacket, lifted him out of the car with one motion, and deposited him on the sidewalk. He put his lips next to the little man's ear.

"Fix it. And then, by heaven, you'll start it."

The big man kept a grip on the tail of his jacket while he followed the little man to the front of the car. He gave the little man slack enough to lie on the street in front of the car and disengage a metallic-looking device with wires from under the engine. He handed it to the big man, who redeposited him in the driver's seat.

"Now start it."

The little man could hardly get a grip on the key with his quivering fingers to give it a twist. When he finally managed it, the faithful Corvette engine sprang to life.

The big man hauled him out of the car and plastered him against the hood while he ran his hands quickly through his pockets. He pulled out a wallet and rifled through it one handed, pulling out a driver's license with his teeth. He took a wad of folding money out of another pocket and flipped through it until he found something of interest. He held it up to show me that inside of a role of American bills was a wad of ten euro notes.

His final plunge into the rear pants pocket produced a passport. The big man handed it to me. I saw that it was issued by the Republic of Ireland.

The big man turned back and lifted the little man off the hood of the car with two hands and held him close enough to whisper, "Who sent you?"

Sweaty beads covered the small man's forehead that had gone from bleached white to crimson red. No words came out. He just shook his head violently. The tall man put his lips practically on the ear of the small man.

"That question was for you, you cowardly little rat. Who sent you to do his dirty work?"

Through all of his shaking, the little man found a voice with a heavy Irish accent. "I can't. Please. Whatever you do to me is nothing to what he'd do to me. I can't."

The tall man kept his grip while he looked to me. "He's probably right. What's your pleasure, Mr. Knight?"

I was still recovering from the thought of what would have happened if I had just bumbled out of the club and started the car myself. I walked up next to the small man, who was still held by my tall rescuer. I said in the calmest voice I could muster, "You'll deliver this message to whoever the hell sent you. Are you listening?"

He looked from the big man into my eyes. I was comforted to see that the look of fear had not diminished.

"Memorize this and say it to whoever it is verbatim. 'I don't give a damn about anything but getting that child back. Unharmed. You have nothing to fear from me or the girl's mother as long as we get her back.' Did you get every word of that?"

He nodded vigorously with a hint of relief in his eyes and looked back at the man who still had him in his grip. I pulled his attention back with a rap on the shoulder.

"That's half of it. Here's the rest. 'If that girl is harmed in any way, you'll have trouble you can't even imagine.' Have you got that message? All of it?"

His head was nodding affirmatively with every ounce of energy he could muster.

"Then deliver it. You're on borrowed time, little man. Use it well."

When the big man's grip eased, he got his legs under him and ran down Beacon Street like he was training for the Irish Derby.

Tom Burns's man handed me the little weasel's driver's license. He looked around to be sure we hadn't picked up any spectators. He gave me the best piece of advice I'd had since kindergarten. "Try to stay out of trouble, Mr. Knight."

I dearly wished I could follow it, but I knew it was not in my future.

I got into my Corvette, thanking God and the tall man that it was not scattered all over Beacon Hill, and me with it. I checked the passport and driver's license before starting up. If they were legitimate, the little man was Padraig Noonan of 412 Gardner Street in Dublin. The spider's web had just expanded across the Atlantic, and still no sighting of the spider.

CHAPTER TEN

Colleen was halfway out the door when I pulled up in front of the house. Even the tunnel traffic on the way back to Boston was light at ten thirty at night. We parked in a garage on Boylston Street. I walked her to the top of the long escalator at the entrance to the Park Street station of the MBTA.

The bells of the Park Street Church sounded eleven o'clock exactly. What I was about to do went against every alarm in my system. I could hear the ghosts of John Hancock, Paul Revere, Samuel Adams, and, for the love of Pete, the real Mother Goose, all keeping vigil in the Old Granary Burial Ground next door, warning me against it. I agreed with their forebodings, but it still seemed the better part of valor to follow the directions of the kidnappers to the letter. That meant sending Colleen into the pit alone.

I handed her the briefcase holding ten thousand dollars. My final words were, "Just wait down there. Let him come to you. I'll be right here if you need me."

I watched the long down escalator swallow her up, while I stood frozen at the top, looking into the small illuminated area visible below and listening for any sound.

Four and a half minutes went by after Colleen disappeared from my view. I was pacing with antsiness, when the interminable silence below was split by a gunshot. I ran three steps at a time down the moving stairs. A third of the way from the bottom, someone passed me in a long black raincoat and black brimmed hat running the steps on the up side of the escalator. He was holding the briefcase. My first impulse was to jump the divider and tackle him. The second impulse a fraction of a second later overruled the first. Get to Colleen.

As the black raincoat flew past me, I could see no face, but a voice hissed out the words, "You bollixed it, Knight. You've yourself to blame." The accent was Irish, but the voice was not Scully's.

It took all my willpower not to try to run him down. My first priority was still Colleen. When I reached the bottom, I looked to the left. She was slumped against the wall. I got to her in three seconds. It was actually a relief to hear her sobbing. I lifted her up.

"Are you hurt, Colleen?"

All I could hear through the sobs was, "He said we'll never get her back."

"What else?"

She just shook her head and sobbed against my shoulder. I looked around for some hint of what went wrong. I caught a glimpse of a gray sleeve on the tiny counter of the information booth across the room at the foot of the escalator.

I left Colleen just long enough to run to the booth. The sleeve belonged to the MBTA uniform of a man slumped between the seat and the wall. He was a man in his thirties with dark black hair, a small goatee, and a red oozing hole in the center of his forehead.

I could feel my legs begin to weaken. I rested my head against the glass for just a moment to pull it together. The picture suddenly opened up. He shouldn't have been there. At that time of night, the MBTA leaves the booth unmanned. That was why they had set the time at eleven.

The man in the booth had to be one of Tom Burns's men. Mr. Devlin must have alerted Tom. The man was there to keep an eye on Colleen so she wouldn't be totally unprotected. The man in the raincoat must have taken him by surprise.

I phoned Tom. It seemed best to let him notify the police rather than get into a question-and-answer session with them when there were no answers I felt comfortable giving.

There was a bottomless empty, drained feeling in both of our hearts as I drove Colleen home in silence. Whatever hope had buoyed her up was gone. I had no idea whatever of any next step that could inspire one drop of optimism.

The next day, I met Mr. Devlin at police headquarters for a session with our client Hector Vasquez. We had to press on with the preparation of a defense, first because of our commitment to the client, but a close second, because I still had a notion that the fixed race and Erin's kidnapping were part of the same plan. The only factor I couldn't allow myself to compute was the possibility—or likelihood—that Erin was now more of a problem to them alive than otherwise. The kidnapping had escalated to murder, the murder of Danny Ryan. That wouldn't go away with the return of Erin. She was now excess baggage.

Billy Coyne met us and took us to an interrogation room. He left us alone with Hector. Mr. D. gave me the lead.

"Hector, we've got to pull some things together. Let's start with the big one. Who was behind the fixing of that race?"

Hector forced a blank look on his face. "I don't know anything about a fixed—"

"And we could say 'Poor Hector. He's just a little innocent lamb caught up in a big meat grinder.' We could leave here with a head full of bullshit and almost guarantee you a life sentence. You couldn't give the prosecutor a better gift than our trying this case with our heads in a dark place."

I had his attention, but still no words flowed.

"Understand the rules. Whatever you tell us in this room can go no further. You have the attorney-client privilege. And you've got something better than that. You've got Mr. Devlin's and my word that it will never get out."

He looked from one of us to the other with an expression I couldn't read.

"What, Hector? Speak."

He looked down at his folded hands on the table and just shook his head.

"Listen to me. I spoke with Vinnie Hernandez and Alberto Ibanez. They say it's time to get this monkey off your backs. I think they can get the other jockeys to go along. But someone's got to make the first move. Given the circumstances, it should be you."

I think I touched something that set off a debate in his mind. He still looked down, but his face showed the struggle that was going on inside. His words were just mumbled.

"You don't know what's going on."

"No, I don't. But I seem to be taking one hell of a pasting finding out."

He looked up and saw the face scabs from my meeting with Scully.

"I'll tell you what I've learned so far. Paddy Boyle is everyone's hero and King Rat at the same time. I get the idea he's some kind of Irish godfather in South Boston. He's got a thug named Scully who does some of his dirty work. I think he's the one who has all of you jockeys in his pocket so he can call the outcome of a race before it's run. That's what I think. But I don't know it, so I can't use it to find out who knocked Danny out of the saddle. I'm assuming it wasn't you, which is giving you one hell of a benefit of the doubt. Now I need a little give on your part. Your turn."

He was starting to sweat, which in this case was a good sign.

"Tell me, Hector. Are Boyle and Scully the problem?"

The struggle was cutting lines in his forehead. "If I say it, they'll find out. They'll know it came from me."

"If you don't say it, and I stir the pot with those two, they'll assume it anyway. They know you're our client. Where else would we get the information?"

Now he really went into the jitters.

"You don't know what he's like. Scully. Some of us have families. You have to leave that part alone, Mr. Knight."

"Nothing would please me more. But I can't. What do you know about Danny's daughter, Erin?"

He looked surprised at the jump shift. "What do you mean?"

"I'll lay it out for you. She's been kidnapped. She was taken before the race. You said Danny was acting funny. Did he say anything about it?"

Hector went into a complete shutdown. He just froze up. I knew it would take verbal dynamite to get what I needed. I nodded to Mr. Devlin and stood up. I put all my hopes into one exit speech.

"Get this, Hector. I may be stumbling around in the dark, but I'm going to go on stumbling till I find that little girl. If that causes Scully and the rest to assume the word came from you, then the chips will just have to fall as they may. I won't mention your name, but you're no dummy. I'll do my best for you, even without your help, but my number one is Danny's daughter."

Hector's eyes were the size of half-dollars when Mr. D. and I headed for the door. We didn't look back. It was Hector's voice that stopped us at the door.

"Mr. Knight. Please. Come back."

"Not unless there's a reason."

He waved us back to the chairs. "What do you want to know?"

"Who's behind the race fixing? Is it Boyle?"

His voice started in a whisper, but it was enough. "Yes."

"Was Scully the contact with the jockeys?"

"Yes. He brought a couple of others the first time. I don't know their names. They roughed a few of us up to show they meant business."

"When was that?"

His voice was getting stronger. "About a year ago."

"How often did they make you fix races?"

"First it was every couple of months. It's been every month for the last four months. It's getting more frequent."

"Same time each month?"

"Yes. So far. Always around the fourteenth."

I looked at Mr. D to see if that rang any bells with him. He just shook his head to let me keep rolling.

"How did they pay off the jockeys?"

He looked around out of instinct, although there were just the three of us there.

"Scully gave me the money. I gave it to the jockeys he told me to."

"Not all of them?"

"Only the ones with horses that had any chance of winning."

"The day Danny died. Was that race fixed?"

"Yes. I was supposed to win."

"Was Danny in on the fix?"

There was a hesitation I didn't understand, but he answered the question. "No. His horse ran like a cow in the workouts. He didn't have a chance."

I still wondered how Black Diamond turned into a speed horse overnight. I made a mental note to follow it up.

"Now to the most important part, Hector. Did Danny tell you about the kidnapping of his daughter before the race?"

"No. Like I told you. He just acted funny. He was jumpy, tense. We didn't talk to each other."

"Did he say anything at all about Erin?"

"No."

I looked to Mr. Devlin to see if anything was overlooked. He just shook his head. We left with little more than we came in with, but at least the spotlight was clearly on Boyle and Scully.

The rest of that Tuesday went by like molasses. I was filled with an emptiness that ran deeper than any I've ever known. Even Danny's death took second chair to an almost hopeless concern for little Erin.

I busied myself with phone calls and coffee breaks. There was a brief due in a week in another case, but I couldn't focus enough gray cells to put it together.

Just before Julie left for the day, she took a phone call. She came to the door of my office to say it directly.

"He didn't give his name. He didn't want to talk to you. He just wanted me to give you a message."

"And the message was?"

"Michael, I don't like this. I got chills just listening to that voice. I think you should ignore it."

"Julie, I can't ignore it if I don't hear it. What's the message?"

"He just said, 'Tell the lawyer. Last pew, right side, Saint Anthony Shrine, Arch Street. Tonight, six thirty.'"

"That's it? Did he mention the name, Erin?"

"That's all of it. He hung up. If you want my advice, which you don't, don't go there."

"No Problem, Julie. I know who it is. He's harmless."

I never lie to my secretary, except when it's necessary to subdue her mothering instincts. This time, it took a bit of method acting. I was sure it was Scully, and no one had called him "harmless" since he left the crib.

By six thirty, the sun was well down. The Franciscan Friars who administer what is locally know as the Church on Arch Street a few blocks from our office had said the last Mass for the day. The back of the church was in a hushed darkness and empty except for a few late drop-ins and homeless dozers.

I welcomed the comforting peace that pervades that church. It was an antidote to the sense of personal dread I felt for both myself and Erin. I took a seat a couple of pews from the rear on the right side and settled into an internal communication with the Lord to whom I prayed for something to break the standstill.

Five minutes into the first rest I'd felt in days, a low voice behind me that sounded like gravel and sandpaper brought me straight up.

"Sit down, lawyer. Keep lookin' straight."

I did. "What is it, Scully? Are you going to kill me here in church?"

"You'll probably be dead before this ends, but not at my hand."

Since my question had not been rhetorical, the answer un-clenched my fingers a bit on the front of the pew.

"Then what do you want? Like you said, you're holding the cards."

"Not me. I'm not your problem. I want out."

I went from the last prayer I thought I'd say on this earth to a state of total confusion.

"Out of what? And what have I got to do with it?"

"Just listen. I'm no choirboy. I've done things that might shock the father over there in the confessional. But I've got my limits."

"Such as."

I could hear him shifting around on the pew behind me. He leaned forward until I could feel his breath.

"I had no part in kidnapping the girl."

"Really. Wasn't that you staking out the Ryan's house the day I came there?"

"I followed orders. I was told to watch the woman to see if she went to the police. That's all."

"Whose orders? Boyle didn't even recognize the Ryan name. I thought you worked for him."

"I'll say what I've got to say, and no more. Boyle had no part in the girl either."

"Then who did? Who am I dealing with?"

"I don't know all of it. And that's the truth. I can give you a name. That's my part of the deal."

"What deal? Why the change? The last time we met you nearly decapitated me."

"I want no part of the doin's with the little girl. But you with your nosin' around. You'll suck me into the whole business till you brand me a kidnapper and worse. Like I said, I want out of the whole thing."

The ground was shifting under me so fast I could hardly catch up. At that moment, I only knew I'd promise anything for a name that could lead me to Erin.

"What do you want from me?"

"They say you're an honorable man, lawyer. I've asked. I want your word that I'll not be tarred with things I've never done."

My conception of Scully was rocked by his use of the word "honorable." I knew there was something below the surface that hadn't come out yet.

"You have my word in exactly those terms. If what you said about Erin is true, you'll have nothing to fear from me."

"Fair play. Then I'll give you what I've got, little as it is, and remember I've done it."

"Where is she?"

"She's not here. The day she was taken, they took her out of the country for safekeeping."

"Where?"

He leaned still closer. "I'm just sayin' what I picked up from their talk. They took her to Ireland. Dublin."

That was a numbing blow to think of her that far away. "Who took her?"

"I'll give you a name. It's all I have. I heard it last night. Seamus McGuiness. Killarney Street, somewhere in the north of Dublin."

"Who are these people?"

I heard a stirring behind me as he stood.

"I've said what I came to say. But I'll give you this. You'd be better off against ten of me than any one of them."

I heard him move away. I spun around and grabbed the end of his coat.

"What happened, Scully? Something happened to turn you around."

He looked back at me. "I'll have no part of their doin's. That little girl—"

"What? What did you hear about Erin?"

He jerked his coat out of my hand. He sidestepped to the end of the pew. I thought he was going to leave without a word. I pierced the silence with a whisper that must have been heard at the altar.

"Scully, if I find her, will I find her alive?"

He turned around. He looked me in the eye, and he drove a dagger through my heart with one word.

"No."

CHAPTER ELEVEN

I got up Wednesday morning with a headache, a cold, and a decision. The cold was the result of walking through a drenching, chilling rain on nearly every paved street in Boston the night before until I could come to a decision. It came in two parts. The first part was that I clearly lacked the stone-cold callousness it would have required to take the last vestige of hope away from Colleen. Could I, on my worst day, summon the nerve to tell her that she would not even be able to kiss her baby one last time and lay her to rest with God? That she was just gone? I don't think so. It may come to that, but not today.

That led to the second part. If only to give her the chance for that last goodbye, I had to find what they'd done with Erin's body. That meant that the decision to go to Dublin was a fait accompli.

Since I was still awake at five thirty a.m., I substituted a shower and a breakfast of Motrin and black coffee for a night's sleep. I knew that any flight to Dublin would leave in the evening. That gave me the day to pull together any leads I could squeeze out of my slim sources for cracking the shell in a foreign country. I was working around an appointment at eleven, and missing that one was out of the question. Colleen had arranged for a funeral service for Danny at their parish church—family only. That included me.

By six a.m., I was at the backstretch at Suffolk Downs. I still could not shake the feeling that Black Diamond's part in that race was linked to the kidnapping of Erin.

I caught Rick McDonough right after his briefing of his exercise riders. I held two cups of that good rich mud they serve for coffee at the backstretch shack. That was enough to sidetrack him to the rail for a couple of quiet words.

"How's Danny's wife, Mike?"

I couldn't answer, just thinking of how completely devastated she'd be if she knew that both Erin and Danny were lost to her. A simple head shake conveyed the word that she was not on top of the world.

Rick just looked into his coffee cup. I knew how deeply this tough old cowboy was wrung out by Danny's death.

"I need some information, Rick. I'm probably stepping on toes, but I have to do it. This is for Danny."

The old man turned around and leaned against the rail. He looked me dead in the eye. "To hell with them all. For Danny. What do you want to know?"

"Black Diamond. You said he was sent over from Ireland. Where in Ireland?"

"There's a place west of Dublin called The Curragh. It's in County Kildare. Lot of horse farms there. This one raises just Thoroughbreds. It's a small operation as near as I can tell. I don't know a hell of a lot about it."

"What's it called?"

"*Dubh Crann* Stables. It means Black Tree."

"You speak the language, Rick?"

I got the first half smile. "I got trouble enough with English."

"Who contacted you?"

"His name's Kieran Dowd."

"What does he look like?"

"Dammed if I know. We did the whole thing over the phone. I don't think he ever came over here."

I walked over to lean on the rail beside him so we could lower our voices.

"What was the deal, Rick?"

He wiped his face with a hand grown oversized from a life of pulling on reins and halters. I'd seen him make that gesture every time he was wrestling with a decision.

"They deliver the horse. I train him. Enter him in that race on MassCap day. That was it. We keep a third of the winnings and anything we can make on a bet. It looked good at the time."

I moved even closer, because this was the touchy part.

"Rick, what was good about it? His breeding is mediocre, to be generous. His workouts were the pits. I could practically beat him on foot."

He gave me a sideways look with a trace of a grin that died as soon as it was born.

"You don't know what we've been through, Mike. This stable's on its last legs. These are not the days of Miles O'Connor. Look down that row." He pointed his chin to the stables. "There's not a one of them that's not nursing swollen knees, biting shins, hot ankles. I can't run any of them more than once in six weeks. When I do, they barely cover the hay bill."

He shrugged.

"I'm not griping. It's the life I chose for the good days and bad. But this deal came out of the blue. I thought maybe lightning could strike."

I could have said, "Based on what?" I could have asked out of what miraculous depth the Diamond pulled the burst of speed he showed in that race. But I'd asked it before and got no answer.

It was around nine thirty when I caught Mr. D. on his way out of the office.

"I'm walking up to Federal Court, Michael. Walk with me."

He caught a good look at me in the elevator.

"Good Lord, Michael. Have you been to bed this week?"

"It's just a little cold. It'll pass. I need your help with something."

He gave me his immediate you-name-it nod, and then his serious look. "This involves little Erin, doesn't it? Any news?"

The question tightened the bands around my heart again.

"Yes." I just shook my head.

"Dear God, you don't mean—"

I could only nod.

"Have you told Danny's wife?"

"Not yet."

"How did you hear?"

I filled him in on my meeting with Scully.

"Can you trust his word?"

"About as far as I could throw City Hall. But I think he was on the level this time. That's what I want to talk to you about. I have to go to Dublin."

If it were anyone else, I'd have had to paint the rest of the picture. Mr. D. understood without words. He just said, "When?"

"Tonight."

"What do you need?"

"I need to get together with Billy Coyne. We both know he's holding back on what's really behind indicting Hector. I still think there's a connection with Erin. He might have something that could give me some leverage over there."

We reached the street. Mr. D. was going to cross Franklin toward the Water Street entrance to Federal Court. He stopped before crossing and took out his cell phone, one of his few concessions to the twenty-first century. He hit one of the numbers on speed dial. While it was ringing, he looked back at me.

"Meet us for lunch, Michael. Twelve thirty."

"Will he do it?"

"I'm going to invite him to Locke-Ober's. My treat. He'd have had lunch with Osama Bin Laden on those terms."

The funeral service for Danny at eleven was brief, but about as personal as you could get. As an orphan, Danny had no family. Nor did Colleen on the East Coast. It was just Colleeen and me and Father Mack, who had known Danny and Colleen since he had married them. The brevity of the service was Colleen's request until she was up to arranging a more inclusive memorial service. There may have been a shortage of people, but there was no shortage of tears, prayers, and memories.

True to Mr. D.'s prediction, Billy Coyne met us at Locke-Ober's for lunch. I watched him savor the last morsel of his lobster Savannah in silence. He slowly wiped from his lips the evidence of the best meal that public servant had had in recent memory and sat back.

"Now, Lex. Will you tell me what it is I've been so elegantly bribed to disclose?"

The word "bribe" could be used in jest with ease between those two old warhorses since neither was susceptible to the slightest breach of ethics the word suggested. It did, however, bring down the curtain on the continuous flow of Irish banter that had pervaded the meal. The low tone of Mr. D.'s voice opened the second phase.

"Billy, I want you to listen with both ears to what Michael has to say. I want you to consider who's saying it. You know you can trust my word to the limit. I'm putting my word behind what Michael's offering."

The ball was squarely in my court, and I couldn't afford to whiff on it.

"Mr. Coyne, I'm going to tell you something I swore I wouldn't divulge to anyone. Last night the rules changed."

I poured across the table everything I knew about the kidnapping of Erin and finished with the final word of her death. His eyes were riveted on mine. They were cold as stone when I began. By the time I finished, they reflected the empathy for Erin and Colleen he was sharing with the two of us.

"I'm going to Dublin tonight. At least I can try to bring her body back for burial before I break it to Colleen."

Billy looked over at Mr. Devlin. Mr. D. nodded and put his seal on everything I'd said.

"So what do you want from me, kid?"

I knew I'd graduated from the "kid" ranks with my senior partner, but not quite yet with Billy Coyne. No matter. He sounded ready to deal as long as Mr. D. backed me up.

"Mr. Coyne, the indictment of Hector Vasquez is pure bullshit. Forgive the term in this fine restaurant. You have a shoestring for evidence, and your shock and dismay at the fixing of a race at old Suffering Downs was an Academy Award performance. I'm not criticizing you. Can we just admit that you and the D.A. have bigger fish to fry? You want Hector to take a plea bargain or witness protection or whatever to flip on someone higher. I won't insult your intelligence by making that a question."

Billy looked at Mr. D. He tilted his head in my direction. "Your junior partner's picked up a bit of the old Devlin piss and vinegar, Lex. Do I have to take on two of you now?"

"Just listen to him, Billy."

I was back in the spotlight.

"I need to know whom I'm up against when I get over there, Mr. Coyne. What's really going on?"

Billy took a few seconds and then called the waiter for a refill of coffee all around. When he finished, Billy asked him to close the door of the private room Mr. D. had reserved. That done, he took a minute in silence before he spoke, and then it was to Mr. D.

"I could lose one hell of a lot more than my job for this, Lex. Are you familiar with the Irish mob in South Boston?"

"I'm from Charlestown, Billy. Same as you. I never had to deal with them."

"But you've heard of them. They're every bit as dicey as the Italian Mafia in the North End. Would you agree?"

"I've heard."

"I'm sure you have. Then let me tell you this. The people your junior partner is asking about would make the Southie group look like Sister Agnes's Knitting Society. That's what I'm after."

"Spell it out, Billy. It'll go no further."

Billy drained half of his cup of coffee before the words started to flow.

"The IRA. The Irish Republican Army."

"You don't mean they're still—?"

"Sit there, Lex. Keep quiet and listen. God knows I shouldn't be saying this. So let me get it out. There were two wings to the IRA. The political wing that held talks with the English reps for years to end what they called "The Troubles." There was also the militant wing. They were the ones trying to bomb their way into a united Ireland, north and south, separate from England. There were people in that part of the IRA who could blow up innocent civilians, women, children, whoever, to get what they wanted. I've heard they exploded enormous bombs in London. It's been said they fired mortar shells at Ten Downing Street. They blew up parts of towns in Northern Ireland. Let me say this by way of understatement. They were one hell of a tough lot. I'll leave it to your imagination."

"But the two sides worked out a peace over there, Billy. It's been years."

"True. It goes back to the nineties, early two thousands. The political part of the IRA and an outfit called "Sinn Fein," "Ourselves Alone" they call themselves. They took the peace-making approach with meetings with the Brits. Some of the meetings went on in secret, while the other wing was said to be still killing innocent people. That's another story. Listen to me. During those years of the troubles, there were people of Irish descent in this country, in Boston, who were supporting the militants over there with money and weapons."

"So I've heard."

"It was illegal to support a terrorist group, but we've had a hell of a time routing them out. For the most part we couldn't."

"What's that got to do with now?"

Billy held up a silencing hand. "Now the peace sets in. The Good Friday Agreement. There's no so-called patriotic cause for these terrorists. There's no place for them in the current government, north or south. So what do they do with their skills? We hear a number of them turned to pure crime. Why not? They had organization, training, and a whole country to prey on."

"That's Ireland. What does that have to do with you?"

"I'm getting there. The wealthy Irish here who sent money and guns over before to support the cause had been guilty of a serious crime. Now they're ripe pickings for blackmail. That's how some of the gangsters over there keep the flow of money coming from this side."

Mr. Devlin turned to me with one of those penetrating looks without words that said he was not delighted with my getting caught in that crossfire. I had no desire to debate it.

"Mr. Coyne, how do you tie this to Hector Vasquez? He's about as Irish as Pancho Villa."

"I don't have all the pieces, kid. Yet. I'm sure in my bones that Paddy Boyle has had IRA connections for years. I'm also sure he's up to his neck in the kind of racketeering that includes race fixing. How are the two connected? I'm working on that."

"And if you can get Hector Vasquez to flip, you think he'll add a piece to the puzzle."

He looked back at Mr. D. "There you are, Lex. Cards on the table. One whiff of this gets out of this room, I lose my leads, probably my job, maybe my legs."

Mr. D. just shook his head while we both absorbed more than we'd anticipated.

"Not all of them, Mr. Coyne."

The eyes were back on me.

"Not all the cards."

"What do you want, kid?"

"I need a name. When I get to Dublin, I need some entry point. What you've said will never come up, but I need to know where to start."

Billy sat back in the chair looking at his cup of coffee. I knew he was calculating the possible fallout on two sides of the Atlantic from mentioning one name at that table.

"Mr. Coyne, consider this. This is the truth. Hector had nothing to do with Danny's death. I wouldn't have taken the case if he did.

He won't plead guilty and he won't flip. This is not defense lawyer posturing. That's how it is. On the other hand, if you give me a lead, I can run it down in places you can't go. I give you my word, I'll give you everything I get. We're on the same side in this. Different reasons, but the same side. If you're going to put your eggs in one basket, I'm a better basket than Hector."

I could feel his eyes drilling straight through to my innermost thoughts. If he were dealing with Mr. Devlin, he'd have jumped in. But this "kid" was a different gamble. I could almost hear the moment of decision when his chair came forward and he was four inches from my face.

"Seamus McGuiness. You want to play chicken with the devil? There's a name."

I looked at Mr. D. to see if he remembered that that was the name I got from Scully. I could see that it registered.

"Who is he, Mr. Coyne?"

"He's a player from the old IRA days. He floats between Dublin and Boston. To do what? I'd like to know. I only know he has connections on both sides of the Atlantic."

"That's a start, Mr. Coyne."

I started to stand up. He stopped me halfway.

"Sit down, kid, or I'll have your death on my conscience for the rest of my life. Dammit. I'll give you one more piece. I've been working behind the scenes with the *Garda Siochána*. That's the Irish national police. Superintendent Dermot Phelan. He's in security and intelligence. He handles cooperation with foreign governments on terrorism and organized crime. I'll give him a heads up you're coming."

"Thank you, Mr. Coyne."

I held out my hand to him. He looked straight at me when he took it.

"You've got us both out on a limb, kid. God help you. And God help me if you're less of a man than your senior partner."

CHAPTER TWELVE

The sun was high enough to light up the greenest countryside I'd ever seen when my Aer Lingus flight set down at the Dublin Airport, about seven miles north of the city. I breezed through immigration and customs with my one carry-on and looked for the quickest ground transportation. Julie had booked me into the Gresham Hotel on O'Connell Street in the heart of the city.

My eyes were bleary from a second night without sleep. Sleeping on a plane is an art I've never mastered. Bleary though they were, I caught sight of an unexpected sign in the hands of a man in a Gresham Hotel Uniform that simply said "Michael Knight." I blessed Julie and resolved to boost her salary.

In less than five minutes I was in the backseat of a limousine. In less than six minutes my eyelids dropped and I was in the land of Nod.

I was jostled out of the sweetest sleep I'd had in days by the rumbling of the limo over a rough surface that turned out to be cobblestones. We cruised around a circular driveway that led to the front of what looked like a small country estate surrounded by nothing but green fields.

The driver opened the limo door. I reached for my overnight bag before getting out.

"You can leave it, Mr. Knight. We'll not be long."

There are people whose bearing, clothes, and even haircut just smack of "government employee." That was the cut of the tall, middle-aged man in narrow pinstripes and highly shined shoes waiting in the doorway. He smiled, introduced himself, and bid me welcome to Ireland. Without a wasted second, he led the way at a quick march to an office in the rear of the house. In that brief minute, I got the impression that Superintendent Dermot Phelan was comfortable in his capability and nobody's fool.

When conversation began behind the closed door of his office, I sensed that he attributed the same qualities to Billy Coyne. Billy had been true to his promise to alert the superintendent to my arrival.

"Will you have a cup of tea, Mr. Knight?"

To one who starts every day with a double jolt of Starbuck's caffeine-drenched special, the offer of a cup of tea was like offering tofu to a carnivore. On the other hand, when in Rome—or Ireland—

We were into the second cup of tea, diluted with milk yet, and some mutual sizing–up conversation by the time Superintendent Phelan seemed to reach the decision to take Billy Coyne's word and put a certain amount of trust in this disturbingly young colonial sitting in front of him. From then on, it was full-cruising speed with no wasted words.

"I understand you're looking for a child—I'm sorry, the body of a child, Mr. Knight. Your Mr. Coyne was explicit. I offer my condolences. I'm afraid I can offer little else."

That brought the tea back up into my throat.

"That's a bit of a disappointment, Superintendent. Billy Coyne thought you could give me a starting point."

"And I can. And I will. What I'm saying, Mr. Knight—"

He looked at me with an expression that said he was looking for the softest way to explain the brick wall I was up against.

"—is that there'll be precious little good you can do with it. We've been trying to break this gang of thugs for eight years now. They're tight, tough, and well experienced in the art of terror. Forgive the question, Mr. Knight. How old are you?"

"Twenty-nine, Superintendent. In years."

He smiled, "I appreciate the distinction. I've gathered myself that you're more experienced than the years imply. Nonetheless, you'd have to have lived through what we have during the past two decades to understand what you're up against."

"Superintendent, I want you to know I have no grand illusions of accomplishing world peace or eliminating terrorism. I'm here to find a child's body. No more."

"And that's what worries me. That child may be one thread of a sweater that won't unravel as easily as you may like."

I forced down one more swallow of the tea before answering to give the impression I was duly weighing his words.

"I'll give you my word, Superintendent. If I find I'm over my head, I'll pull out. I have no intention of sending two bodies home."

He smiled a benign silent smile.

"You said you could give me a lead, Superintendent."

"And so I shall. You could do worse than to talk to Ten Sullivan. I'll give you the address."

"Strange name. Who is he?"

He leaned back. "Ah, now there's a question. If nothing else comes of your quest, you'll have made the acquaintance of a man worth remembering. Where do I begin?"

He held out the teapot for a third refill. If eternal relations between Ireland and America depended on it, I could not have swallowed one more ounce of it. He seemed to understand.

"I'll tell you where he got the name. He was a fighter, a boxer as you call them, back in the days when it was a thing of honor. You had two men with gloves, toe-to-toe, each testing the mettle of the other. None of this kicking and butting like two animals in a cage you see on the telly today."

"And his name?"

"Ah yes. When Sullivan was in the ring, shortly after the bout began, his opponent would invariably be flat on his back. The next thing he'd hear would be the ref counting him out. '—eight, nine,

ten. Sullivan,' with the referee holding up Sullivan's hand as the winner. One of the sportswriters picked it up. Whence the name, 'Ten
Sullivan.'"

My turn to smile. "Was this recent?"

"Oh heavens, no. He hasn't stepped into the ring as a fighter in
three decades. He's been fighting a different fight."

"And that is?"

"He runs a gym in the north section of Dublin. He's used the
respect people have for him as a fighter to try to save the kids from
the muck they find on the streets. Especially during the times of
the Troubles. He kept a lot of young lads from throwing their lives
into that bottomless pit. Not all, but a good many. He's still at it.
Nowadays it's the drugs, and the rest of it. The people in that neighborhood all but pray to him as a saint. Even among the kids, his
word goes. He's more powerful than the parish priest."

"That's interesting. You say Billy Coyne told you why I'm here.
The little girl. Would he know anything about that?"

"If it happened in Dublin, especially north of the river, Ten's your
best bet."

I could see his expression sharpen. The smile was less pronounced.

"And that's where a certain amount of discretion enters, Mr.
Knight. It's a pleasant chat we've had. But I should tell you this. If
it weren't for your Mr. Coyne, we'd never have had it. When he says
I can rely on you not to muck about in Garda business, I take him
at his word."

"I think I'd better be sure what that means, Superintendent."

"Then let me speak plainly. This meeting never happened. You'll
not need to mention my name. I'll have contacted Mr. Sullivan before you do. Then it's just between you two. "

"Thank you, Superintendent."

"To be perfectly clear. You'll not mention my name or the Garda,
or any such connection. It's taken years to establish a certain rap-

port, shall we say a working relationship with Mr. Sullivan. It thrives on secrecy. I'd be very disappointed if your business, significant though it is, disrupted that relationship."

The words were civil and softly spoken, but the manner left no room for a flexible interpretation.

"I understand perfectly."

"Good." The bright joviality was back. "There it is then. The limo will take you to your hotel. Good choice, the Gresham. Grand old lady since back in the eighteen hundreds."

He was on his feet for a handshake with one hand and the offer of a slip of paper with the other. The limo driver appeared, and I was in the backseat of the limo in the time it would have taken to pour another cup of that anemic liquid.

I checked into the Gresham, which lived up to its reputation for classic grandeur in spades. I changed into jeans and sweatshirt without unpacking. Since this was, in no sense, destined to be the jolly tourist's frolic in Dublin, I got down to business.

The paper I got from the superintendent gave an address on Sheriff Street, a few blocks north of the River Liffey. I took a cab to the corner of Amiens and Talbot Streets and walked from there. It seemed less conspicuous to arrive on foot.

The neighborhood was gritty working-class and less. You could almost breathe in the poverty and hard times that shaped the lives of those confined there by life's circumstances.

A brick-and-wooden building in the middle of the block sported the name in pealing paint letters, "Sullivan's *Nua Saol* Gym." The words in the Irish, I later learned, mean "New Life"—an interesting glimmer of optimism in a setting not otherwise glowing with joy.

I walked in past a couple of exiting teenage boys with gym bags. Their nods in my direction relieved some of the uptight apprehension I carried in with me. Inside it resembled any of the boxer-training gyms in South Boston or Dorchester, from the ancient wooden floor giving off the vapors of decades of sweat to the elevated canvas-covered ring that had absorbed a saturation of sweat mingled with blood. You could smell, almost to the point of tasting, the pain of young fighters dreaming of punching their way out of the poverty.

I passed through six or seven stripped-to-the-waist teenagers, focused on pounding a rhythmic cadence on light and heavy punching bags. Straight through toward the back, I saw the man I figured I was looking for. Two skinny Irish-looking redheads were circling and jabbing at each other in the ring, while a box-built, white-haired man in sweat clothes leaned on the ropes with his back to me. He was yelling instructions, curses, and encouragement at each of them in turn. His hands flew out in jabs and uppercuts as if he were carrying out his own orders.

I watched from a bench until another older assistant at ringside hit a bell with a hammer. The boys dropped their oversized gloves to their sides and just panted. The white-haired man climbed up into the ring and grabbed both boys by the back of the neck.

"Listen to the two of you. You sound like steam engines. You'll both jump ropes for fifteen minutes. And if I ever catch a smoke in your mouth, I'll stuff it up your nose. Lit. Do ya hear what I'm sayin' to ya?"

Both boys nodded. Between gasps they said, "Right, Ten. Okay, Ten."

"So why're ya standin' here like there's nothin' to do?"

They were both out of the ring like they were being called for supper. I came up beside the ring.

"Mr. Sullivan, see you a minute? Michael Knight."

He turned around and looked at me with eyes that seemed accustomed to sizing up newcomers in the first look.

"Let's get this straight. I intend to call you Michael. You better damn well call me Ten or we'll never get to know each other."

"Ten it is. It's my pleasure."

"Don't jump to conclusions, lad. I know why you're here. You'd have a softer go if you came for boxing lessons."

I looked him in the eyes and I smiled for some reason, "I guess we can't choose our missions in life, Ten."

"Sure we can, Michael. It's the measure of a man that he chooses the tough ones."

He jumped down off the ring more nimbly that I would have expected of a man his size and age.

"Come into my office. Let's talk. Would you like a beer?"

"It would sure beat a cup of tea."

Now he was smiling. "Don't sell the tea short, Michael. The Irish have built a nation on it."

I had no chance to make a comeback—even if I could have thought of one. A boy younger than any in the gym ran up to him. I thought he was holding back tears. Ten took him by the shoulders and bent down to him.

"Did your mother send you, Tim?"

The boy nodded, but said nothing.

"Same thing?"

The boy nodded more vigorously. Ten lifted him and sat him on the side of the ring.

"Stay here till I get back, Tim. C'mon, Michael. We'll talk later."

I followed a few paces behind while the big man strode in giant steps through the door and down the street. He was walking, but I had to jog to keep up. We went four blocks, turned right on Garner, and did three more without slackening the pace. I was twenty feet behind him when he stopped in front of a pub. He waited for me to catch up, panting like a racehorse. He was scarcely breathing above normal.

"You might consider gettin' yourself in better condition."

I wanted to answer, but I had all I could do to breathe. I followed him into the pub. He scanned the line of men at the bar until he locked onto one at the far end. I was right behind him when he reached the man leaning on both elbows with one fist around a shot of whiskey and the other with a grip on a pint of dark brew. There was a small stack of paper euros in front of him.

Ten said one word in a tone that could barely be heard, but it straightened the man to attention.

"Patrick."

He turned a ruddy face with a day's growth of beard to face his caller. If the man was buzzed a second before, he was sober in that instant. Ten said what sounded like a few sentences to him in a level tone. I thought my ears had gone sour until I realized he was talking in the Irish.

The man grabbed the money from the bar and backed away until he could turn and fairly ran out of the pub. I heard Ten call the bartender to the side. I was close enough to hear him say, "Whatever he owes, put it on my tab, Clancy. And a tip for yourself."

The bartender smiled, "Thank you, Ten."

"And Clancy." The bartender turned back to him. "If you ever serve Patrick again on payday, I'll be lookin' for you."

The smile was gone, but Clancy expressed his comprehension with sincerity.

Ten turned back to me. "Well, do you think you're up to the walk back to the gym?"

"I can handle it, Ten. Would you mind telling me what you said to him in Irish?"

Ten rubbed his chin and looked at the ceiling. " Oh I just said, "Now Patrick, wouldn't it be a better thing for you to pick up what's left of your paycheck and bring it home to Kathleen?"

He walked down the bar to the door to the greetings by name of every man in the room. Before I followed, I asked the man who was standing next to Patrick, "What did he really say?" It brought belly laughs from everyone at the bar within hearing.

"What he said, Yank, if you want a literal translation, was 'Patrick, if you're not runnin' that pay home to Kathleen by the time

I count to two, I'll shove that whiskey so far up your arse you can gargle with it.'"

I couldn't help asking, "Is Kathleen Ten's sister or something?"

"Not at all. She's just a woman in the neighborhood who'd have nothin' on the table if Patrick pissed it away on the sauce."

I heard a voice from the door. "Michael, are you comin'? We've business."

I was on my way to the well wishes of all the men at the bar, who, to a man, simply called me "Yank." It was good spirited, though to a born Red Sox fan, the name "Yank," short for "Yankee," was a bit jarring.

CHAPTER THIRTEEN

Ten popped the caps on two Killian Red ales and passed one across the weathered desk in his office at the back of the gym. The groan of the wooden chair when he leaned back testified to the steel in every ounce of the man's frame.

"Tell it to me, Michael."

I answered with everything that bore on my search for Erin, and why the trail had led me to Dublin without a clue as to where to begin the search.

He soaked it in without a word. When I finished, he rocked forward in the chair and rested his elbows on the desk. I was taken back by the similarity of his manner to that of my senior partner.

"I'm sorry for your pain, Michael. We've got good men in this country. It's those years of the Troubles that's hardened some of them till I'm ashamed to admit they're Irish."

"I don't know where to start here, Ten. I have one name. Seamus McGuiness. Killarney Street."

His eyebrows went up a notch.

"And what have you heard of him, lad?"

"Practically nothing. I got the name from a man in the States, Vince Scully, who may or may not have been in on the kidnapping depending on whether or not you'd bet a cent on his truthfulness."

"What did he tell you about McGuiness?"

"I asked him about a lead to find Erin's body for her mother's sake. He gave me McGuiness's name. That's it. What can you tell me about him?"

"Ha!" He was up on his feet and pacing. "I can tell you this. If you went strollin' down Killarney Street askin' questions about Seamus McGuiness, you'd come back with your head under your arm. If at all."

He sat on the edge of the desk on my side, looking down at me.

"It's best you know you're in turbulent waters. The peace is on us, and we all love it. But there's still a layer of violence in some places just below the surface. You're a clever fella, but you don't look to me like your American—what's his name, Rambo."

I stood up to be eye-to-eye with him.

"You've got that right. I'm no Rambo." I added, "Unfortunately, that's irrelevant. I can't go back without word of the little girl. I've got to give her mother at least that."

"Or die tryin'. Is that it?"

"I'd rather not. But I can't quit either."

He broke the moment with a laugh and a shake of his head on the way back to his chair. He was grinning when he spoke. "Dammit, Michael. What do they feed you over there? You're a scrawny beanpole of a lawyer. You can't run a block without gaspin' for air. And you want to take on the toughest fighters three decades of war could turn out. You're either soft in the head—or—maybe tough-headed when the chips are down." The grin was gone. "Either way, there's no point in being suicidal."

"I hope you're about to suggest an alternative."

He ran his hands through a shock of white curly hair and sat back down.

"Maybe. I can go places and ask questions that you can't. Not and live."

"Would you do it?"

"Go back to your hotel, Michael. Have a pint or two tonight and get some sleep. You look like you need it. I'll call you there tomorrow."

"Thank you, Ten. I don't think—"

"I'm not finished. For the sake and the love of God, don't go Ramboin' around on your own. Do you hear?"

No problem. It was my every wish.

I walked the eight blocks back to the Gresham Hotel on O'Connell Street. A quick change of clothes, a catch-up call to Mr. Devlin, and I was back downstairs by about nine p.m. for what I realized was my first meal of the day. The Gresham earns every one of its four stars in every corner, but nowhere more deservingly than in the up-scale Writer's Bar. I slid onto a seat at the classic bar in the elevated section that looks out onto Dublin's lifeline, upper O'Connell Street.

The cushy luxury of coasting into a sirloin beef baguette, in the fine company of a draft Guinness with its micro frothy little head, and absolutely nothing on my mind but a long night of rejuvenating unconsciousness had me near comatose. I could look out on the ebb and flow of tourists, businessmen, laborers—the entire amalgam that gave O'Connell Street its pulse—without one disruptive thought.

For some inexplicable reason, I fastened on a pair of twenty-something young men crossing the street. The uninvited notion that I might have seen the pair around Sullivan's Gym earlier nudged my mind out of neutral.

They seemed somewhat out of their element when they came in the front entrance of the Gresham, and disturbingly out of place when they came into the posh Writer's Bar. I could see in the mirror behind the bar that they were scanning the crowd. Alarms went off when they seemed to focus on me and take a direct line in my direction. Some self-preservative notion said it was time to take defensive action.

When they walked up to the bar on either side of me, I forcibly suppressed the urge to bolt screaming into the lobby. I simply raised the Guinness to my lips and slowly sucked in the snowy foam on top.

"Mr. Knight."

The one on my right was the spokesman. I kept looking at the Guinness.

"And to what do I owe this pleasure, gentlemen?"

"It's a message. From Mr. Sullivan."

That did it. I pressed the button I had my finger on in the left pocket of my sport coat.

"And the message is?"

"He wants to see you. Somethin' come up. We'll take ya."

"Excellent. I'd be pleased to see him. And where are we off to?"

"Like I said. We'll show ya."

"The pleasure will be mine, gentlemen, as soon as I finish this delightful pint. Would you care to join me?"

The one on the left raised his hand to signal the bartender, but the one on the right grabbed his arm in mid-motion. "Another time, perhaps. We don't want to keep him waitin'."

The one on the right got a grip on my elbow and started moving me off the bar seat. With one jerk of the elbow I smashed his fingers into the bar. He winced, but made no sound.

"I'm terribly sorry. I must have slipped. I think I mentioned it once. When I've enjoyed every drop of this delightful stout, I'm in your pleasant company. Please, have a seat."

He was flummoxed. The Writer's Bar was not the place for a tussle with someone better dressed than he was. He compromised by leaning against the bar. The one on the left took the seat. I forced a tone of voice that suggested to our fellow bar mates that we'd just all gathered for a friendly nightcap. I needed another five minutes.

"That's better, gentlemen. I don't think we've met. You know my name. And yours?"

One look from the one on the right silenced the one on the left.

"I'm Pat. This here's Tom."

"Pat and Tom. Good solid names. And you say Mr. Sullivan sent you to fetch me?"

"Yeah. We'd better move. He's not one to be kept waitin'."

"No. I got that impression. Nor is he one to see a good Guinness go to waste."

I sipped on the stout while I made inane conversation for another five minutes. Pat, the brighter of the two by half, was getting antsier by the second. Before he reached the exploding point, I called for the check, signed it, and slid off the bar seat.

With one on each side, we walked in lockstep out the front entrance into the bustle of O'Connell Street. The three of us were as close packed as sardines as we turned right and kept formation through the walkers. We turned right again on Cathal and zigzagged onto Brugha Street. With every block, the number of pedestrians diminished, along with my confidence in survival. I kept up a running commentary of street names that sounded like a tour director. My companions had long since lapsed into total silence.

By the time we approached Gardner Street, we were the sole bit of life on a street that could have used a great deal more illumination. I felt like a lobster that's backed into a trap and can't back out. Both arms were in a grip that felt like a vice.

When our little parade started to make a right turn into an alley that was black as the pit of Hades, my legs stopped moving. I knew I had made a fatal mistake of confidence and vowed never again to take a smart-ass approach to a dangerous situation, assuming there would be an ever again.

The grips tightened, and I felt myself being dragged into the alley. Twenty feet inside, I heard a distinctive click and caught sight of one tiny glint of light. I said the last prayer I thought I'd ever say on this earth as I realized that the tiny beam of light was reflected off the blade of a knife.

I tightened every muscle I could control, not knowing where the blade would enter. The rigidity made the blow I felt the more stunning when I hit the pavement in a dead drop.

My eyes were closed and my ears were ringing. I lay still, fighting off the effects of shock. Slowly it broke through my mental shell that I had never felt the sting of the knife. My next sense was that there was a massive bulk lying still beside me. That was followed by the revelation that I could move, and the best direction was away from that mass beside me. I somehow got to my feet, off balance because of the darkness. I was aware of scuffling around me. I wanted to run to the miniscule bit of light back at the opening of the alley, but the attempt to run only tumbled me over another mass at my feet.

My total confusion lasted a half second before an arm around my shoulder led and half carried me over whatever was on the ground to the mouth of the alley.

We came out of the alley into the dim light of McDermott Street as I was beginning to get my legs under me. I heard a familiar voice beside me that I knew was either Saint Peter at the Gates or Ten Sullivan. It turned out to be the latter.

"Dear Lord, Michael. You do attract a seedy lot."

I realized I was still taking breaths as if they were my last. Somehow I got out the words.

"God love you, Ten Sullivan. I know I do. What happened?"

"You're a clever Yank. I was still at the gym when you called."

"Thank God. I dialed the number you gave me when I saw those two come into the Writer's Bar just in case. When I knew I was in trouble, I kept the phone in my pocket and hit the call button."

"How did you know those two weren't from me?"

I cracked the first smile of the rest of my life.

"They called you 'Mr. Sullivan'. I figured if they were your boys, it would be Ten."

"And you'd be right."

"How'd you get here, Ten? I never saw you from the time we left the hotel."

"You led us. I took a few of the boys with me. You were smart enough to leave the phone on and give us a running itinerary. By the time you got into that alley, I had my boys ahead of you and behind you."

"And thank God. Who were those thugs?"

"Don't worry. They'll not bother you again."

"Were they connected with McGuiness?"

"That's for me to worry about. I told you I'd make inquiries."

"Not to be ungrateful, but are your inquiries going to keep the flies away in the future?"

He smiled. "Leave it to me, Michael. I've done all right by you so far."

I refrained from saying that my coming closer to the eternal crossover than I ever hoped to was not "doing all right."

CHAPTER FOURTEEN

I woke up at eight the following morning with a number of previously unknown muscles rebelling and the distinct impression that for me, the Emerald Isle's reputation for gracious hospitality had its exceptions.

Two favorable hints of a better day ahead were my first glimpse of sunshine since I'd arrived in Ireland and a buffet breakfast that would bring joy to a lumberjack at the Gallery Restaurant in the hotel. I took note that two relatively normal meals in a row, could be habit forming.

I was into my fourth cup of coffee when I got the call from Ten. He told me to watch for a blue MINI Cooper in front of the hotel. This time, the driver would be from him.

"Where am I going, Ten?"

"It's not the most pleasant of errands you'll be on, Michael. But you knew that. I wish I could undo it all for you. At least I asked the questions and got the answers that you couldn't. That's as far as I can take it. I can't give you justice. Just information."

What miniscule hope I had left in the tank that somehow I'd find Erin alive drained out the bottom. It caused a silence that Ten read rightly.

"I'm sorry, Michael."

"You did what you could. I'd still be floundering."

"Talk to Feeney. He knows you're comin'. I'll be at the gym."

I needed that morning sunshine to keep my spirits high enough to put one foot ahead of the other. I knew that whatever unthinkable revelation the day was about to bring would have to be broken ultimately to Colleen. But one thing at a time.

I was there at the curb when the Cooper pulled in. The driver was somewhere between forty and sixty with a face that indicated a life in the ring—a life for which he had apparently not been particularly well suited. Between a misshapen jaw, an angular nose, and a brogue as thick as beef stew, I could scarcely understand a word he said. The blessing was that he was more into driving than conversation.

He wove through the heavily trafficked streets of Dublin to a section of small roadways above the North Circular Road. It was about ten o'clock when he pulled up to the curb at the side of St. Margaret's Avenue. The small sign in front of the door read, GRIMES & FEENEY FUNERAL HOME.

My driver said his first two words since we left the hotel. "I'll wait."

I took the cue and walked to the door. The chimes were answered by a tall, gaunt figure in black. He had a nose that hung over his upper lip and eyes that had become practiced in professional mourning. He looked like a raven that was on the verge of giving or receiving bad news.

"Good morning. I'm looking for Mr. Feeney."

He answered with a single mournful syllable, "Aahhh," and a bowing invitation to cross the threshold.

Once inside, I fully expected the door to creak when he closed it. It didn't, thank God.

"Mr. Feeney, my name is Michael Knight. Mr. Sullivan suggested that I see you."

"Uh-huh." I read it as expressing his own personal grief that I was there about past rather than future business for the house. He led the way to a sedate office. Once seated, I took a stab at beginning one of the most difficult conversations of my life.

"Mr. Feeney, I'm looking for a child around two years old. Her name is—or was—Erin Ryan. You may not have been given that name. I guess the best way to ask it is this. Have you buried a little girl like that in the past week?"

"Mmm. You understand, Mr. Knight, that we carefully guard the confidentiality of our clients. It is the hallmark of Grimes and—"

I sensed I was about to be smothered in funereal bullshit. It was not what I had the mind-set or time to endure patiently. It seemed the moment to play my only trump.

"Mr. Feeney, I believe you're acquainted with Mr. Ten Sullivan. With all due respect to your professional crap, let's cut to the chase. Mr. Sullivan has put his very personal interest behind your answering my questions truthfully. Let me try it again, and for the last time. Did you bury a two-year-old girl recently?"

He was sitting on the edge of his black leather chair with a rigidity that suggested that my direct approach had rammed a poker to the hilt where it would do the most good. He was struggling vainly to continue playing a role that would do me the least good.

"Mr. Knight. There is no call—"

"Mr. Feeney. There is call. The child was murdered. You may well be an accessory to the murder. You can either answer my questions without excessive posturing and it will stay between us. Or you can bid me an incriminating farewell on my way to the nearest office of the Garda. Your call. Quickly."

The rosy tinge of his Irish complexion was paper-white. He looked up at me as I rose out of the chair for effect.

"I do believe, Mr. Knight, that our company handled a matter such as you suggest. I, personally, had no—"

"Tell me about the girl. Everything. Leave the denials out of it. How old? What did she look like?"

He fumbled in a drawer for a file card with hands that practically vibrated. He pretended to read from the card.

"She was apparently two years old. She had reddish-blonde hair. What more can I say?"

"When?"

"She was brought to us last Friday. They wanted the burial immediately. We were able to inter the body the following day. There was to be no service."

That part stung particularly. I knew how Colleen would take it.

"What was the cause of death?"

He checked the quivering card. "My only indication is 'terminal illness'."

"When you embalmed the body—I assume you did."

"Oh yes. Quite legally."

"Right. Were there any identifying marks?"

"You mean?"

"Birthmarks? Be specific."

"Why, ah, yes. There was a heart-shaped birthmark on the left side of her neck. I'm merely reading—"

That did it. That pulled the last plug. He babbled about having no personal part, but I could hardly hear a word he said. I had to get it together. Where do I go from here? Do I dig to find out who was behind it? I don't think so. Would it bring Erin back to us? Would it relieve me and Colleen of facing a conversation that would rebreak both of our hearts? The only thing that mattered was getting Erin's body back home for a real burial by her family—with a funeral Mass.

I stood up. "Thank you, Mr. Feeney."

"I must assure you, Mr. Knight. The body was simply delivered to us. Payment was made. It was most irregular. Completely anonymous. I have no idea—"

I have no conception of what Irish laws were violated by Grimes & Feeney, nor did I care. Whatever they did was probably done under threats I couldn't even imagine.

"It doesn't matter, Mr. Feeney. You have nothing to fear from me. I have just one more question. Where is she buried?"

He seemed sufficiently calmed to answer the question. "She's buried in Glasnevin Cemetery. It's in the north of Dublin County on Finglas Road. Where there was no service and we didn't know her faith you understand, we were limited. She's in a row reserved for young children."

"Thank you, Mr. Feeney. I'll be going there directly."

"I'll call ahead. It's the largest cemetery in Dublin. You'll need directions to the gravesite. Just go to the office. I'm truly sorry for your loss, Mr. Knight."

I had the feeling that he meant that last sincerely, which induced me to take the handshake he offered.

True to his word, my driver, Finbar O'Neil, was waiting. He knew the cemetery, and Ten had put him at my disposal for the day.

Finbar was still no conversationalist, for which small favor I thanked God. He wove through the streets of northern Dublin and had us there in twenty minutes. The office directed me to what was obviously a freshly made burial site.

I walked alone to the edge of the new sod. I'm not one for visiting the physical remains of people I've loved. I'd rather visit their immortal souls in prayer. But in this case, I had a message to deliver.

I stood washed in the memory of those tiny arms around my neck, of those dazzling greenish eyes that danced with bubbling joy, of that smushy little nose that she'd burrow into my cheek and giggle until I knew that of everything He did, this was God's greatest achievement. I could scarcely believe that all of that was now sleeping in a box beneath the earth.

I knelt down on the sod beside her grave, and I said it aloud. "As God who's holding you now is my help and my judge, Little Erin, I'll take you home."

CHAPTER FIFTEEN

Ten Sullivan was in the ring refereeing and coaching at the same time. He called a break when he saw me come in the door and pointed back at his office.

"How'd it go, Michael? I think I can tell by lookin' at ya."

"You've been good to me, Ten. But I need one more favor."

"Such as?"

"I need a lawyer. Probably a solicitor, at least to start."

"Start what?"

"I have to take her home. Her mother needs at least that. I probably need a court order to exhume the body and whatever forms are necessary to send her home."

He bent back in the chair. "Whew! You're a little out of my area."

"Mine too. I don't know where to begin. That's why I need an Irish lawyer who does."

He was up on his feet. "Well I don't have one in my back pocket. Why all the fuss anyway? Understand, I'm not making little of the death of the child. But why disturb the body now?"

"Lot of reasons. Some closure for her mother. The right way of doing things. There wasn't even a funeral Mass."

"Then have a Mass. Have it here. Or there."

I shook my head. "I could give you ten more reasons, but there's only one."

"And it is?"

"I made a promise."

Ten looked at me and started to say something. Then he looked at me again, and he thought better of it.

"It'll take a bit, Michael. I don't run into a lot of solicitors here in the gym. But I know those who do. I'll have a name for you by this evening."

I lay on the bed in the Gresham while I brought Mr. Devlin up to speed. He was unusually quiet. I knew the final reality of Erin's death was hitting him too.

"Do we have someone in Boston who can handle the legalities of getting her home from Ireland, Mr. Devlin?"

"I'll check till I find the best one. I'll have the information for you when you get back. Which will be when, Michael?"

"Probably a couple of days. I'll have to find a solicitor on this end."

I knew that wouldn't take two days, but another plan was rattling around. It was too vague to debate at that point.

"Michael, have you talked to Colleen?"

That one stung. "No. I wanted to be sure first. Now that I am, I can't do it over the phone. I have to be there."

He accepted that without adding to the guilt I felt for postponing the inevitable.

The day was wearing on and I was wearing down by late afternoon. Ten called with the name and number of a solicitor. I called and made an appointment with him for early the following morning. Then I called the concierge to arrange for the rental of a car.

"I'll have it here at the hotel in the morning, Mr. Knight. I take it you'd like a nice mid-sized or a compact."

"No. More like a Lexus or Jaguar."

"Ah, you have good taste. But on our wee Irish country roads? Are you sure?"

I was. And not for the ego or the comfort. It was part of a plan that was becoming less vague as I thought about it.

Eoughan Tynan's firm of solicitors had an office on Great Georges Street by the corner of Parnell Street. It was about eight blocks from Ten's gym, next to the James Joyce Center—a decided upswing from Ten's neighborhood. He did me the professional courtesy of slipping me into his appointment book at eight in the morning.

When we met, I thought I was looking in a mirror. He was about my age, my height, and my coloring. If I could have mastered the brogue and Irish law, we could have swapped places.

I introduced myself and massacred the pronunciation of his first name. He smiled and steered me to something close to "Owen." I knew I liked him when he sized me up as a coffee drinker and made the appropriate offer.

"Ten gave me the bare outlines. What exactly would you like to do about the little girl's body?"

I gave him all the details.

"I want to bring her body home to her mother for burial. I'm a criminal defense lawyer in Boston. This is truly out of my bailiwick."

"Right. Well, it's not something I see every day either. The question is where to start. I think we have two hurdles. First we have to have the body exhumed. That'll require a court order. With no one opposing it, that shouldn't be too difficult. The second is to release the body to you as attorney for the mother, and transportation back to Boston. That will require another court order. That will depend on establishing your client as the birth mother of the little girl. That can be done through a DNA match, since I assume she has no identification here. Thank God this is not happening fifteen years ago."

"I assume you'll need to coordinate with an attorney in Boston for the DNA matching. My partner's looking into it. I'll have a name for you by the end of the day."

"Good. Then we can start right now. I'll need a sworn statement from you setting out the facts as you've told them to me. Are you comfortable with that?"

I liked his get-to-it approach. My comfort level with accomplishing at least that much for Colleen was rising. I agreed.

"Excellent. Then let me get the girl in here for dictation."

I could tell that my spirits were climbing out of the basement when I entertained the random thought that if I ever referred to my secretary, Julie, as "the girl," I'd have her resignation on my desk and a pot of coffee in my lap.

I arranged to get back to Eoughan with the name of the Boston attorney by evening. His parting words were an admonition that Dublin courts plod at about the pace of the Boston courts. While he thought it could be done, immediacy was not in the cards. No matter, it was underway.

It was about nine thirty and still a sunny morning when I got behind the wheel—on the right side—of the first and probably the last Jaguar I will ever drive. I felt twinges of disloyalty bordering on cheating on my Corvette. I fought off the emotion of love-at-first-sight with the Jaguar with the self-admonition that "It's just a car." The echo came back from my subconscious, "But one hell of a car."

I followed the directions of the concierge to the N7 and then the M7 through the rich, green, fertile, and storybook beautiful countryside of County Kildare west of Dublin. Rick McDonough, the Boston trainer of Black Diamond, had said that he had been shipped from a breeding stable in an area called the Curragh. I still had responsibility for the defense of Hector Vasquez, and I still believed that Danny's death was somehow tied to the Diamond's losing that race.

Curragh, it turns out, means a plain or down. This one is about eight miles square, some twenty-five miles southwest of Dublin. It's no accident that the area is rife with stud farms and training facilities. The soil is unusually rich. It produces pastureland that is apparently the best for Thoroughbred racehorses. The concierge at the

Gresham said that horse races had been held there as early as the first century, and the Irish Derby is still run there annually.

I checked a local phonebook for the address of the stable Rick mentioned, and within half an hour of entering the region, I was at the gate of a stone-walled facility with the name posted: Dubh Crann Stables.

I pulled up to the guard at the gate. He came out of his little enclosure with an attitude that said that he functioned more as a blockade than a reception committee.

Before he could speak, and without removing the mirrored sunglasses I donned for the occasion, I said without looking at him, "I'm here to see Kieran Dowd."

I remembered that as the name of the man who arranged for Rick McDonough to train Black Diamond. It was a slender thread, but the only one I had.

I could see the guard eyeing the Jaguar. I stepped out of it to give him a full view of the conservative Italian wool suit I wore for the occasion. I bought the suit a year previously for a price that could only be called obscenely outrageous, but it had been my ticket of admission to some dangerously impenetrable places over the year. The whole package was put together to suggest that this was not someone to blow off without a hearing.

His attitude relented slightly when he asked, "What name?"

I still didn't look at him. "It doesn't matter. He doesn't know me."

"I need a name."

I glanced at him casually. "Mention Seamus McGuiness."

It was the only name I'd gotten from Vince Scully.

The guard walked away and spoke into a phone attached to his little guardhouse. Whether the car, the suit, or the name, tripped the trigger, I have no idea, but the heavy electric gate swung open. The guard pointed out a cobblestone drive that led to a row of stables.

"You'll find Mr. Dowd just beyond the stables at the exercise track."

I drove over the cobblestones to within six feet of a totally bald man, probably in his fifties, looking intently at a stopwatch. He was leaning his short, chunky frame against the middle rail on the outside of a racetrack that would have been the envy of Suffolk Downs. A small number of Thoroughbreds were engaged in breezing, galloping, or cooling out in different sections of the track.

I spoke through the open window of the Jaguar. "Mr. Dowd, I think perhaps we can do business."

He looked at the car and then at me. His entire expression was a question mark.

"You want to work with me?"

"No."

I got out of the car. He all but felt the Italian wool with his eyes. I took off the sunglasses and made eye contact.

"I may want you to work *for* me. I like what you did with Black Diamond. You may be of use to us."

He smiled and turned back to the horses on the track. "I don't know what you're talking about, young man."

I walked to the rail beside him with a smile as if at a private joke. "'Young man' is it? I guess that'll do for now."

He looked back at me with a squint. "Who the hell are ya?"

"I take it you've heard of Seamus McGuiness."

"Do you work for Mr. McGuiness?"

"No."

His curiosity was turning to aggravation. "Then why're ya takin' up my time?"

"McGuiness works for me. I occasionally find him useful."

His stunned look lasted only an instant. He pulled out a cell phone. "And suppose I call Mr. McGuiness. He'll back you up, will he?"

I looked down at him with every ounce of detachment I could muster. "No, Mr. Dowd. He'll say he never heard of me in his entire life."

He had that stunned look again. I went on. "Go ahead. Call him. I want to hear this. If he admits to the slightest recognition of me or anything connected with me, it'll be the last time you'll be able to speak with him on this earth."

He slowly closed the cell phone. "What's your name anyway?"

I shrugged. "What's the difference? There's no one you can check it with. Do you want to stop playing name games and hear what I'm here for?"

He just gave me a blank look.

"Good. Then here it is. You have a fairly tight operation, Mr. Dowd. What's your first name?"

"Kieran. And what is your name?"

"It still doesn't matter, Kieran. I'm impressed with how you handled Black Diamond. That was a good test. But you should know you're wasting your time."

"I'm what?"

I bent down and picked a stick off the ground. I drew a horizontal line in the dirt below us, and handed the stick to Dowd.

"Go ahead, Kieran. Write the amount you made on the deal with McGuiness for Black Diamond."

He just looked at me. I grabbed the stick back and wrote below the line, × 10. I handed it back to him. "Go ahead. It's easily erased. It's just dirt. Write the number."

He took the stick and wrote 50,000 euros. It was probably a lie, but no matter. I took the stick back and did the multiplication times 10 and wrote 500,000.

He looked me straight in the eye, this time with a combination of curiosity and greed. "What're ya talkin' about?"

"McGuiness is chicken feed. You can't get blood out of a turnip. And you can't get interesting money out of Suffolk Downs."

"And what're ya suggestin'?"

"I'm suggesting you'd do well to serve the interests of someone with contacts at every major track in the United States."

"You're talkin' about purses for winnin' races."

"Of course not. You're still thinking about chicken feed. I'm talking about wagers placed at the maximum odds with every syndicate in America. That takes connections."

"And you have the connections?"

"So far we're just breezing here. I'd like to see a level of interest on your part."

"Meanin' what?"

"Your operation can be improved before we throw the real dice. I need details. Let's talk about Black Diamond."

I got an instantaneous twinge in the stomach. I might have started reeling him in before I'd really set the hook. I was getting nothing but confused looks from Kieran.

"I'm waiting, Kieran, and I've never been known for patience."

"Let me think about it, mister."

"You see that gate I drove through. In ten seconds you're going to see the rear end of this Jag drive through it again. It's the last you'll see of me personally. I have to admit, though, I'm not comfortable leaving you with this much information and no commitment."

Kieran was no dimwit. He read fluently between the lines. I could see it register in his eyes.

"What do you want to know?"

"Let's start with the obvious. Black Diamond had no breeding and dismal workouts when he left Ireland. Somehow he acquired blazing speed during that race. Fill me in."

He looked around although we were the only ones in sight. "He had the speed all right, if not the breedin'. We knew it from the time he was a colt. He's another Seabiscuit. With just as much heart. If the real times got out, he'd have been even-money odds. Less."

"So?"

"So we let the racing press in here to clock him when we wanted to. We'd run him till he was tired, cool him out, and saddle him up again. Then we'd bring the press boys to the rail, and he'd put on a show. He never gave less than all he had, but by then he didn't have much. They'd report the slow times in the racing press."

"And what about Suffolk Downs? He had to be breezed and galloped there. Why wasn't he noticed?"

"I don't know. All I know is this side of the pond."

"And again, how much did McGuiness pay you?"

He stuck to the lie. "Fifty thousand euros."

That was what I came for. He answered the question I didn't ask. I needed confirmation that it was Seamus McGuiness behind the whole Black Diamond business. I could feel one more piece of the puzzle slip into place.

I left Kieran Dowd with the vague suggestion that I'd be in touch with him when I had all the ducks in a row—whatever that meant.

CHAPTER SIXTEEN

It was near six when I got back to the hotel. One call to the Boston office served to bring Mr. Devlin up to date and to ask Julie to book me onto the morning flight from Dublin to Boston. Mr. D. gave me the name and number of an attorney with one of the large law firms on Federal Street who handles international civil law. I was surprised and pleased to hear that it was a law school classmate, Charlie DiSilva, a smart lawyer and one I could trust.

Not to lose time, I called Charlie from Dublin and gave him the background and what I needed. He wanted Colleen's phone number to arrange to take a sample of her DNA to compare it to the child's after exhumation. I gave him the number, but asked him to delay contacting her until I had a chance to break the news about Erin. I put that at the top of my list of things to be faced when I got back.

I also gave both Charlie and Eoughan each other's phone numbers so that they could coordinate directly. Eoughan thought that he could get a hearing on his motion for exhumation within a week. The DNA comparison and motion to release the body for shipment home could take another week.

That done, I invited Ten Sullivan for a last pint or two at Mulligan's Pub on Poolbeg Street on the south side of the River Liffey. It was in the center of the city, but far enough out of Ten's neighborhood that he wouldn't be known by everyone from the owner to the men's room attendant. I needed a bit of privacy.

We were into the third pint by the time I broached anything

related to my other reason for being in Dublin. I had no intention of sandbagging him, but I needed information that would most easily flow in an atmosphere of relaxed companionship.

"Ten, I keep running into this name, Seamus McGuiness." I was looking at his features. "Look at that. Even you flinch when I say the name. Who is he?"

He was smiling when he took a long draught of the bitter ale. "That wasn't a flinch, Michael. Just a surprising shift of subject matter."

He took a long breath that came out in a deep sigh. "What can I tell you about Seamus McGuiness?" He seemed to say it to himself.

"Everything. I need to understand him. He was probably behind the kidnapping and death of that little girl. I can't go after him now. I have too many fish to fry already. But I may need to learn the truth to defend a client."

"Ah, the little girl. I'm sorry for you all on that score. And you could possibly be right about Seamus being involved somehow. But I'll give you this from the heart. It'll shock the piss out of me if you find that he was."

"Really. So far, everything points in that direction. Why would you be shocked?"

Ten waived a big arm at the bartender with two fingers up. The bartender drew two more and brought them to the table. I sipped, while Ten took a swallow that brought the level down by three inches.

"You can't know what it was like during the Troubles, Michael. And I can't explain it to ya. You're too young, and you weren't here. In those times, we could be in church. We could be in a meeting. We could be at home. And you never knew if the building would be blown to hell. It could be kids on the way to school, and a rain of bullets at someone else would cut them to pieces. You're feelin' a loss for the little girl, Michael. Well there was hardly a family that hadn't lost more than one. And that on both sides. Seamus himself lost his wife and two little ones. The hatred was that thick you could cut it with a knife. The only thing you could seem to feel in those days was hatred, and fear, and loss of someone you didn't think you could live without. Shite, Michael, the devil had a holiday every day of the week."

He stopped for a swallow of ale and a quelling of emotions too close to the surface.

"I understand, Ten."

"No you don't. But no matter. What I'm about to tell you is not to be talked about. Not here, or back home, or anywhere. Do you hear me?"

"You have my word."

He nodded as if he put stock in that.

"Seamus McGuiness was a soldier. I'll not say what organization, but he was on the side of the Catholics. He did his share of the fightin'. And I'll not deny that any number of her majesty's troops would be alive today if it weren't for Seamus McGuiness. But there were others in his group —"

He took another pause. I was taken back by how close to the surface old emotions lay in this man of the ring.

"There were some in those days who lost their souls without losin' their lives. And some of them are among us today. No conscience left in them at all. They have nothing left to fight for but their own greed and pleasures."

He leaned over the table toward me. "But not Seamus McGuiness." His eyes almost bore holes through mine. "I'll give you one story, and so help me God, Michael, if you ever repeat it—"

"Never, Ten. My hand to God."

"It was years ago. It was the height of the Troubles. There was to be a Protestant march on a street that divided the two sides. It was to be kept secret until the day of the march, but one of our— one of the boys on the Catholic side got wind of it. There was a meetin'. Some of the boys took their march as a brazen slap in the face, but what to do about it? There were going to be children and women in the march. Most of the boys said to hell with it. Let 'em march. There were others, not many, said no. It's a matter of honor. Shite, there was no honor in any of it. But it's a great word for the killin'."

"Was McGuiness there?"

"Will you let me tell it, Michael? Yes, he was there. He heard the plannin'. A few of them were gonna throw bombs from a certain rooftop to kill anyone, any age, in that crowd of marchers."

"Was Seamus in on it?"

"Not by a damn sight. He faced every one of them to a man. He asked them to their face what the hell they'd become. He asked them, if they could do that to children, what kind of a country they'd be makin'. And it did not one damn bit of good. When they left that meetin', Seamus knew exactly who was going to do what in spite of him."

Ten took another swallow. I could see in his eyes that he was back in those days. I kept the silence until he was ready.

"That next day, the marchin' started, to the surprise of no one. It started in the Protestant section and wound through the streets toward the Catholic border. I could see the men I spoke of at the top of the buildings on the corner. They were ready and waitin' to toss the bombs. I could just see the first of the marchers roundin' the bend up the next block. I said a prayer, 'Sweet Jesus, prevent this.' I'd just said it when the whole damn block shook. There was an explosion a block away. It was an old empty building. No one around to be hurt. Some of the soldiers and police ran to it, while the others disbanded the march and sent everyone home. They all went home with their lives."

"Are you saying—?"

"I'm sayin' there wasn't a man in that group that didn't know it was Seamus set off that blast, and why he did it."

"Did he get away with it?"

"It's not likely you'll ever see it. But if you ever do see his back without his shirt on, you'll know the price he paid at the hands of his own for the lives of the other side."

There was nothing either of us could say for the next minute. We finished our pints before shaking hands in the parting. I recalled the words of Superintendent Phelan of the Garda who put me in touch with Ten Sullivan, "If nothing else comes of it, you'll have made the acquaintance of a man worth remembering."

CHAPTER SEVENTEEN

By late afternoon, I was packed and ready to catch the late-evening plane out of Dublin Airport. My last act at the Gresham was to tip the concierge. Since I'd arrived, he'd been ready with directions, information, chat, or a bit of Irish humor, depending on my need of the moment.

"Safe trip, Mr. Knight. Come back to us. Can I get you a car to the airport?"

He took my bag and saw me off with a smile. On another occasion, the smile would have brought me a glow and good thoughts for what lay ahead. As it was, I sank back into the car seat with the hollow feeling that whatever I'd accomplished in Dublin would bring nothing but the pain of confirmed loss to Colleen. I tried to force myself to think beyond that moment when I'd have to wrench out her last ember of hope for seeing Erin alive. In place of hope I could offer her a funeral. Whatever the hell "closure" meant, it seemed overrated.

I was gently jarred out of my dark thoughts by the voice from the front seat. "Mr. Knight, would you permit me a short detour?"

I checked my watch. "How short?"

"No worries. I'll have you there and time to spare."

I drifted back and just put my mind in neutral until I felt the car pull to a stop in the yard behind a small cottage. Even in the dark, I noticed that we were now well into the countryside with no other buildings or sign of life in sight. I watched my driver get out and open the car door beside me. "I think you should come with me, Mr. Knight."

That gentle invitation put every nerve on combat alert. Four words sprang to mind. "Dear God, not again."

I looked up at him. "Do you suppose you could tell me who's staging this command performance?"

He kept a gentle voice. "Think of it more as an invitation than a command."

Ambush though it probably was, his voice had a calming effect. I followed him into the darkness of a one-room cottage that looked like a scene out of *The Quiet Man*. The only light in the room came from a stone fireplace half the size of one wall with a peat fire that sent warmth through the entire body, as only a peat fire can.

The driver pointed to one of two wooden rocking chairs that faced the fire. It wasn't until I was seated that I noticed the man in the other rocking chair. He looked tall even in a slouch, with a body that was muscular but somehow depleted of the energy to move.

"You'll forgive me for not risin', Mr. Knight."

The flickering light from the fire picked up the deep lines in his face that bespoke suffering from some cause that was not obvious.

"How do you know me?"

That brought a smile that had nothing to do with humor. He took a deep breath before speaking. "You're better known than you know, Mr. Knight."

That brought no comfort. "And do I get to know your name?" I asked, though I knew to a certainty the answer.

"My name, for the little importance of it, is Seamus McGuiness."

I had the quiet urge to check my watch for the flight time, but there was something about that face and voice that grabbed and held my entire attention. I couldn't take my eyes off of him.

"I'm glad we met, Mr. McGuiness. I don't know exactly why, but

I'd have felt I'd missed something if we hadn't. And just in time. I have a flight in two hours."

"I hope not, Mr. Knight."

That was a stunner. "And why would that be? I came here for one reason. I've gone as far as I can with it. I have business at home. Perhaps you're aware of that."

He seemed to force himself to shift from one uncomfortable position to another at great expense to his store of energy.

"I'll not be wastin' your time. God knows there's precious little of it. I'll be askin' a service of ya."

"Mr. McGuiness, I'd probably be willing to do whatever it is you want at any other time. Right now, something's pressing." I had my upcoming conversation with Colleen in mind and no desire to postpone it. I stood up.

"I'll thank you to sit down, Mr. Knight. I'm nearly finished."

"Why me? You have all of Ireland to call on. And I have a plane to catch."

He was seized with a fit of coughing. When he leaned to the side, my eye caught a drop of liquid splashing on a pool under his chair. When I focused, the fire lit up the deep crimson color.

"Mr. McGuiness, you're bleeding. Is there a hospital or a doctor?"

He just waved off the idea and shook his head between coughs. "No time. Why you, you're askin'. Because if you're half the man Ten Sullivan thinks you are, you'll not deny a man's last request."

I must have looked blank, because he forced a grin. "Pardon the dramatics. But I have to settle this now."

The pool beneath him was growing steadily. His strength, such as it was, seemed to be flowing out with every drop of the liquid.

I relented enough to ask, "What's the request?"

He seemed to drop back against the back of the rocker to gather strength for his next words. "I'll ask you to get back in the car. Just go with Mr. Kearney."

"And?"

"That's all I'll be sayin'. Just go with him."

I looked at the man who was apparently Mr. Kearney for illumination. He said nothing.

"I'm afraid, Mr. Knight, that Mr. Kearney knows almost as little as you do. And so it must be. A bit of faith. Just go where he takes you. And quickly, if you would. Not much time."

It went against everything inside of me to leave any man with the life pouring out of him with every new drop of blood. On the other hand it already seemed too late. He pressed me once more with what seemed like the last words he had the strength to speak.

"Go now, Mr. Knight. And God be with you."

"I think God knows I'm completely in the dark, Mr. McGuiness. I'll do what you ask. I'm praying that He's with the both of us."

He smiled a resigned and even contented smile. "In a very short time, I'll convey your prayer to Him personally."

I got back in the car with Mr. Kearney with just one clear thought in mind. There's not a chance in hell I'll make my flight out of Dublin. The many ramifications of that thought bounced around my consciousness as we drove over country roads barely the width of a car. It was at least twenty minutes later when we pulled up in front of what looked from the dark outline to be a church.

Mr. Kearney opened the car door for me, and led the way up the few stone steps to the church door. Mr. Kearney, who seemed to know at least that much of the plan, rapped loudly on the heavy wooden door.

We waited in silence for what seemed like an eternity until I heard shuffling footsteps approach from the other side. The door opened with a creak that bespoke the ancient origin of the church. There was just enough backlight from within to illuminate the bent form of an elderly man in a priest's cassock.

Mr. Kearney spoke first. "Seamus McGuiness sent us, Father. This is Michael Knight from the United States."

The only feature I could make out in the semidarkness was a nervous smile that creased the old priest's face. His eyes scanned my face and then darted over my shoulder for a glimpse of anyone or anything that might have followed us. His voice seemed more energetic than his appearance.

"Come in, come in, Mr. Knight. Quickly. You're a sight I never thought I'd see."

I came in in a state of total bewilderment. He took my hand and shook it with unexpected sincerity. "Would ya come this way now?"

This priest, whose footsteps earlier sounded like the labored trodding of old age, had an urgency when he walked ahead of me. He led me to a room to the left side of the altar and lit a dim light. "If you'd wait here, Mr. Knight. Sit, if you please."

I could wait, but I couldn't sit. His burst of nervous energy had my own nerves on edge as well. I spent perhaps five minutes pacing, wondering what on earth would come through that door when he came back.

When the latch on the door sounded its opening, I spun around. All I could make out was a large woman in what looked like the flowing black robes of a nun. I walked toward her with my eyes straining to make out the form of something in her arms.

We were twenty feet apart, when she set down on the floor a tiny form that stood frozen for a moment. Then it seemed to move uncertainly in my direction. My mind refused to believe what every sense and instinct was screaming inside of me. Somehow, disbelief was suddenly shattered in both of us at the same moment. The two of us ran together so hard that we both just spun in circles when I clutched her in my arms. I held that tiny form so close that I was afraid of crushing it, until I realized that those little arms were holding me just as tightly. Between that face, with its nose burrowing into my cheek, and my own face there flowed an avalanche of tears that I couldn't begin to control.

I was almost afraid to open my eyes to find that it wasn't true, but I knew the touch of that little cheek against mine so well that all doubt was overcome. I was actually standing there holding this angel that I thought was gone forever.

When we could finally separate enough so that I could see her clearly, I realized that the tears were not all mine. When she called me Uncle Mike and said she wanted to see Mommy, I have no idea what kept my heart from bursting.

It must have been five minutes before I realized that there were two others in the room. Even by that dull light, I could see that there was enough eye liquid to go four ways. The first to speak was the priest.

"Mr. Knight, you're a gift from God. Seamus said you'd be here, but I could only pray. And thank God for it. But time is precious now. Arrangements have been made. Sister Margaret, would you get Erin's things ready?"

Sister Margaret took Erin to get her ready. The priest, who introduced himself as Father Flaherty, asked me to sit for a minute. I did, and he pulled a chair up next to me.

"I'll be talking fast. We've made the reservations. You'll be flying home with Erin, but not from Dublin Airport. That could be risky. Mr. Kearney will drive you to Shannon Airport. You'll be there in time."

"Thank you, Father. I'm catching up as fast as I can. What about documents for Erin?"

"We have them for you. We have an American passport for Erin and plane tickets for you both."

"I should cancel my tickets on the flight from Dublin."

"I wouldn't. There are those I'd rather have think you're going through with your original plans. It's a small price to pay."

"That's fine, Father. My mind's spinning. How did—?"

"It's a long story, but I'll be brief. There's a gang from over here in Ireland, I'm ashamed to say, arranged for the kidnapping of Erin. I'm not sure why, but there it is. They brought her over here from America and kept her somewhere in Dublin."

"Was Seamus McGuiness involved, Father?"

"He's been associated with that crowd, I'm sorry to say it, from back in another time."

"You mean—"

"During the Troubles. I have to be brief, Mr. Knight. When he heard that there was a little girl involved in their plans, he'd have no more of it. But he pretended to stay involved in their business. It was he who saw to it that she was well taken care of while she was with them. Then he heard that they were going to do away with her. God help us. That little angel."

I could see that his emotions were reaching the surface. I started to speak, but he held up a hand.

"I have to finish while there's time. Seamus won their confidence. He volunteered to do that terrible thing. They trusted him. He took Erin and brought her to us for safekeeping. Then he staged a burial with the undertaker. Empty coffin and all. It worked until this afternoon. That gang of cutthroats caught on. They forced the undertaker to tell them the truth. Then they went after Seamus. Whatever they did to him, he didn't tell them she was with us. When they were through with him, they left him to die. He managed to call me. He said he'd do his best to get you to take her back to her mother."

"Thank God he got me to go along. He told me nothing."

"He couldn't. He was afraid they'd get to you. He knew you couldn't tell them what you didn't know. For Erin's sake."

"I understand. I should tell you that I think Seamus McGuiness is dead. His body is in the cottage where he met me."

Father Flaherty made the sign of the cross. "God rest that good man. When you have Erin back safe in her mother's arms, say a prayer for his beautiful soul."

"I promise."

"Now on the other end. She's not safe in Boston either. Is there somewhere you could take her?"

When my benumbed mind had begun working again, I'd started thinking about that very problem. I had a possible solution. I used Father Flaherty's phone to call Terry O'Brien. It was about dinner-time in Winthrop, Massachusetts. I hoped she'd be just getting home from work.

It was a brief conversation, much like many brief conversations I've had with Terry when the more exotic aspects of my particular practice of law required it. Why she remained faithful to me when she could have had her pick of stable suitors who never get shot at or car bombed is a mystery to me.

True to form, she listened to my incredible abbreviated tale about Erin and jumped in with her usual, "How can I help, Michael?"

Once that part of the plan was nailed down, I made the call that I could not in my wildest dreams have predicted. I called Colleen. When I got that first full sentence out, she nearly came through the telephone line. Erin was back in the room in my arms, dressed and ready to travel. I put the receiver to her ear. When the two of them heard each other's voices, the cries and the shouts from both ends were so loud that they practically didn't need the phone.

The flight from Shannon Airport went more smoothly than anything had since the day a hundred years ago when I watched that race at Suffolk Downs. Father Flaherty had arranged a separate seat for Erin, but she rode in my lap for the entire trip.

When we landed in Boston, I rented a car and drove directly to the North Shore Shopping Mall in Peabody. Out of an abundance of caution in case she was still under surveillance, I had Colleen drive to the mall, go in one particular door of Nordstrom's and pass through the store to go out another specific door. I was parked directly opposite that door with Erin.

Caution or not, when Colleen came out of that door and Erin spotted her, no power on this earth could have stood in the way of either of them. They were locked in mutual hugs while the entire world disappeared around them. I thought that after the night before, Erin had no more tears left to release. I was wrong.

They could not let go of each other, so I put my arms around both of them and moved them across to my rental car. Once inside, I drove by a circuitous route, again out of caution, to Terry's house on Andrews Street on the shore in Winthrop. She had stayed home from work to be there to welcome them. She had even foreseen the needs of both of them for the essentials of clothing and such and had spent the morning shopping.

I had a few minutes with Terry for an inadequate expression of my thanks for one more life-saving gesture. I made a renewal of my promise of a date free of the kind of violent interruptions that had punctuated, though apparently not slowed in the least, our falling in love.

CHAPTER EIGHTEEN

The old Franklin Street digs looked like the gateway to Heaven. The hows and whys of Danny's murder were still floating out of reach, and the gang of thugs who snatched Erin could still be out there planting bombs in the intestines of my Corvette. But I was on home turf. Given that, I felt I could take on the Chinese army.

After calling off the exhumation, I flew direct to Mr. Devlin's office and shut the door. I watched the breath pour out of him in relief when I told him about Erin. When he could speak, it was not to me, and I could hear "Thank you" in his whispered phrases.

A new day had dawned for both of us. A whole new set of ground rules applied since we were no longer worried about bringing harm to Erin.

We set to prioritizing the questions that needed rapid answers with a preliminary hearing to set a trial date for Hector Vasquez inexorably approaching.

For a first move, Mr. D. got Billy Coyne on the line. Given the breach of security in the D.A.'s office that tipped Hector off to the indictment, Billy preferred to converse over a clam roll at a rustic outlying restaurant north of Boston on Route 1.

We converged in separate cars on the Sea Witch just after two in the afternoon. Our back table was the only one occupied, and if anyone had foreseen our meeting there with a wiretap, they were beyond psychic.

True to my promise, I filled Billy in on every detail of my stay in the land of his ancestors and Erin's safe haven in Winthrop with the hope of inducing him to cut loose some new piece of the puzzle. He listened in rapt, but stony silence to the very end. The only flicker of reaction, other than a steady deepening of the lines in his forehead, came when I painted Seamus McGuiness as a mixed bag of decent and villainous qualities, and finally conveyed news of his murder.

The silence continued through an interminable sipping of his coffee. Mr. D. finally leaned into his field of vision with an impersonation of Billy's flat Boston accent. "And so, Lex and Michael, in view of your selfless generosity with information gathered at no small peril to life and limb, I'll break my damned infuriating silence with a reciprocal sharing of information. How's that for a start, Billy?"

Billy just looked up at Mr. D. as if the sarcasm just floated over his head.

"This is not a Yankee swap, Lex. The kid did all right. But he barely got his toes wet. I thank God about the little girl, but it doesn't change anything."

That stunned the both of us, but Mr. D. had the Irish temper. The volume rose ten decibels and to hell with privacy.

"Damn it to hell, Billy! How can you sit there and say—?"

"Because I know what's going on, and you don't. Damn it yourself. Give me credit for having an ounce of brains and integrity. There's more to this than a fixed race."

"Then for the love of God, man, open up. Who do you think you're talking to, some sleaze-bag informant? This 'kid', as you like to call him, brought home the bacon, and laid it on your plate. That should earn him, and me, a certain amount of trust."

Billy looked straight ahead, but he leaned to within three inches of Mr. D.'s face and dropped the tone to a whisper. "Trust has no part in it. I'd trust you with my life, Lex. And that without a second thought."

That brought Mr. D. back to earth, and a confidential tone of voice. "Then what? Why is there no give here?"

Billy's elbows were on the table and his head in his hands. The struggle that was going on inside was practically visible. He spoke quietly through his hands. "This is big. It goes beyond friendship, trust, professional courtesy, whatever card you want to play. For what it's worth, Michael, you've added a significant piece to the puzzle. You've opened the window another inch."

I was so shocked to be addressed by my name that I had trouble assimilating the rest of the sentence. Mr. D. had no such trouble.

"Then at least tell us what that piece is. Can you give that much? We're defending a murder charge here. A weak one, but nonetheless."

Billy sat straight up, looked at me and then Mr. D., and dropped his napkin on the table in front of him. He spoke to Mr. D., but it was for both of us.

"This city of Boston, this city that you and I love could be in a hell of a fix."

"What—?"

"Don't interrupt me, Lex, or so help me God, I'll be out that door and be happy that I kept my mouth shut."

Mr. D. backed off. Billy dropped his voice three pitches.

"I'll say this and no more. I walked in here believing that the worst I had to worry about was coming from Seamus McGuiness. Now I know that McGuiness was a bit player in a scene that tests my imagination. And that's a bit jarring to say the least."

He just stood up and shook his head. I saw a man ten years older than the one who sat down to lunch with us walk out the door.

So far, the afternoon had produced a plate of the most wicked good, in the vernacular, fried clams west of Ipswich, but precious little illumination about whatever it was that Billy Coyne was dreading. On the issue that involved us directly, I had a firm grip on the obvious—the peculiarities surrounding Black Diamond and his running of that race were tied directly to Danny's murder. The fixing of that race could be laid at the least at the feet of Vince Scully. Anyone else involved was still in the category of conjecture and speculation. That suggested the need for a visit I could happily have avoided for a lifetime.

By four in the afternoon, the Failte Pub in Southie was taking on a cluster of beer-slugging patrons for what the martini and cosmo set on State Street would call "Happy Hour." The buzz and rumble of conversation, in an amalgam of working-class Irish and working-class Southie accents, were rising steadily.

I picked a spot where I could not be seen by anyone coming through the door from Boyle's office and wedged my way to the bar. The suit and tie drew the odd glance, but it always ended in a smile and a nod. The bartender at my end was not the one I'd encountered in my first visit. Hence the amiable "What's yours, Mack?"

I leaned over the bar to be heard. "Sam Adams lager, and a question."

He cocked a sideways ear. "Yeah, Mack. What's up?"

"Vince Scully?"

He checked the clock behind him while he drew the Sam Adams. "Should be in any time. He expectin' ya?"

I gave him a kind of slanting nod with a wink and a smile. It could have meant anything. He seemed to accept it as an affirmative and answered the call of other demands down the bar.

I leaned sideways on the bar and nursed the pint with an eye on the entry. At about four thirty, I saw the familiar figure of Vince Scully start through the doorway, catch one glimpse of me, and back out of sight in the time it took for one sip of the Sam.

While I was deciding whether or not to go after him on foot, I heard the ring of the bar phone through the din. The bartender grabbed it, listened, and said no more than a couple of words before hanging up. He leaned over the bar and beckoned me to do the same. He said in the lowest voice that could still be heard, "Mr. Scully called. He said meet him in the same place. You'd know."

"When?"

"That's the whole message, Mack."

I gave the OK sign and slugged down the last couple of inches of the Sam. Before I could move off, the bartender grabbed my arm and pulled me close enough to whisper.

"He had one last word. 'Alone.'"

Since Scully gave no time, I figured he could only mean right then. The drive from Southie to the last place we met, the church on Arch Street in Boston, took only a merciful twenty minutes just before rush hour. It was also before the assemblage of office workers for the five p.m. Mass.

I found that same dark figure in the last pew on the right side of the church. I slid into the pew directly ahead of him. I kept my voice as low as possible.

"Mr. Scully. You called."

There was a stress in his voice that replaced the tough cockiness I expected.

"What the hell were you doin' in the Failte?"

"I felt like a Sam Adams."

I barely got the words out when he grabbed a bunch of the back of my shirt collar and straightened me up. The voice came out as a strained hiss.

"Don't get wise, you little bugger. What were you doin' there?"

"I came to talk to you."

There was a moment's pause that put the starch back in my probably unfounded confidence.

"What do you want, lawyer?"

"I want to breathe, Scully. Get off my neck and you'll hear it."

He let go of his grip, which gave me an even greater sense that I had more leverage than I thought.

"So talk."

I deliberately paused and slowly turned to face him.

"An even swap. I've got information I think you need. I want information in return. That's the price."

"I'm listenin'."

"I think you got yourself in one hell of a bind. You're tied to that kidnapping. At least as a lookout man. That's enough. In for a penny is in for a pound. You're up to your neck in it. That's how the law works."

Silence. The last time we met, he told me that he thought Erin had been killed. That meant he thought he could be facing a murder charge. So be it.

"But your boss, Boyle, is not involved. That means to me that you've been up to some double-dealing on Boyle that could put your neck on the block when it comes out. And it will come out. How am I doing so far?"

He leaned in two inches from my ear.

"I could put the silence on you right now, lawyer. That's how you're doin'."

I had no idea what he might be holding for a weapon, and that was discomforting. I had one more card to play.

"It'll do you no good. The D.A. knows all about it. It'll be out whether I tell it or not. But that's not what has you shivering in your boots, is it, Scully?"

No reply. I took it as an invitation to press on.

"I just got back from Dublin. I met your friend or associate-in-crime or whatever, Seamus McGuiness. You'll remember tipping me off to his name. I don't think the boys over there took that too kindly."

"What the hell are ya sayin'? Get to it." Definite tension in his voice.

"Good news and bad news, Scully. The good news. You don't have to worry about Seamus McGuiness coming after you. He was killed there yesterday. The bad news. The gang McGuiness was working with probably had him killed. They could be on your doorstep next. I have a feeling they could make Boyle's gang look like a bunch of cub scouts. But you'd know better than me."

He sat back. You could cut the profound silence with a cleaver. I could hear his breathing get more rapid and I'd have bet his forehead looked like the morning dew. I let the pot boil for a minute before speaking.

"Like I said, Scully, I give, you give."

He said it almost in a daze. "What do ya want?"

"Just one thing. Who killed Danny Ryan, and how and why?"

As long as he showed no sign of bolting, I let him consider his options, few as they were. It was the right move. When he spoke, I was dumbfounded. He gave me the mother lode.

"I'll give it to ya, lawyer. The whole thing. Only my way, or not at all."

"And your way is?"

"I want protection. Witness protection program. I want in. You get it for me, and I give you the whole ball of wax. That's it."

It was as if a trapdoor sprung and I fell into a pot of twenty-four-karat gold. I couldn't believe what I was hearing. I also couldn't hesitate or this fish would be off the line. I had to move fast. People were slowly filling up the front pews for the five o'clock Mass.

"Wait here, Scully. I'll make a call."

I went back through the doors to the vestibule of the church and dialed up the district attorney's office. The receptionist recognized my name as being with Mr. Devlin. She put me through immediately to Billy Coyne's private line. He was as stunned by what I had to tell him as I'd been.

"All right, kid. Stay with him. I'll send some plainclothes to pick him up."

"Can you get him into witness protection, Mr. Coyne?"

"Assume yes. Tell him yes. It's a federal program, but I think the feds will jump on this like a cat. Get back there and stay with him."

"One thing, Mr. Coyne. We get the benefit of anything he has to say that clears Hector Vasquez, and the full cooperation of the district attorney's office on that. Right?"

"One thing at a time, kid."

"No. This comes first. I want your word on it now."

"Damn. Now I've got two Lex Devlins on my ass."

"You could do worse. I want your word."

"All right, kid. Vasquez is small potatoes. I can give you that much. Now get back there."

If it were anyone in that office but Billy Coyne, I'd have recorded his agreement. But I knew his word was better than a recording.

I went back through the door into the church and slid into the same pew in front of Scully. I turned my head enough to focus a whisper at him.

"It's done. The D.A.'s sending protection. They'll take you into protective custody. He can get you into witness protection."

I assumed that that brought genuine relief to the stressed-out Scully since the heavy breathing ceased. I did, however, expect some kind of acknowledgment, if not gratitude.

When the silence became annoying, I turned around for an explanation. He seemed to be asleep. I nudged him on the shoulder to get a response. His whole body slowly sank to the right. The light in that part of the church was no great shakes, but even in those shadows, I could see the gaping slash across his throat.

I ran to the outer room and got Billy Coyne back on the phone.

"Too late, Mr. Coyne. He's dead. His throat was cut while we were talking."

I won't repeat the Irish curse that erupted on the other end of the line. When it ended, I said the obvious. "I'll call the police and stay with him till they get here."

"The hell you will, kid. I'll call it in. You get the hell out of there. Now."

"What? Are you telling me to leave the scene of the crime without giving a statement? I'd like to keep my bar membership, Mr. Coyne."

"You did give your statement. To me. I'm the deputy D.A., in case you forgot. I'll tell the police I'm handling it. Now get the hell out of there."

"I don't like this, Mr. Coyne. Deputy D.A., or not. I need a reason to leave."

"I'll give you two, kid. The killer could still be there. You were talking to Scully. Guess who the next target could be. I'll give you another one. I don't want you being interrogated by the police right now. I don't know who I can trust, and in case you didn't hear me the first time, this thing is a damn sight bigger than Hector Vasquez. Now get the hell out of that church—forgive the expression. And be careful. If you get killed, Devlin'll have my ass for not protecting you."

I thanked him for his heartfelt concern for my welfare and took to the street.

CHAPTER NINETEEN

For no particularly good reason, I felt safe in not going underground. Most convincingly, I was right there when Scully was killed. If they wanted me dead, it would have been a simple thing to make it a doubleheader.

Much as it goes against my nature to be up before daylight, I was at the backside of Suffolk Downs as the light was beginning to dawn.

This time it was not to see Rick or the jockeys. I found my way to the three men who drove the heavy metal mesh drags over the track to break up the clods of earth and fill in the hoofprints to smooth the track for the morning gallopers and breezers.

I was still bothered by the exceptionally mundane times for Black Diamond's workouts prior to the race on MassCap day. Kieran Dowd had explained how they disguised his real times from the racing press in Ireland. I wanted to know how they did it on this side and who was directing it.

I had a fair suspicion as to how it was done and figured there was no reason for the track drag drivers to hold back the information. I used the straight approach. After the introductions, I asked if they usually dragged the track right after the last race of the day to leave it ready for the early workouts the next morning. They did.

Then to the interesting question. Did they ever come to the track in the morning and find hoofprints before any of the horses had taken to the track for a workout?

They looked at each other with that kind of half-smiling expression that said, "How did he know that?"

"Yeah. Couple of times. Pisses us off. We leave the track perfect for the first riders. Some yoyo comes along and does this. We figure we could get nailed for it. And who did you say you are?"

"I'll tell you who I'm not. I'm not the guy who's going to get you in trouble. I'd appreciate one more answer though. Can you remember when you found the track like that?"

They put their heads together and came up with two dates over the previous month. I figured their fear of getting blamed for the condition of the track would give them a reliable recollection of the specific dates.

That was the easy part. Now I needed a matchup. I caught Rick McDonough as he was finishing debriefing his first set of riders back from the morning's gallop. This required a delicate touch. I would have bet my Bruins tickets—playoffs and all—that Rick would have no part in the deceptions going on with Black Diamond, but I was not ready to tip him off to what I'd discovered so far.

"Rick, I need a favor, and I've got nothing to give in exchange for it."

He gave me that old-time-cowboy look. "When did I ever ask it, Mike? I look at you and I see Miles. What do you need?"

"I need you to check your records. I need the dates you breezed Diamond with the track press reporting the times."

I could see the curiosity in his eyes, but he just ran his calloused hands over his head and walked back to the stall he used for an office. Five minutes later I had two dates. It was like pieces of a jigsaw puzzle slipping into place when the two dates squared with the dates the track conditioners found hoofprints on the track in the morning.

That was it. Much like what had happened in Ireland, someone galloped Black Diamond around the track the night before he was to breeze for a clocked timing to be reported in the press and condition books. The Diamond apparently always gave everything he had, but on those mornings, he was running on tired legs.

That left two major league questions. Who did the night riding, and more importantly, on whose orders? I was not ready to tell Rick he had a traitor in the stable. I had no idea how he'd react, and since lives were already being spent, the timing from there on out could require delicacy.

One thing I'd have bet on. The night rider was one of Rick's stable crew. The security on the backstretch of Suffolk Downs is rigid. If anyone not connected to Rick's stable had gotten into the area at all, which was unlikely, he would certainly have drawn attention saddling up, galloping around the track, cooling out, and stabling Black Diamond.

I watched Rick ride his big roan gelding onto the outer edge of the track to watch the next round of workouts before I wandered down the row of his stables. It was easy to strike up a jovial conversation with Rick's stable hands. The Spanish flowed easily and like most Latinos I've known, they were quick to exchange laughs.

As seamlessly as possible, I guided the conversation around to who pulls the night shifts. I knew Rick's concern for his horses well enough to know he'd always have one of his own crew awake in the stable area all night.

We joked about who got stuck with the overnight duty. It turned out that it was usually settled by a gamble on short straws. We had a few laughs, and I heard the name Manny Gomez pop up with some snickers about his love life. Since Manny was hot-walking a horse away from the group, the jokes at his expense came readily. I joined the laughter and nudged the conversation further.

It turned out that Manny had used a demanding girlfriend as an excuse for swapping night shifts with the others on a few occasions. That could be pay dirt.

I sauntered down the row of stalls to the one with the name of the horse Manny was hot-walking and slipped into the stall. When Manny finished and walked the horse into the stall, I caught him by surprise. This time, the direct approach was less likely to produce the quick results I needed.

I had two edges up on the conversation. I could do it in Spanish, and I was Hector Vasquez's lawyer. Both could help in implying that I was in with whomever was pulling Manny's strings. I added a low tone that couldn't be heard outside of the stall to emphasize the conspiratorial nature of the conversation.

"You've been doing great, Manny. The big guy's pleased. Nothing to worry about. He needs you to do something else."

I could see him freeze up, but I did an internal high five when I saw him go to the front of the stall and look up and down the row before turning around. It seemed a good moment to go with the assumptions I made about who had been controlling him.

"We've got some trouble in the organization, Manny. Mr. Scully had to be taken out of the picture, if you take my meaning."

I was locked onto his eyes for a reaction to the name. What I read was intensified tension, and no trace of a look that said, "Who the hell is Mr. Scully?" On with the show.

"There'll be a new contact, Manny. We're breaking in a new man. We need to keep him on a short leash for a while. You know, just to be sure. Loyalty is everything, right?"

"I don't understand. What do you want from me?"

"Me? Nothing. I'm just delivering the message. The big guy wants this. When our man contacts you for another night ride, you call me just to confirm it? You got that, Manny? Here's my number."

I gave him a card with just my cell phone number on it. He looked at it without speaking, and I knew he needed more incentive.

"Two things, Manny. You listening?"

"Yeah. What?"

"He would not be pleased at all if you didn't show your loyalty in this. Not at all. You understand?"

"Yeah. *Comprendo.*"

"That's good, Manny. The other thing is he rewards loyalty. There'll be more in it for you this time. A good bit more."

That part seemed to sit well. Between the carrot and the stick, I figured I had a chance of learning who Scully's replacement would be in the gang that was manipulating Black Diamond. I left feeling that we had at least one duck in a row—to bend a metaphor.

On my way out, I passed by the rail where Rick was still astride the roan, watching and clocking his horses.

"Any new plans for Black Diamond, Rick?"

He looked around. "You looking for a tip on a horse, Mike?"

"Not any horse. I've become sort of a fan of the Diamond."

He looked back at the track. I knew there was a certain close-to-the-chest secrecy to the plans for entering horses in particular races. If it had been anyone else, he would have kept his silence. Just before I started to move away, I heard in low tones.

"Next Friday. Sixth race. Five and a half furlongs."

That was jarring. Unlike other trainers at Suffolk, Rick never ran his horses back with less than three weeks rest.

"Who made that call, Rick? That wasn't yours."

He looked down at the pommel of his saddle. I could see his teeth clenching.

"I just get him ready the best I can. The rest is out of my hands."

I leaned over the rail to get as close as I could. "Rick, this is for Danny. I need this more than I can tell you. It could go a long way to making things right. Is it the Irish bunch that's calling the shots on the Diamond?"

He looked back at me with that tough, stone-faced look and I just prayed for a crack in the wall. It took ten seconds before I got a slight nod. I had to press on.

"Rick, I know I'm pushing it. But I'm asking for Danny and Colleen, and even Miles. He'd back me on this. Someday I'll tell you why. I need a name. It's not Kieran Dowd. He's just the trainer over there. Who's giving you the orders?"

He looked me in the eye and the stone wall was up again. I knew I was asking him to betray one loyalty for the sake of another one.

"Rick, you don't know this. Two men have died so far. Three, counting Danny. It has to end. I think I'm the only one who can make things move, but I need that name. I give you my word. Your name won't come up"

I could see the struggle in the deepening grooves in that leathered face, and I hated being the one who put them there. I knew I'd lose some of the trust between us if I pushed him, but there was no time and no other way.

"Damn it, Michael!"

"I know, Rick. But we need it. Don't let Danny's death go for nothing."

That stung. He turned his head in the other direction. He was gripping the pommel with both hands, and I was losing hope of breaking the code of loyalty of this old cowboy.

I was half a second away from relenting and letting him off the hook, when I heard the whisper.

"Sweeney. Martin Sweeney."

I locked it in my memory. "Is he connected with Dubh Crann Stables?"

He looked at me as if I had gone beyond anything our friendship entitled me to. There was both defeat and anger in his voice when he barked out, "Yeah."

He pulled the reins and dug his heels into the roan's side to canter down the track away from me.

CHAPTER TWENTY

It seemed that at least ten thoughts were struggling for front-and-center time as I drove to the gate from the backstretch. The most pointed was a pang of remorse for putting a painful wall between me and Rick. That was the first bridge I'd try to mend when this thing finally resolved.

When I reached the gate, one burning desire rose to the top of all the other issues. I turned right on Revere Beach Parkway toward the ocean with the intent of taking another right on Winthrop Parkway. I figured that since I was close, I had time to stop in and check on Erin and Colleen without making a call on a possibly compromised cell phone. I could also see Terry for long enough to insure that she still remembered what I looked like.

I was just settling into the joy of anticipating those two possibilities when my cell phone rang. It was too soon for Manny to have heard from Scully's replacement, and only a small handful of people I'm close to have my cell number. That's why it was jarring to hear a completely unfamiliar voice with a pronounced Boston Irish accent.

"Keep drivin', Knight."

"It's my every intent. What's your interest?"

"You'll find out. Stay on the parkway. Bear right ahead there at the fork."

Whoever it was knew where I was and where I was heading. When it finally clicked, I checked the rearview mirror. There was a blue Chevy Impala about ten feet from my rear bumper. The driver had his cell phone to his ear. More disturbing when he put down the cell phone was the handgun the size of a .357 Magnum he waved out the window and pointed at my gas tank. When he knew he had my full attention, he put down the gun and picked up the cell phone.

"Keep on straight, Knight. Take a right on Bennington."

That did not sound promising. Bennington led back to Belle Isle Park. At that early hour of the morning, it would be just the two of us and the ducks. And he had the only gun.

I decided to change the odds. I dropped the Corvette down one gear and just continued at the same speed to where Revere Beach Parkway bends left at the fork. At the last second, I whipped the wheel to the left and floored it.

The Corvette, true to its breeding, leaped an additional thirty miles an hour. The Impala barely made the turn and came barreling after me. I eased off on the speed just enough to let him keep me in sight.

I made a three-quarter turn around Eliot Circle on two wheels and floored it again on Revere Beach Boulevard. The Impala labored to close the gap, but I stayed far enough ahead of him to prevent an accurate gunshot.

When I was within a hundred yards of the Castle-Mar Motel, I cut back on the speed and let him catch up. In a few seconds, he was back on my rear bumper, screaming demands into the cell phone in colorfully blistering language, but so far he hadn't fired a shot.

My fits and starts were not quite as random as he must have thought they were. I had a clear recollection of two expensive chats with Revere's finest on that stretch of road just past the Castle-Mar. I prayed that they were creatures of habit.

Fifty feet from the Castle-Mar, I hit the gas pedal, but this time only fast enough to exceed the speed limit and still keep him on my tail.

We blew past the Castle-Mar at sixty with only twenty feet between us. For the first time in my life, I thanked God for the Revere Police Department when I saw the red and blue flashing lights fall in line behind the Impala. I knew the police couldn't stop both of us with one squad car, and they were more likely to go for the car closest.

The screaming siren sounded to me like Beethoven's *Third Symphony*. I could see the driver of the Impala scrambling to get the gun far under the driver's seat before pulling over to the curb. His face was bright red, and it turned two shades deeper when I succumbed to the urge to wave out the window.

There was one last thing to do. I turned a sharp left, and then another left onto Ocean Avenue. I cruised past the backside of the Castle-Mar and took two more lefts. That put me back on Revere Beach Boulevard. I dropped the speed to within the speed limit and drove past the spot where a nearly seven-foot traffic officer seemed to be taking serious exception to the language coming from inside the Impala.

I resisted the urge to honk the horn and wave on my way by, since my primary purpose was only to catch the license number of the Impala. That done, I got on the phone to Tom Burns.

"I need some of that Tom Burns magic."

"Ready and waiting. You sound out of breath."

"Just playing a little cartag with one of the boys."

"You need help, Mikey? I have people ready to go."

"No, Tom. I'm good. At least for the moment. I need you to run a license number for a name and address. Can you do that?"

"What's the number?"

"Mass. tag, 49560. My guess is Revere or East Boston."

I based the guess on location on the fact that Manny Gomez must have phoned his gang contact as soon as I left the stall. His contact put the Chevy driver on my tail and gave him my cell phone number. That meant the Chevy driver lived close enough to Suffolk Downs to get there in the five or ten minutes I was talking to Rick.

The thought crept into my consciousness that the Lord might

have dropped a possibility into my lap that should not be ignored. Before I could act on it, I needed three things—a name and address from Tom Burns, a plan that could result in my surviving, and enough solid sustenance to get me through what I had in mind. A stop in the nearest Dunkin' Donuts had possibilities for all three.

Ten minutes and two chocolate-covereds later, Tom called.

"Got a pen, Mikey?"

"You're golden, Tom. Shoot."

"Kevin Murphy. You're on the money about the Revere address. Forty-two Walden St. It's a little street off Beach Street. You got it?"

"No sweat. I know Beach Street."

"Then you know that neighborhood. You need backup?"

"I want to try a soft approach first. Another face could throw it off. If it doesn't work, I'll thank you to send in the marines—or the coroner."

I needed one more piece. I called my diminutive gossipmonger in South Boston, Binney O'Toole. From the sound of his voice at that hour, I caught him in mid-hangover.

"Binney, a moment of your valuable time. I need to tap your expertise."

"And it couldn't wait till a decent hour, I suppose."

"Right again, Binney. I need information on one Kevin Murphy. Lives in Revere."

"Oh, for the love of the saints, Mikey. Do you get a man out of a sound sleep to ask about the likes of Kevin Murphy?"

"I do, Binney. And it sounds as if you have a bit of information to share."

"I wouldn't count on it. I remember the last little chat we had. Gave me the trots for three days, it was that distressing."

"It also gave you a handsome jug of the Tullamore Dew. That could happen again if I think it's worth it."

There was a slight pause and a distinct change of tone.

"And what can I tell you about our Mr. Murphy?"

"Everything you know."

"Little there is worth tellin'. The truth of it is he's a bagman for Doyle's outfit. Has been for the past thirty years I've known him."

"Meaning what?"

"Sure what do they teach ya in law school, Mikey? Your education's been neglected."

"Then educate me. Do it well and I'll call your favorite bartender and see that there's a green jug waiting for you."

I could hear him lick his lips.

"Ah, then. Bagman 101. He's just that. He carries the bags of cash from Boyle's bookies, loan sharks, extortionists, and the rest of it back to Boyle's office."

"And gives it to whom?"

"I'll deny that I said it. He gives it to that blackheart, Vince Scully. That's the half of it. He also carries bags of cash the other way to Boyle's politicians, police, judges. He's an errand boy, but he's one they can trust with the bags of cash."

"Is that it? Because that's not worth half a jug. What else?"

There was a second's pause. "Well, there might be somethin'. What bartender did ya say?"

"I didn't. Give, Binney."

His voice dropped to a near whisper.

"I shared a drop or two a couple of weeks ago with your friend, Murphy. He was well into his cups. He spilled a little word between us. It seems that every couple of weeks, they send him to the North Station. There's a locker key left for him in an envelope at the newsie's shop. Always the same locker. Five twelve. I remember 'cause it's me birthday."

"And—"

"He said he opens the locker and takes out a leather valise. Always the same."

"What's in it?"

"Ah, that's why he mentioned it. In a whisper, mind you. It has him puzzled too. He assumes it's cash, but he never opens it.

Wouldn't dare. The orders are to take it direct to Mr. Boyle himself. No one else."

"What else, Binney?"

"On me mother's grave, that's all I know. Now can we discuss this other business?"

We picked a bar in the bowels of South Boston. I called and left word with the bartender that I'd be in before the day ended to pay for a jug of the Tullamore Dew. He agreed to hold it until Binney got there. We hardly finished the conversation, when I heard Binney's out-of-breath voice in the background, looking to collect his Dew.

By the time my Chevy driver parted ways with the speed cop on Revere Beach Boulevard and parked in front of forty-two Walden Street, it was a little after eight a.m. He looked about fifty, five foot five or six, and the kind of pudgy that makes everything he wears look as if it were mail ordered. His balding pate was like a mood ring—the color indicated the state of his emotions, which at that moment, were still in the red zone.

He lumbered up the flight of stairs to the porch that ran across the front of the house. He was out of breath, and his hand quivered enough to require three stabs at the door lock with a key. I was sitting on one of the lounging beach chairs that adorned the porch facing the door.

"Good morning, Kevin."

I gave it my cheeriest tone. He leaped just high enough to take the porch light off its mooring. The key flew out of his hand and somehow landed at my feet. I picked it up while he tried to catch his breath. I expected to see him pull the handgun out of his belt, but he had apparently left it in the car.

A crotchety, elderly sounding female voice with an Irish accent came from upstairs.

"What did ya break now, Kevin?"

"Nuthin', Ma. Go back to sleep."

"I heard—"

"It ain't nuthin', Ma. I'll fix it."

"Why can't you get in at a decent hour like your brother? I can't—"

"Go back to sleep, Ma."

The upstairs mother was another gift from God. Kevin was unlikely to get raucous with me on the front porch as long as his mother's hearing held out.

I got up and walked over to Kevin with a take-out cup of steaming Dunkin' Donuts coffee in each hand. He had probably been rousted out of a sound sleep by whatever gang member took Manny Gomez's call, and absolutely nothing had gone right since. He just stared at me with an expression that said he was almost too worn down to be pissed off.

I handed him one of the coffees, and said, "Kevin, why don't we sit down and talk things over? Better yet, you just drink the coffee. Let me talk. Let's see if I can make sense of this thing."

Kevin looked as if he were too confused by the morning's events to make a clear decision to sit or stand. He probably got the early call to corral me because he was the only one who lived closer to Suffolk Downs than the boys in South Boston.

He finally sat down across from me and began slurping the coffee without a word.

"This work with a gun. It's not your line of work, is it, Kevin?"

He looked up at me over the rim of the coffee cup.

"The hell do you know about it?"

"Well, Kevin. May I call you 'Kevin'? You don't seem too good at it."

No response. Back to slurping. My tone went from bright and cheery to sharp and threatening.

"I want you to listen to me. You've had a bad day so far. In your most frightening dreams you can't imagine how much worse it's going to get in the next few hours. You listening, Kevin? You don't know it, but after this morning's little farce, you're in it up to your little red ears. You don't begin to know what trouble is. Shall I lay it out for you?"

The slurping stopped, but his mouth hung open and his eyes were riveted on mine.

"Here's the deal. Mr. Boyle says you're a bagman for his organization. He says you're a good-faithful employee. He feels he can put a lot of confidence in you. What do you think of that? I bet you didn't know how Mr. Boyle felt about you."

I couldn't hope for anything affirmative yet, but I got a very valuable negative. No denial. In fact, the slight relaxation of the folds that were creasing his forehead said he was pleased to hear it. From the look of Kevin, and the tone of his mother upstairs, it was probably the first compliment Kevin had heard since he was toilet trained.

"Do you ever get to talk to Mr. Boyle personally?"

Silence. Another slurp of coffee.

"This is a conversation, Kevin. I have a reason for asking. Do you ever see Mr. Boyle face-to-face?"

Another slurp. "Sometimes."

"You see, this is why he values you, Kevin. He values loyalty more than anything else on earth. He's told me that a dozen times. Did he give you that impression?"

The chances were good that the only words Boyle ever spoke to him were curses or orders. Nonetheless.

"Yeah. I guess."

"I agree with you, Kevin. Now I'm going to tell you something that's not for publication. Did you ever meet Vince Scully?"

The mere name put the wrinkles back in his forehead. I didn't need an answer.

"See, Vince Scully took up with another gang behind Mr. Boyle's back. Mr. Boyle heard about it. I was with Vince Scully last night. They slit his throat wide open from ear to ear."

I added the appropriate gesture.

Vestiges of shock and fear grew in Kevin's beady little eyes. He'd probably thought of Vince Scully as invincible.

"Now, here's the deal. When you threatened me with a gun this morning and tried to force me to go to Belle Isle Park, you were acting on the orders of a man who's also turned traitor to Mr. Boyle. That makes you part of the conspiracy."

I figured whoever took Scully's place as Manny Gomez's contact had to be linked to the mob that controlled Black Diamond and kidnapped Erin. And those were definitely not Boyle's troops.

"I'm thinking of the gaping slit in Vince Scully's throat. I can't help wondering how Mr. Boyle will react to your working for his enemies."

"The hell I am! I'm just doin' what I'm told!"

He was on his feet. His telltale pate was passing through magenta. His voice was up two octaves. That triggered a raspy voice from upstairs.

"Kevin, will you for the love of—?"

"Yeah, yeah, Ma. Go to sleep."

He pulled his chair over and leaned about six inches from my face. He was down to a hissing whisper.

"What the hell am I supposed to do? I get a call before the damn sun is up. He says he's callin' for Mr. Boyle. I do what I'm told."

"Just sit down, Kevin. Cool down. Have some coffee. There's a way out of this. Just relax."

The last thing I wanted at that particular moment was for Kevin to go into cardiac arrest.

"I'm the only one in Boyle's outfit who knows about this. It's distinctly in your interest to have me keep my mouth shut. Are we in full agreement?"

He saw the possibility and nodded.

"Then tell me one thing, and my lips are sealed. When is the next time you go to the North Station?"

His eyes bulged. I think the thought of disclosing information about his most secret mission frightened him almost as much as the specter of Scully with his throat slit. Thank God, the operative word was "almost."

He leaned closer. "If this gets out—"

"It won't. When? Say it."

He wiped away brow sweat with his sleeve.

"Tonight. Five o'clock."

I patted him on the shoulder. "Thank you. That'll be our little secret."

I started down the porch steps, when a thought struck home. I caught Kevin as he was opening the front door.

"Oh, one last thing. Who called you this morning?"

He looked to both sides and hustled over to me in three quick steps. He was spitting the words out between locked teeth.

"What the hell more you want from me? I don't even know who the hell you are."

"Sure you do. I'm the one you tried to kidnap this morning at gunpoint on orders from a traitor to Mr. Boyle. I'm the one who's keeping you alive, remember?"

He just froze.

"Who was it, Kevin?"

Another look both ways. It came out in a hiss. "Sean Flannery."

"And what exactly did he have waiting for me at Belle Isle Park?"

"I don't know. I swear it. I was just supposed to get ya there."

"Uh-huh. But chances are it wasn't an invitation to a tea dance. Right?"

"I gotta get in."

He was back across the porch and through the door before I could get another syllable out of him, but that was enough. I remembered Sean Flannery as the stakeout who relieved Vince Scully in front of Colleen Ryan's house after the kidnapping. I couldn't help wondering, *"Mr. Boyle, how many traitors do you have in that rat pack of yours?"*

CHAPTER TWENTY-ONE

Like it or not, it was time to move into the big league. We'd been dismissing Billy Coyne's major sweat over something bigger than Hector Vasquez as Billy's problem, not ours. It finally dawned on me that that kind of thinking could be dangerous. If we kept limiting our concern to an isolated piece of the puzzle, we'd go on blundering like mice in a maze that only see as far as the manipulator lets them see.

I went into Mr. D.'s office to make my pitch that afternoon. He dropped what he was working on, stretched back in his oversized desk chair, folded his arms over his suspenders, and gave me the go-ahead nod.

"Point one, Mr. Devlin. Someone in Ireland went to great lengths to conceal Black Diamond's natural speed. Why? No-brainer. So they could ship him to the United States and make a killing on his first race. Suffolk Downs is a good choice. It's a small-time track. Mostly mediocre, unpredictable horses. If a long shot comes in out of nowhere, it's not like it doesn't happen every day. They pick Mass-Cap day when all the attention is on the big race. Nobody much cares what happens in the early races. It's a perfect setup all around. Black Diamond has long odds, twenty to one, and that's no surprise given his reported workout times and poor breeding. They can bet the farm. How'm I doing, Mr. Devlin?"

"No disagreement yet."

"Then let's play another line. That same race happens to be fixed by Boyle and the Boston mob for Hector Vasquez's horse, another long shot, to win the race. There's no indication that the Irish gang behind Black Diamond let Boyle in on their scam. On the other hand, since Vince Scully appears to have been secretly working for both mobs, he undoubtedly informed the Irish mob behind Black Diamond that Boyle had the fix in for Vasquez's horse. In fact, that may be why the Irish mob picked that particular race for Black Diamond. Boyle didn't put the fix on Danny because Black Diamond didn't seem to be a threat, based on his workout record. So if the other jockeys pull their horses to give Vasquez's horse the win, it's a genuine lock for Black Diamond. The Irish mob knows Black Diamond can beat Vasquez's horse on natural speed like he's standing in cement."

Mr. D.'s eyes were closed, but I knew it was all going in. "Perfect logic."

"All right. Now here's where the logic goes sour. On the day of the race, the Irish mob behind Black Diamond goes to the extreme length of kidnapping Danny's daughter. Why? To get Danny to win the race on Black Diamond? No. He was going to do that anyway. It had to be to get him to lose the race. Why? After all they went through to make a bundle on Black Diamond's first race, why would they want Danny to lose? It makes no sense. For some reason, all of a sudden on the day of the race, both Boyle and the Irish mob had the same interest. They both wanted Danny to lose the race."

"I'll give you this, Michael. You're right. It defies logic. At least on what we know so far."

"And it gets worse. When Danny squeaked Black Diamond through on the rail at the eighth pole, he was apparently going for the win in spite of everything. So either Boyle or the Irish mob had to knock Danny out of the saddle to keep him from winning. That throws us two more curves. Which mob was it that caused Danny's spill? Or was it both? And, even more perplexing, how did they do it?"

"You're assuming, of course, that there's not a simple answer to that last question. I might add, one that does not defy logic."

I knew what he was getting at. I just looked at him.

"You don't want to hear it, do you, Michael?"

I knew that he was suggesting that the simplest answer would be that our client, Hector Vasquez, used his whip to jab Danny out of the saddle. Nothing in the films showed that he didn't. But to accept it would be to concede that Mr. Devlin was right in the debate that began the day I met him. I'd be admitting that clients do lie about their innocence to get the lawyer to fight harder, and therefore a lawyer should never build a defense on a belief that the client is telling the truth about his innocence. Mr. D. called it an invitation to being blindsided. As he says, the jury has to presume the defendant is innocent until proven guilty; defense counsel doesn't.

"Face it, Michael. If Vasquez is guilty, and if we can't establish reasonable doubt, which, by the way, is looking more difficult all the time, our best service to the client may be to get the best bargain for a guilty plea. Heaven knows the D.A. is panting to cut a deal for the testimony of Vasquez against Boyle's mob."

"True, Mr. Devlin. But if he is telling the truth, and he's not guilty, even with probation, which is not likely, it would mean a criminal-felony record and probably loss of his jockey's license. That's assuming Boyle's people let him live long enough to ride again anyway."

Mr. D. just held up his hands and shrugged. I think it was a comment on my gullibility.

"Besides, I want to try one more approach before suggesting a guilty plea to Vasquez. There are too many jagged edges to this thing."

"What kind of approach?"

I could hear a perceptible protective shift in Mr. D.'s tone—protective of me. To avoid unwanted limitations, I decided to keep it vague.

"It's still a bit sketchy. I'll keep you up to date."

"Damn it, Michael! Every time you do that, I get another ulcer. These are not boy scouts we're up against. What are you up to now?"

"A walk in the park. Nothing my mother couldn't handle."

I neglected to tell him that the kind, loving, caring woman of faith he knew as my mother had had an upbringing in a neighborhood in Puerto Rico that could rival marine boot camp.

He took a few seconds to digest the mother comment. His respect for her cooled the heat of the moment. He went back to being quietly strategic. I made a mental note to remember that little ploy.

"There's another reason we have to get this game together soon, Michael. We have a preliminary hearing before Judge Peragallo this afternoon at four. I got a call from his clerk this morning. I want you there. He's going to be looking to set a trial date. Angela Lamb'll be trying to pressure us into a plea with a trial in the next couple of weeks. It's fish or cut bait time."

I must have had a look that conveyed my reaction to a two-week trial date.

"What is it?"

"We need more time. At least three weeks. I may have to go out of town for a bit."

"There you go again. Where are you going this time? If you get yourself hurt, your mother and I'll both have your head on a platter."

His phone rang. He answered it and handed the receiver over to me. I thanked God it was my secretary, Julie, rescuing me with word that Tom Burns was on my line. After I left Kevin Murphy, I had asked Tom to have a man keep an eye on locker 512 at North Station and tail anyone who made a drop there.

"Shall I transfer it to Mr. Devlin's office?"

"Not on your life, Julie. I'll be right there."

I remembered the question I had left hanging.

"Possibly Ireland, Mr. Devlin. What could happen to me in the land of your ancestors?"

It was an exit line, delivered over the shoulder as I passed quickly out of his office to take the call.

I closed the door of my office and picked up the phone.

"Go, Tom."

"Pay dirt. Got a pen?"

"Shoot."

"That could be a prophetic phrase. This even has my head spinning. Your man dropped the valise in locker five twelve. He left the key at the news shop. My man followed him back to his office."

"Right. Which is where? And who is it?"

"Top of the Fidelity United Trust Building on State Street. Are you hearing this?"

"Tom, you're dragging this out. Who is it?"

"This is not just dramatic effect. I want your full attention."

"You have it. For the love of Pete, who is it?"

"Colin Fitzpatrick."

He paused for some reaction from me. I had none.

"Refresh me."

"CEO of the largest investment firm in New England. He burps and the stock market gets indigestion. You listening, Mike? This man is a walking pillar of power and money."

"I hear you."

"Not when you say it that way. I'm talking power beyond anything you can imagine. Want a translation? Whatever the hell you're planning, back off."

My little bucket of confidence in what was shaping up as a plan was being drained by the gallon. I needed at least to bluff my way into a false sense of optimism.

"Like they say, Tom, the bigger they are—"

"—the harder they squash little gnats like you."

I took a deep breath. "I'll be all right. In the words of Sir Galahad, 'My strength is as the strength of ten, because my heart is pure.'"

"Oh shit, Mike. That's the kind of crap that could get your parts in six different suitcases."

When I stepped out of the building onto Franklin Street, Tom's words were slowly seeping into my sense of reality. I'd been able to dismiss the almost bombing of my Corvette outside of Daddy High-tower's as a once and done incident. I'd even been suppressing the thought of what I could have walked into in Belle Isle Park. But I'd never heard Tom speak like that, and we'd come through some hairy tangles together. His tone, even more than the words, was stripping away my mental firewalls.

On the walk to the garage, I could actually feel myself fighting down a good case of the jumps every time I melded into a sidewalk crowd, rounded a corner, or, in particular, contemplated turning the key to start my Corvette. Each of them brought up a little volcano of stomach acid.

I had to block it out or I'd be useless to everyone. I remembered the wise words of John Wayne. "Courage is being scared to death, and saddling up anyway."

On that note, I saddled up and drove to Suffolk Downs.

Alberto Ibanez rode a roan gelding in the second race and came in fourth. I caught the attention of his groom just after Alberto had handed him his saddle and straps to get ready for the next race. The groom hesitated, but finally walked close enough to me to take a slip of paper I held close to the rail. There was no one close by, but eyes were everywhere.

I was standing by the rail in the paddock when the jockeys mounted up for the next race. Alberto was on number six, and when he rode by me on the way to the post parade, he never looked in my direction. He just smiled at some imaginary person across the pad-dock from me and mouthed the word, *"Viernes."*

As he rode past, I kept my eyes glued on his hands while he tied the traditional jockey's knot in the reins. I knew what I was looking for. His only hand motion that had nothing to do with the knot was a quick flashing of four fingers close to the horse's mane.

I could suddenly sense the distinct clicks of a couple of puzzle pieces dropping into place. My note to Alberto had said that the time we talked about was now. I needed to know when Boyle was going to fix the next race. Alberto had cautiously told me in Spanish that it was to be Friday, the fourth race.

It was no trick to get the phone number of Fidelity United Trust. The trick was to penetrate the web of protective isolation provided by the staff surrounding Colin Fitzpatrick himself.

I resorted to my fallback. When in doubt, fly direct, and tell the truth—to some extent.

I worked my way through a series of holds and transfers from clerks and underlings with patience and determination until I hit the highest level I could reach with the unvarnished truth—Mr. Fitzpatrick's appointments secretary. To go the final distance, the truth needed a bit of varnishing.

Ms. Paxton's creamy-smooth tones sugarcoated the steel-clad blockade she maintained against anyone who presumed to invade the privacy of the man himself.

"Ms. Paxton, My name is Michael Knight. I'm a junior partner in a firm that is totally irrelevant to the business or pleasure of Mr. Fitzpatrick. And yet, I would like you to push that little button in front of you to interrupt his doings with the financial giants of the world in order to shoot the breeze with me."

That was the truth. And clearly the truth would have gotten me a disconnect faster than I could blink. Obviously, I didn't say that. Instead, I repackaged the truth and took a slightly different tack.

"Ms. Paxton, my name is Michael Knight. I'd like you to tell Mr. Fitzpatrick that I'm going to lunch now."

"I'm sure he'll be absolutely delighted, Mr. Knight. Should I alert the city desk of the *Globe*?"

I liked her already.

"No need. But there's more to the message."

"Are you about to disclose your dinner plans as well?"

"You're too kind. Insignificant as my little message sounds, it is more important than you can imagine that you tell Mr. Fitzpatrick immediately that I will be having a sandwich on the bench in the Public Garden in front of the swan boat dock."

"I'm sure he'll be thrilled for you, Mr. Knight. Must I convey the type of sandwich?"

"Kind of you to think of it. But no. That won't be necessary. Just one more detail though. And this is the crux of the message. I have news regarding a certain Seamus McGuiness that's more important than any stock quote he'll hear all day. Will you convey that?"

"I shall interrupt his conference call with the German and Swedish ambassadors immediately to inform Mr. Fitzpatrick of your luncheon plans."

"Ah, Ms. Paxton, I detect a note of levity in your voice. And to be perfectly honest, I could fall in love with you for it. Any day but today. You know that tired, overused expression a matter of life or death? Clichéd as this will sound, this is exactly that. But you won't have to explain that to Mr. Fitzpatrick."

CHAPTER TWENTY-TWO

Within fifteen minutes, I was seated alone on a bench in the Public Garden. It would have been a center of tourist activity if it were swan boat season. Summer tourists from far-flung regions like to see where *Make Way for Ducklings* took place.

As it was, I sat warding off a chill, looking at the quiet pond where my parents and those of practically every other Bostonian had treated their children to the gently paddled cruise around tiny islands, throwing bread in the direction of ducks smart enough to swim in their wake.

The chill was partly weather and partly the jitters, wondering what I'd say to this behemoth of finance if he did show up, which was looking less likely every minute. Passersby were few at that time of year. I matched every one of them against the profile I had formulated for Mr. Colin Fitzpatrick. I was praying that the name, Seamus McGuiness, would penetrate the air of triviality with which our Ms. Paxton would deliver the message—if in fact, the message got through at all.

Twenty minutes and half a sandwich later, I noticed the brisk pace of a tall, pinstriped suit, tailored impeccably to a man with snow-white hair and an air of self-confidence and New York urgency about every movement. The whitish, pinkish tint of his clear skin clearly bespoke a Celtic ancestry.

His eyes remained fixed on the pond, but there was a deliberateness about his taking a seat at the far end of my bench. He simply sat in silence.

My gaze also stayed on the pond. Between bites of sandwich, I broke the silence softly.

"Mr. Fitzpatrick, I presume."

I hoped he caught the allusion to Stanley's greeting to Dr. Livingston to set a high tone to the conversation. Apparently not.

"What is it this time?" The tone was heavily salted with something between anger and disgust.

"This time, Mr. Fitzpatrick?"

"What does McGuiness want now? I can guess, but I'll give you the pleasure of telling me. How much?"

I slid a paper bag with the label of Zaftig's Delicatessen across the bench. I had dispatched Julie to the bowels of Brookline for two of Zaftig's world-famous corned beef specials. He cast a disdainful eye on it, but never moved.

"Corned beef special on rye, Mr. Fitzpatrick. Even New York can't beat Zaftig. Surely I haven't met the first Irishman who didn't like corned beef. I'm not McGuiness's man."

He looked across at me. A slight tint of surprise joined the anger and disgust. "Then who are you?"

"I'm probably the one person on this globe who can offer you the possibility of relief from the monkey on your back. I have no connection with McGuiness."

"Then this is not about money?"

"Actually it is, in part. But it's not about extortion."

He looked back at the pond as if to cut me out of his sight. You could practically taste the loathing for me and all he thought I represented.

"Really. And what do you call it?"

I gave it a few seconds. "Why don't we stop playing the naming game and get to the point, Mr. Fitzpatrick?"

He just nodded, but he was radiating a seething heat.

"McGuiness is dead."

That brought a slightly startled look in my direction.

"And I suppose you take up where he left off?"

"I've told you twice now. I'm not connected with McGuiness."

"Then who the hell are you? And what do you want? As if I didn't know."

"What I want is ten minutes of your time. Where we go from there is your choice."

For the first time, he looked *at* me instead of *through* me. On the other hand, we were clearly not buddies.

It was showdown poker time—all the cards faceup. He was a man who played for high stakes as a profession. Intuition told me that if I strayed one inch from the truth, I'd sever the thinnest of all possible threads.

I laid out everything I knew, beginning with Danny's fall and ending with all I'd learned in Ireland. Then I got to the thin-ice part.

"Here's what I think. For some reason beyond my understanding, you sent a lot of money over to Ireland to support the IRA during the years they were bombing innocent people in London and Northern Ireland. It probably went back to the eighties and nineties. That was a major crime in this country—supporting an illegal terrorist organization. That was then. The so-called cause must have ended when England and Ireland reached a peaceful agreement in the late nineties. My understanding is that it's been all diplomatic relations since then. I've read that even Gerry Adams tried to squelch the bombing and shooting wing of the IRA. Am I right or wrong so far?"

"You have a warped view, but I'm listening."

"Then let's get personal. You still send shipments of money to those thugs over there. They don't represent a cause anymore, except their own bank accounts. So now it has to be extortion. They've probably got you by the throat. You keep paying or they turn you in for supporting an outlawed rebel gang in the old days. It sounds like a never-ending gravy train."

He looked at his watch and stood up.

"Young man, you had my curiosity. Now you're just annoying. You clearly have no idea whom you're dealing with." He walked toward me until he stood nearly touching my knees. "If you think you can jump on that gravy train, let me put it straight. No room for doubt. If you ever contact me again, or anyone else on this subject, I'll crush you into tiny pieces. Disbarment will be the least of your worries. Do you hear me?"

I stood up. Our heights brought us eye to eye. It took every ounce of will to look into those pools of hatred and not blink.

"I hear you, Mr. Fitzpatrick. Now you hear me. This morning, you personally took a valise of money to the North Station. You put it in a locker and left the key with the man at the newsstand. It will be picked up by one of Boyle's men and delivered to whoever replaces McGuiness. From there it goes to those Irish thugs, probably some of what's left of the IRA."

The details brought the seething heat in his eyes to a boil. I had to hold fast against an avalanche of temptation to cut and run.

"The locker number was five twelve. I can prove all of that. And if you can pry your ears open, I'll tell you for the fourth time. *I'm not here to extort your money.*"

He might have heard me for the first time. Anyway, he froze in place.

"Then what the hell do you want?"

"Exactly what I said. I want ten minutes. Stand, sit, stand on your head. I don't give a damn. But listen to me. You may be surprised."

The fire in his eyes could have ignited a conflagration. But he stood there for a full ten seconds making a decision. Swallowing orders from this juvenile delinquent must have gone against everything he'd been conditioned to in half a century. But he was still there. I waited until the internal blaze subsided.

"We could do this more easily sitting down, Mr. Fitzpatrick. We don't have much time."

The decision did not come easily, but he sat down in the middle of the bench.

"They say 'the enemy of my enemy is my friend.' On that score, I'm your friend. I'm convinced that to defend the jockey I told you about, I have to crack the wall of that Irish mob that controls the horse. I have reasons to believe it's the same bunch that's been extorting you."

He just stared at me in silence, but the steam pressure seemed to be slightly diffused.

"I want your help, Mr. Fitzpatrick—and thirty thousand dollars."

That brought his head around, and the steam was back.

"Just sit there, Mr. Fitzpatrick. I said I want it. I'm not demanding it. I'm going to explain why I need it and what I'll do with it. Then you make the choice. You're in or you're out. If you opt out, it's the last you'll see of me."

He still looked suspicious, but he hadn't moved. I took it as an invitation to get to the details.

Before I lost him, I explained quickly how I'd begun to see the pieces of the puzzle fit together. I laid out how I planned to use his money in as much detail as I'd been able to work out. The payoff line was that if I could pull it off, I might have the answer to who killed Danny, and he might have the extortionists off his back.

When I finished talking, he leaned back. For the first time he looked at me as if he were sizing me up without a preconceived prejudice. I only knew that he was still there, and he wasn't glaring at me like the embodiment of Satan. I was the first to break the silence.

"Mr. Fitzpatrick, could I ask you a question? Answer it or not as you wish."

"What?"

"I think you're a good man. I'm literally betting my life on that. Back then, how could you give money to the terrorists in the IRA?"

He shook his head. I think it was at the incongruity of his bothering to explain anything to this juvenile. He stood up and looked back at me.

"Do you have any Irish blood in you, Knight?"

"I do. My paternal grandmother was Irish. Her parents came over from County Waterford. My Irish blood is usually at war with the Puerto Rican blood on my mother's side."

He half laughed, which was a first. His body language was still speaking tension, but for the first time he was speaking the words rather than spitting them out between his teeth.

"Do you know when it started? What the Irish call the Troubles?"

"No."

He sat again on the edge of the bench. He checked his watch against whatever was pressing him to just leave.

"Why do I bother? You obviously couldn't care less. On the other hand, maybe you should understand why your great grandparents probably risked their lives on a famine ship to come over here."

"I'm interested."

"Then listen. Two kings fought for the English crown and control of all Ireland in sixteen ninety. The Battle of the Boyne River in Ireland. Every hear of it?"

"Not really."

"I thought not. The Catholic King James was beaten by the Protestant King William. Most of the people in the south of Ireland were Catholic. From that time on, they were subjugated in their own land. William and the rest of the kings of England that followed him took the best land from our people to give it to their English favorites. Your ancestors and mine were reduced to the poverty of dirt-poor farms and heavy taxes paid to the lords of the manors. I'm compressing a hell of a lot of history here."

"I understand."

"I doubt it. But I don't have time to give you the whole picture. I'll tell you this, though. If there's a drop of Irish blood in you and you haven't heard of the potato famine, I'll say to hell with you and leave now."

He looked me in the eye.

"Don't leave. I've heard of it, but that's about all."

"Then listen. Ireland was still a colony of England in 1845. Eight million people, and half of them living in abject poverty. Our people. They lived on dirt farms so poor that all they could grow were potatoes. It was literally all that kept them alive. There was no other food. One day they woke up and a blight spread like wildfire across Ireland. Every potato they pulled up was black, diseased, and shriveled. And that left nothing a man could feed his wife and children, let alone himself. It lasted five years."

He stopped for a minute. I could see in his face that he was feeling the pain of the people he was one with. There was bitterness in his voice.

"Over a million, Knight. Can you conceive of that? Over a million of those people died the slow death of starvation. Women, children, the lot. Another million left Ireland on the famine ships to try to save their lives. Your great grandparents were probably among them."

"I had no idea it was that bad."

"Well then try to understand this. There was no reason for it. There was plenty of food in Ireland at the time. There was so much surplus food in the hands of the English king's people who owned the land in Ireland that they were exporting wheat and grains for profit all through the famine. That, while over a million people in the same country died of starvation."

There was nothing to say. We both sat in silence for a time.

"That was the start of it. The oppression of the Irish went on until the need to be free of the king of England drove them to fight an impossible insurrection to take back their country. They had the example of our own American revolution against England to give them hope for the impossible. The Easter Rebellion in nineteen sixteen was the start of it. It was bloody and it failed. But it was the turning point. Michael Collins led the fight in the streets of the cities and the towns until he was killed himself. Did you ever hear of Michael Collins?"

"I've heard the name."

"He was the George Washington of his day for Ireland. Anyway, in nineteen twenty-one, Michael Collins and his group met with the then British prime minister. The English were exhausted by

World War I. They had no stomach to keep fighting the Irish. They finally gave Ireland home rule as a dominion in nineteen twenty-two. The Irish Free State, all but six counties in the north. Mostly Protestant. They chose to remain a part of England. Still do."

He looked out over the swan boat pond.

"They share an island, Protestants and Catholics. But the hurts on both sides run so deep and so fresh—the violence on both sides, killings and bombings, not just the soldiers, but innocent people, children. There's not a family, especially in the north where Catholics and Protestants live close together, that doesn't have its dead to mourn and to keep the hatred alive."

He paused in his thoughts. I used the silence to ask what I might never get another chance to ask.

"If Ireland got home rule in nineteen twenty-two, why did the fighting between Catholics and Protestants go on?"

He looked at me as if I hadn't heard a word.

"What the hell do you think? The king signs a proclamation of independence and everyone lives happily ever after? The Irish people were still dirt poor. The English still owned the land. The power in a Catholic country was still in the hands of the Protestant English. The oppression didn't disappear because the king found a pen. That's why the Irish Republican Army came into existence. They fought the battles to make independence for the Irish people a reality. And yes, damn it, I supported them. My mother and father came over in nineteen forty. They had tales to tell of what life over there was still like. They saw to it that I got an education here. I made some money, and I did what I could."

He looked at his watch and stood up. I was about to lose him but for one last question.

"So how did it change? How did it go from support to extortion?"

He sat back down. I could feel a different kind of pain come back in his face.

"The time came. It was in the nineties. Even Gerry Adams. He led a group called Sinn Fein, "Ourselves Alone." He realized that the best course was nonviolent negotiation with the English. He and his outfit had meetings, some of them secret with the English, even while the violence continued. After a while, the violence of the paramilitary wing of the IRA became counterproductive. Eventually the negotiations led to the peace agreement of nineteen ninety-eight. The IRA agreed to lay down their arms."

"What about the bombers and shooters in the IRA. How did they take it?"

"That's the shame of it all. They became irrelevant to the cause. But they were still men of violence. And they were well organized as a paramilitary group. Many of them turned their skills to crime. Bank robberies, holdups, whatever."

"And extortion?"

"I tried to cut off any support when the peace agreement was signed. But the violent ones had a grip on me. I could go to jail for the rest of my life because of the support I'd given them before."

"And you've been paying ever since."

He stood up, and I did too. The biggest question was still hanging in the air. I dreaded the moment, but I had to ask it straight out. I held out the bag I had offered him before with the corned beef sandwich from Zaftig's.

"Mr. Fitzpatrick, I have to know. As my senior partner says, it's fish or cut bait time. Not to be dramatic, but I may be staking my life on your decision. Are you in or out?"

He looked into my eyes as if he were searching for an answer. Could he sanely risk his freedom, possibly his life in the hands of this underage Don Quixote with the implausible scheme?

It took what seemed like an age, but he took the sandwich out of my hand and left with two words.

"Call me."

CHAPTER TWENTY-THREE

I was actually buoyed up by what I took as a positive result from the meeting I'd dreaded with Colin Fitzpatrick. At the same time, I was deeply feeling the weight I'd taken on these uncertain shoulders, and all on the strength of a "plan" that now seemed barely a hypothesis. In other words, the jitters were back with a vengeance.

I had a rare few hours free of any other commitments. I indulged in the intoxicating prospect of spending those hours with Terry O'Brien and aimed the Corvette toward Winthrop. That also carried the prospect of checking on Colleen and little Erin.

I was through the tunnel and into East Boston when I got a cell phone call from my faithful secretary. Julie may be on the short side of twenty-three, but she never lets that stand in the way of acting like my surrogate mother.

"Michael." I know that tone of voice. It always precedes a lecture. "Who are these people you're dealing with?"

"I don't know, Julie. Give me a hint."

"Someone who's very upset says he wants you to call him immediately."

"That could describe twenty people I've met in the last week. Narrow it down for me."

"Easier said than done. I think he was calling from Ireland. But it could be Iceland. That accent was thick as pea soup."

"It's Ireland. Who was it?"

"The best I could get out of it was something like Paedar something."

That rang no bells. "What number?"

I jotted the numbers down as Julie read them.

"I'll call now. By the way, would you book me on tomorrow night's flight to Dublin. Make it one way. I'm not sure how long this will take."

I got another shiver when I realized I'd have to survive what I had in mind to get to use a return ticket.

"Michael, are you doing something risky again? I think I should get Mr. Devlin on the line."

"Not a bit of it. I'm fine. I'm flying over to catch the running of the Irish Derby. It's just a little fun thing. No need to trouble Mr. Devlin."

My warped view of the truth is that the Lord perhaps sanctions the use of its opposite as an escape hatch from certain uncomfortable conversations. i.e., no harm, no foul.

I pulled into a Dunkin' Donuts parking lot and dialed the number Julie gave me. The voice that answered sounded as if he had his hand over his mouth and the phone to muffle the sound.

"Mr. Knight. Thank God. I wasn't sure she got the message."

"I'm sorry. She didn't get the name. Who is this?"

There was a pause as if he was looking around before he spoke.

"I have to make it quick. My name is Paedar Kearney. I'm the driver who took you to the priest when you picked up the little girl."

"I remember. What's wrong?"

"Dear God. I had to let you know. I came back to the house. I found Father Martin. They tortured him somethin' fierce. He's dead."

The words rang through my mind. *My God in Heaven. What kind of people are these?*

"How about the sister? She was there at the time."

"Nowhere to be found. I suppose they've taken her. I have to call the Garda. I needed to let you know first. They were probably tryin' to make Father Martin tell them where the little girl is. I don't

know if he told them anything. Or the sister. The little girl can identify them."

I squeezed every memory cell I had to recall whether or not I had
mentioned where I was taking Erin and Colleen. I couldn't be sure.
The best thing I could do was to assume that the thugs had the information and move.

I called Terry immediately. I thanked God that she answered.
She could tell from my tone that I hadn't called for a chat. In the
nearly six months we'd been a couple, I'd been in enough threatening scrapes that brought her within reach of the danger to react
quickly.

I told Terry to pack a few necessities and have Colleen do the
same. I'd be there in fifteen minutes. She knew I had reasons, and
there were no questions.

I took time for a quick call to Tom Burns. I gave him the bare
outlines. He caught my tension and the reason for it.

"It'll take me half an hour to get there through traffic, Mike. I'll
make a call. Damn it. I've offered you a gun twenty times. Why the
hell—?"

"No, Tom. We'll debate it over a Guinness someday. I'm out of
here."

With no traffic at one in the afternoon and a heavy foot on the gas
pedal, it took me sixteen minutes. I skidded to a stop on the short
gravel road to the beach that was Andrews Street. Terry's car was
there. The house seemed peaceful.

My relief at finding the scene quiet lasted right up to the time I
saw the outside kitchen door standing half open. Terry always kept
it closed against bugs.

I was caught between caution that said go slow, and the panic
that was driving me to rip through the house in search of Terry. I was
so distracted by worry that I was inside the kitchen before I realized
that something else was missing. That set my alarms off full tilt.

There was no barking. Terry had a Shetland Sheepdog. Kelty and I had bonded from day one. I couldn't drive up the street without hearing that glad-to-see-you bark at the door. But not this time.

I got as far as the dining room before getting the answer to one question. It nearly brought up my lunch. Kelty was lying there with a bleeding cut on the top of his head. My heart was in freeze-frame for them all. Kelty must have felt my presence because I saw him start to move. I ran to him as he was struggling to get up on his front legs. I held him for a few seconds until he could get his hind feet under him.

He was still unsteady, but I held his head in my hands and whispered to him. "Where are they, boy? Where's Terry? Where's Mama?"

I've told Terry twenty-nine times that that dog is smarter than both of us put together. He was weaving, but he made a direct line for the stairs. By the time he hit the top step, he was at full speed. I wasn't far behind.

He ran and leaped at the closed door to the bedroom. It didn't budge. All I could hear was Kelty's frantic barking. There was no sound from inside.

To hell with caution. I didn't even turn the knob on the door. I just smashed it open.

My heart went into overdrive. I saw Terry on the bed and Colleen and Erin on the floor. They were all bound hand and foot. Gray tape covered their mouths.

I ran to Terry first and tried to get the tape off of her mouth without taking the skin off of her lips. Before I could pry it loose, I heard some kind of gargling sound from her throat. I looked at her eyes. They were looking over my shoulder with pure panic.

I spun around, just in time to take a blow on the chin from what I later learned was the butt of a rifle. The room passed in an instant through gray to black. After what was probably a few seconds—or minutes, it passed back through gray to the fuzzy image of a man standing in the hallway.

When the image cleared, I could see that he was on a cell phone. At that point I had nothing to fight with. I struggled to form one clear thought in a head that was splitting with gongs and cymbals.

The first rational thought I had was why the hell did I keep refusing Tom's offer of a gun? That was a dead end—but then not completely. It brought to mind something Tom said on the phone. He said he was making a call. To whom? I could only make one guess.

My second rational thought was that this thug must be acting for the Irish gang that kidnapped Erin. He was here to finish the job. On the other hand, since he was on this side of the ocean, he might be one of Boyle's men, like Scully, who was double-crossing Boyle for the Irish mob. So what does that do for us?

I decided to grasp at two straws at the same time. The thug was yelling into the phone in the hallway. I figured he was talking long distance to Ireland. He seemed to be asking what to do about the two women with Erin.

With as little movement as possible, I reached into my coat pocket for my cell phone. I used 411 in a whisper and got a connection to Paddy Boyle. The thug in the hall was so into his weak connection with Ireland that he couldn't hear me.

I can seldom remember being more relieved to hear a human voice on the other end of a phone line. Boyle was his usual gracious self.

"Yeah. What?"

I said in the loudest voice I could muster, "This is Michael Knight. Just stay on the line, Mr. Boyle. You're going to hear something interesting."

That time the thug in the hallway heard me. He came back into the bedroom with the rifle aimed at my left eye. I recognized him as one of the men at the bar in Boyle's pub.

I held my cell phone up to him. I knew Boyle could hear everything we said. I put it on speaker.

"It's for you. It's your boss. It's Paddy Boyle. You work for him, don't you? I've seen you in the pub. What's your name?"

"What the hell're you talkin' about? Gimme that thing."

He grabbed for it, but I pulled it back to get a few more words in. Truth be told, I was stalling for a miracle.

"No name, eh? Mr. Boyle'll know you anyway. About thirty, six feet, sandy curly hair, Red Sox T-shirt with Johnny Damon. Scar on the right side of your face."

I could hear Boyle screaming into the phone, "Casey! Is that you? What the hell's goin' on over there?"

Casey, if that was his name, was stymied. With Boyle on an open phone, and me narrating a situation that he clearly did not want to have to explain to Boyle, he didn't know if he was afoot or on horseback. But he did have that damn rifle.

I still needed time. I got Boyle to stop the flow of obscenities long enough to get in a word.

"Mr. Boyle. Your man, Casey, here says he'd like a word with you. Shall I put him on?"

What he said in more flavorful words came down to, "Put him on!"

I held the phone out to Casey. He looked at it as if it were a coiled cobra. He couldn't refuse Boyle. He grabbed the phone, but there was no time to speak. The gravel in the road in front of the house growled with the skidding sound of cars pulling up in front of the house. I knew in my heart that they were Winthrop police cars. I also knew they were there because of Tom Burns's call.

I raised my head enough to see out the window facing the beach. Armed uniformed police were running up the beach side toward the back and both sides of the house.

Casey dropped the phone. Whatever he feared from Boyle was trumped by the closing circle of police. He bolted down the stairs and ran through a side door into the narrow space between houses. He covered less than twenty feet before he was boxed in by police with weapons drawn.

It took another fifteen minutes to carefully untie and ungag the three girls. There was no time for the comforting they needed. While they threw some clothes into suitcases, I took Kelty downstairs to wash the blood off the cut on his head, and show him with hugs and treats what I thought of him. I blocked out the thought of what would have happened if he hadn't found them in that bedroom.

At some point, the thought of the pre-trial conference with Judge Peragallo penetrated through everything else going on in my mind. I called Julie. In the most unperturbed voice I could manage, I asked her to see if Mr. Devlin could have the hearing put off until the next morning.

The five of us piled into Terry's Escalade, thrown-together luggage and all. I figured at that point we could drive direct without evasive action. It wasn't likely that either gang could get a tail on us that fast.

Two hours later, we were deep in the pine woods of New Hampshire on the dirt road that led to my family cottage on Milton Pond. We had picked up food and other supplies for an indefinite stay on the way through the town of Milton. The cottage had been recently winterized for stays through cold weather, and if seclusion was a key factor, it had it in spades.

I stayed while the girls were settling in with unpacking and planning something to eat. Little Erin was with Kelty on the beach in front of the cottage making a sand castle.

I stressed a few final points with Terry and Colleen before leaving. No phone calls out on the cottage phone. No charges on credit cards. Both of those could be traced. If I had to call, I'd let it ring twice, hang up, and call again. Answer no other calls. I'd have a trusted friend from town deliver a rental car in the morning so they could get into the town of Milton for shopping, but no farther.

They took it in like troopers. By the time I was ready to leave, the morale in their little group seemed astoundingly good, considering what had happened within the previous four hours. There were kisses and hugs all around, including Kelty.

Terry walked me to her car, which I'd be using to get back to my Corvette. We just held on to each other with no words for a long time. I know we were both wondering if life would ever give us a time together to just feel love for each other in unbroken peace. We could only hope and pray for it some day. But not this night.

CHAPTER TWENTY-FOUR

The next morning, I decided to use the two-ring code to call the Milton cottage. The girls were into pancakes and New Hampshire blueberries and coming through like troopers.

The most definite word I had to give them was to hold tight until I called them with the all clear. Only the Lord knew when that would be.

I could hear the worry in Terry's voice that could only come from a deeper love than I deserved, considering what I'd put her through. I made a mental note on the balance sheet that I owed her love and peace by the ton. The former I could promise. The latter, for the moment, was out of my hands.

Julie's cell phone message told me that the pretrial conference before Judge Peragallo was set for nine thirty. I had breakfast in a little hole-in-the-wall on Arch Street that I'd never been in before—just to break any routine that could have been noticed. I entered the courthouse through the jurors' entrance, thanks to a buddy on the security desk. It started me wondering where the line was between caution and paranoia.

Our little menagerie gathered in the judge's chambers with His Honor presiding from behind a magnificent walnut desk. Judge Peragallo was young for the bench—mid-thirties, but something of a wunderkind as a trial lawyer. He had the reputation for shooting straight down the middle. He could match any lawyer in front of him in intelligence, and he had caught on quickly to the subtle tricks

of older practitioners who walked into his courtroom with an eye to
playing on the youthfulness suggested by his boyish features. They
frequently walked out with their heads tucked under their arms. He
was nobody's fool.

The cast of characters included: Mr. Devlin and myself on the
side of right and justice, and D.A. Angela Lamb and Billy Coyne
representing the prosecution.

The judge set a brisk tone after barely clearing the good mornings.

"Counsel, when can we bring this to trial? Keep in mind, we
have a man sitting in jail."

Angela, never one to let a point pass unscored, was on her feet
as if a spring came through her chair.

"Your Honor—"

"No need to stand, Ms. Lamb. We're in chambers."

She was down as fast as she'd been up. What she lacked in
courtroom savvy, she made up in obsequiousness.

"Your Honor, the people, as always, are on the side of swift justice. The people stand ready—"

I'd been before Judge Peragallo before. I'd noticed that when he
got the slightest whiff of bull crap, his eyelids came down slightly
and his level of intolerance climbed on a steep vertical curve. He
spoke softly, but the edge was there.

"Ms. Lamb, the people are out doing whatever the people do on
a Tuesday. Let's keep this thing real. What does the D.A. want?"

Angela flushed as if she were in an instant tanning salon. Bluff
and posturing were clearly her best, if not only weapons. They generally served her well. In fact, she was likely to ride those two qualities into the next higher elected office as long as Billy Coyne was
competently sitting first chair for the district attorney's office in the
courtroom.

Mr. Devlin stepped into the breach before Billy could come to
her rescue.

"If I may, Your Honor—"

"You may, Mr. Devlin. Please."

"Thank you. I imagine our esteemed district attorney was about to claim readiness to try this case in the next five minutes. That would give us swiftness. I'm afraid it would be a far cry from justice. There are complications. May I point out one of them."

"I'm all ears, Mr. Devlin."

"Then perhaps Your Honor would entertain a motion. The defense would like to move for disclosure of the names and addresses of every eyewitness to this so-called murder the prosecution intends to call."

Angela was still off balance and this nearly tipped her out of the chair. Her personal need to recoup face trumped her greater need to call in reinforcements, to wit, Billy Coyne. Her voice rose half an octave.

"Your Honor, that's out of order. We've had no notice that this would be turned into a motion session. There are matters of security, protection of witnesses. We're not prepared—"

Mr. Devlin cut in. "No, Your Honor, I can see that Ms. Lamb is, as she says, not prepared."

Mr. Devlin was leaning back in his chair with a composure that nicely counterbalanced Angela's increasing flustration, to coin a word. Billy Coyne had lines in his forehead that projected near panic at what the loose canon in a pantsuit to his right might say next. Judge Peragallo was reading every expression with a faint but increasing smile. He looked to Mr. Devlin with anticipation.

"Well, Judge, I'll take her off the hook. If witness security is her worry, I'll withdraw the motion."

Angela almost sighed in relief. Judge Peragallo's focus remained locked on Mr. Devlin as if he knew that that was not the last shoe to drop.

"On condition, Judge, that the district attorney play fair with this court and the defense and admit here and now that she has no wit-

ness whatsoever who can testify to what caused Mr. Ryan to plum-
met out of that saddle. Surely that doesn't put any prospective witness in jeopardy."

Judge Peragallo's smile was in full flower when his attention
shifted back to Angela. His distaste for officiousness was matched
by his appreciation for a subtle, legitimate ploy of counsel.

"Ms. Lamb, the ball would appear to be in your court."

She got as far as a strained, "Your Honor—" when Billy launched
a lifeboat—more for the case than for his superior.

"Judge, do you mind if I make a request?"

Judge Peragallo seemed to welcome getting the case back in the
hands of two professional trial counsel.

"I wouldn't mind a bit. I might even welcome it."

"Perhaps not when you hear it. I know you have a full docket.
May we have just five minutes for a brief conference?"

"You may. Take ten minutes if we can get this case scheduled
for trial."

Billy all but took Angela's arm and led her out of chambers and
down the corridor. Mr. Devlin and I followed them outside. We gave
them some distance to get their act together. It was a study in body
language to see Angela's arms flailing while Billy applied soothing,
calming hand motions to quell her little tantrum. In a matter of minutes, Angela's steam had been expended, and Billy seemed to be
doing the talking. Eventually she gave Billy a rigid nod, and they
headed in our direction. Billy took Lex aside, but I could hear their
conversation.

"You got your point across to the judge, Lex. What do you want
out of this?"

"We need three weeks. Why the hell not? Other than Angela's
grandstanding, there's no reason to rush it. Vasquez is not going anywhere. Let's get the right result out of this case."

"All right. Let's go back in."

I stopped Billy before they opened the door. "Mr. Coyne. We
need to talk about things that can't be said here."

He looked at me, for the first time I could recall, more as if I was an attorney than a gofer on a high school summer job.

"When?"

"It has to be today. Lunch?"

He looked questioningly at Mr. Devlin.

Mr. Devlin picked it up. "The Marliave, Billy. Noon. And yes, the tabs on me. Next time you pick it up, or I'm going to claim you as a dependent."

Our little troop marched back into the judge's chambers. The judge seemed relieved when Billy did the talking for the prosecution.

"Defense has no motion on the table, Judge. We agree to trial in three weeks."

The judge slapped the desk in approval as he bolted upright and headed for his courtroom.

"Done, gentlemen—and lady. Three weeks."

Tony took our lunch orders in the upstairs private room of the Marliave. As always, we left the choice and personal preparation of food to his culinary talents. His friendship with Mr. Devlin went back a couple of decades. Tony's son and another teen-ager had pulled an ill-advised heist of a delicatessen in the North End that netted them more cash than they thought existed in the world. Unfortunately, they had tapped into a drop site for the Boston Mafia's numbers racket for the week. The police were the least of the kids' worries.

Mr. Devlin used some personal contacts with that North End organization. He arranged to have the money returned with no pulverized kneecaps. From that day on, neither Mr. D. nor anyone in his company had ever seen a printed menu at the Marliave. We were like guests in Tony's home, and no other hand touched the preparation of the delectable repasts he set before us.

An added feature was that when Tony had served us and closed the door on the way out, we had privacy that I would trust beyond anything the FBI could offer.

Once served, Billy began the veal and pasta and the conversation at the same time.

"And so, gentlemen. What's this superb lunch going to cost me?" Mr. Devlin set the agenda in clear terms.

"The lunch is on me. No strings. The rest is purely professional. But we're a hell of a ways past sparring with each other for information. Michael's life has been in danger since we got into this thing. And mostly because we didn't know the good guys from the bad. Now he tells me he's going back into the lion's den. He's going back to Dublin. Heaven knows I'd stop him if I could, but his mind's made up. Are you listening, Billy?"

Billy's face was showing tension from whatever conflict was going on inside. We waited, but nothing broke the silence until Mr. D. erupted.

"By damn, Billy, if Michael goes over there, he's going with every bit of information you can give him. We'll share everything he gets with you. You know that. Now for the love of God, open up. What is he really up against?"

Billy looked from one of us to the other. I studied his face. I thought there was one moment when his eyes went from troubled indecision to a kind of peace.

He pushed his plate back and slowly wiped his mouth with his napkin. He leaned in close with both elbows on the table. He looked straight into my eyes.

"All right, kid. I'll give you what I've got. I pray to God it doesn't get you killed. Or anyone else."

We both leaned in.

"I told you about that group of thugs in Ireland, the leftovers from that paramilitary group that did the bombing and killing when there was a so-called cause. They're still there. The only cause they fight for now is themselves. They've been hardened by years of war in Ireland. They're a well-trained band of terrorists, and they're organized. They make what we call the Irish Mafia in South Boston,

Boyle's crowd, look like pushovers, which, by the way, they're not."

"So why are the thugs over there your problem, Billy?"

Billy's jaw went tense.

"We have information from the inside. They have ambitions of crossing over. They have plans to take over Boyle's mob here. "

"What about Boyle? He's not going to cave-in to them."

"Just listen. These terrorists are thugs, but they're not dumb. They've been setting this thing up for the past year. They plan to attack Boyle from the inside and the outside. They've been winning Boyle's men over one by one with promises of big money once they take over. You've run into a couple of them, kid."

I nodded. I was thinking of Vince Scully and Sean Flannery who were in on the kidnapping. There was also Casey at the house in Winthrop.

"Well, there are more than you know. We don't know yet how deeply they've penetrated Boyle's mob, but we know that Boyle's under attack without even knowing it."

Mr. D. leaned in to ask it quietly.

"And what if they do take over, Billy? How will that be different from the way things are with Boyle running the mob?"

"In about a dozen ways. Let me give you a few. For starters, this city'll be awash in drugs. That Irish gang has supply connections that Boyle couldn't dream of. And they're miles ahead of Boyle in pushing the stuff. That's one reason they can promise Boyle's men big money down the road."

We both sat in silence, absorbing what Hector Vasquez's case had put us into. Billy picked it up.

"I'll give you another. Style. There's one hell of a difference between Boyle and that bunch. Boyle has the local police and judges and politicians in his pocket because he bribes them. That Irish bunch does it with beatings and murder. And kidnappings. These are terrorists first and criminals second."

I was beginning to get a grip on why Billy had played it so close to the chest and why the weight of it was bearing down on him. I could see from Mr. D.'s expression that it was getting through to him too.

Billy took the volume down another notch. "Something else. Once they're in control of crime in South Boston, it won't stop there. They'll move in on the Italian Mafia in the North End, and then the Russians. It's already in their plans. It's strange to say it, but we have something like peaceful coexistence between the ethnic gangs right now. When these Irish terrorists move in, we'll have the mother of all gang wars in this city."

Billy had us stunned into silence, getting our heads around what he'd been dealing with since before we started pounding on him for information about a fixed race at Suffolk.

Mr. D. was the first to break the silence. "I'm assuming this is all more than guesswork. Where did you get the information?"

"I have a contact over there. My counterpart in the Irish Garda. He's concerned too. If they tap into a money source over here, they'll have more power over there too. We've been working together for a year. He's been able to place a couple of moles in the terrorists' organization. They're not high up yet, but they've fed us some critical information."

Billy looked at his watch. He started to get up. "I have to empanel a jury."

Mr. Devlin caught his elbow. "The jury can wait five minutes. Why haven't they made their move already? What's holding them up?"

Billy sat down and looked straight at Lex.

"They're waiting till the time is right."

"And what would make it right?"

"Money. A lot of it. They need a war chest to buy enough of Boyle's men to assure the transition. That's what we're getting from our inside men. I should say man. One of our men over there was killed last week."

My heart froze. "It wasn't Seamus McGuiness, was it?"

Billy looked at me. He hesitated before answering.

"No, kid. He wasn't one of ours. Don't ask me any more names."

Mr. Devlin got back on track. "How do they plan to get it?"

"They have some plan that's supposed to give them a windfall. They're counting on it before they make their move."

"What's the plan?"

Billy shook his head. "I'd give one hell of a lot to know. If they pull it off, they'll be coming in force. We'll have more blood in the streets of Boston than any time since Prohibition."

Billy stood up. "I have to get to court. I don't have to tell you, gentlemen, I don't want anything I've said in confidence to come back to haunt me. You have my trust."

I stood up with him. "Before you go out that door, Mr. Coyne, I need one thing. I have to go back to Dublin. I may need to cross paths with the people you're talking about. Can you give me one name I can trust?"

He looked me square in the eye for a few seconds. It was like giving his life's blood.

"I'll give you one name. So help me, if you screw this up—"

"Look at it this way, Mr. Coyne. I can do you more good than harm. I can go places you can't."

He took my arm and pulled me close enough to whisper it. "I've been working with Superintendent Phelan of the Garda. You met him last time. You can talk to him just like you talk to me. We fill each other in on everything. Maybe he'll give you a lead. Maybe not. He'll be just as worried about you screwing up the investigation as I am. Probably more. It's his country. Tread lightly, kid."

CHAPTER TWENTY-FIVE

The overnight flight gave me thinking and planning time, and precious little sleep. I caught a cab from the Dublin Airport to the Gresham Hotel. As far as I knew, no one dangerous was aware that I'd be coming back to Ireland. I registered in my own name as a gesture of defiance to my creeping paranoia. The warmth of the welcome from the concierge and desk clerk on my return made it feel like a homecoming.

When I walked into my room, the little red blinking light signaled a phone message. It was brief.

"Mr. Knight, a car will pick you up at the side entrance to Toddy's Bar. Noon."

There was no name of the caller. To go, or not to go, that was the question. On the other hand, why the hell would I endure a night flight, crawling with every fanciful premonition my overstimulated imagination could plague me with, and then pass up the only promising lead I could scrape up? Even I knew the question was rhetorical.

Toddy's is a bar off the lobby of the Gresham. The side door opens onto Henry Street. On the dot of noon, I was standing twenty feet down the block in a doorway across the street from the side door to Toddy's. I wanted the first look. No need to press my luck.

Within five minutes, a Mercedes stopped at the curb where no other cars stopped. An older gentleman, whom I estimated I could outrun or outfight if need be, got out of the driver's side and stood on the sidewalk.

When I approached the car, he immediately opened the door to the backseat. He'd already conveyed two thoughts, neither of which was comforting. First, he knew me on sight, although I didn't recognize him. The second was that there was to be no chitchat on the drive or he would have put me in the front seat. A third thought that occurred after he closed the door behind me, was that even if I could outrun and outfight him, what if he had a gun?

All disturbing thoughts aside, the drive was uneventful. Within twenty minutes, we pulled up in front of the country estate I recognized from the first visit. Superintendent Phelan was in the doorway as before.

We shook hands, and he gestured me back toward his office. I noticed him cast an eye around the grounds as I went by. We took the same seats as previously. This time the offer was coffee. He had read and remembered my reaction to Irish tea.

Once served, he cut straight to the chase. The jovial, Irish sense of smiling hospitality seemed a thinner layer this time. A deep concern for handling extremely sensitive information was showing through more clearly.

"Mr. Knight, I'm surprised to see you back. I thought you achieved your goal and more the last time."

It was a question. How much of an answer to give was another question. I hedged.

"I take it you've been in contact with Mr. Coyne."

He took the deflection with a slight smile.

"Let me make this easier for the both us, Mr. Knight. Your Mr. Coyne and I are more than in contact. We have a common enemy. I think you know who that is."

"If you're saying we can speak plainly, Superintendent, then let's. Neither of us has the time or the temperament for tap dancing."

That brought a full smile. "Perceptive, Mr. Knight. You go first."

Smile or not, I made a note never to play chess or tennis with this dude. I had no desire to be the first one in the pool, but he had neatly put me in that position. To scotch up now on disclosure from my side could raise a barrier of distrust between us that would stifle cooperation on his part. The trick was to disclose enough to make him a confidant, and still withhold enough to keep my word to Billy.

"My interest comes down to this. A jockey was killed in a fixed horse race in Boston. My partner and I represent another jockey who's accused of his murder. The horse the supposedly murdered jockey was riding was bred and trained by the Dubh Crann Stables here in Ireland."

He nodded as if he was hearing nothing new.

"There was an elaborate scheme by the Irish group to mislead the betting public about the speed of the horse. I could give details."

He waved off the details. He was clearly frying bigger fish than race fixing.

"The twist is that the Irish group had a perfect setup to win a large amount on his first race. Long odds, mediocre competition. And yet they went to the extreme of kidnapping the jockey's daughter to make him lose the race. When the jockey appeared to be going for the win in spite of it, somehow they knocked him out of the saddle so the horse would be disqualified."

He slightly raised his eyebrows and hands together in a gesture that said, "An interesting tale, but why does this concern me?"

I sensed he was three jumps ahead of me. So why did he need me to spell it out? My guess was that he wanted to know how much Billy Coyne trusted me with. I knew then that it was all the way or nothing. I'd come too far for "nothing."

"You mentioned a common enemy, Superintendent. You have a criminal organization of former terrorists over here. They're your problem. Billy Coyne has reason to believe they're planning to import their organized criminality into Boston in spades. That's his problem. You must be concerned that if they tap into a major source of money in America, they'll have the resources to strengthen their grip in Ireland. Whence the 'common enemy.'"

He leaned back and looked at the ceiling. I sensed that no barriers had gone up yet.

"And why is this your problem, Mr. Knight?"

"I live in Boston."

He just shook his head. My mistake. No dodges.

"After two weeks, we're no closer to learning who actually knocked the jockey out of the saddle or how. If we don't cut that knot, a jury could convict our client of murder on circumstantial evidence. I believe we have to crack open the organization behind the race fixing and kidnapping to get the answers."

"Mmm."

"I also believe the organization I need to crack is the same one you refer to as the 'common enemy.'"

I let it lay there. So did he. The problem of how much to disclose was now on his side.

In about five seconds, he sprang forward as if he had reached a decision.

"Mr. Knight. I have a conundrum. Mr. Coyne and I share it. You're a bit of a joker in the deck. He and I have spent a year infiltrating this group with the hope of dismantling it. You could easily derail our efforts with one misguided step. We can't afford that. There's too much at stake for both of us."

My heart temporarily arrested while he sipped his infernal tea.

"But then, Mr. Knight, Mr. Coyne made an apt point. You can go places and do things that our positions prevent us from doing. On the strength of that, I'm going to show you a tiny crack in their wall."

My heart restarted and leapt at the same time. I started to speak, but he cut me off.

"Don't thank me. I'm going to give you the name of the man whom we believe to be the current head of this organization. It's dangerous information. It could easily get you killed. If you thank me for it, you'll double my pangs of conscience."

He wrote something on the back of a business card and led me to the door.

"Mr. Higgins will drive you back to the Gresham Hotel."

When we shook hands, he slipped the card into my hand.

I continued to clasp his hand for one last burning question.

"What constraints go with this information? What are my limits?"

He placed his other hand on top of mine. The smile was genuine.

"Just this. Don't get yourself killed, Mr. Knight. I'm beginning to like you."

On the drive back, I diverted Mr. Higgins with a request to drop me at the Hertz car-rental office on South Circular Road. On the way, I checked the business card the superintendent had given me. On the back, he had written the address of a pub, McShannon's on Fowne's Street. No great shock. The Irish seem to have a proclivity for doing business in the back rooms of pubs.

The name written above it in clear print was, "Top Man—Martin Sweeney." It brought back the troubled look on trainer Rick McDonough's face when he gave me that same name as the man who was pulling the strings on Black Diamond.

I committed the information on both sides of the card to memory and burned the card at the first opportunity. A card with both names could prove an embarrassment or worse if the wrong eyes found it.

The clerk at the Hertz office was tickled beyond measure to be able to lease the Jaguar to me again. He all but offered to drive it for me.

My first stop was the Gresham to throw a few essentials from my luggage into a plain paper bag and drive west out of Dublin.

Within an hour, I arrived at the Keadeen Hotel on the Curragh Road in Newbridge. It is an exquisite gem, awash in flowers, and set in undulating green country close to places I needed to be in the next two days.

I checked in with the name Dave Robicheaux. How many people in Ireland would recognize James Lee Burke's Louisiana detective? And if they did, the very literate Irish would be more amused than suspicious.

I used the next two hours to stop by the National Stud Farm a few miles away. I needed a cram course on Thoroughbred breeding practices in Ireland where Black Diamond was sired and born.

I was always bugged by Rick's account of Black Diamond's uninspired breeding. What nagged me was that world-beaters from undistinguished sires and dams pop up once in a great while, but not often. Speed is most frequently passed on from champion stock. Considering the whoopla that went into concealing Black Diamond's speed, if it were that important to me, I'd start with proven bloodlines.

I took the public's tour of the National Stud Farm, but I needed more particular information. I cornered Mick, the lifelong horseman who gave the tour. I told him I was writing a novel, and true to the nature of the literature-loving Irish, the floodgates of information opened.

The part of his information that mattered to me came down to this. The breeding of Thoroughbred racehorses can only be done legally by putting a stallion and mare together at the proper moment in an enclosure Mick referred to as the "honeymoon suite." Artificial insemination is banned because of the possibility of confusing or falsifying the lineage of the foals.

Three witnesses watch nature take its course—one from the owner of the mare, one from the owner of the stallion, and one from the Irish National Registry. DNA samples are taken of the mare and stallion for possible later comparison with the DNA of the foal. Then, in Ireland, a tiny electronic chip with all of the lineage information is inserted behind the ear of the foal. Before the horse runs in any race in Ireland, the chip is scanned to verify that the horse is not a ringer.

This was new to me. The chip method has never been adopted in the United States. Before every American race, a track official checks the number tattooed inside the upper lip of every horse on the way to being saddled in the paddock to verify the identity of the horse. The registry of tattoos is kept by the Jockey Club.

Before parting company with Mick, I laid the ultimate question on the line. "How could someone get around the system in Ireland? Let me put it straight. How could someone falsify the lineage of a Thoroughbred?"

Mick gave this simple Yank an indulgent grin and cut him off at the knees.

"Don't try it, lad, even in a book. It's impossible."

I gave him a grin, a nod, and a handshake, but I was thinking, *"Ah, Mick, nothing is impossible if you put enough money and clout behind it."*

CHAPTER TWENTY-SIX

It was a little past four in the afternoon when I drove the Jaguar, for which I was developing a guilty affection, up to the gates of the Dubh Crann Stables. I had apparently burned no bridges on my last visit. The guard swung open the gates with nothing more than a wave.

I mouthed a two-word question through the window, "Kieran Dowd?" He pointed to a paved, one-lane path that led to a large stable that was only slightly more spotless, sterile, and luxuriously appointed than the lobby of a Four Seasons Hotel.

I pulled the Jaguar up crosswise at the open door of the stable, skidding to a stop. There was a point. It's like the answer to the question, "Where does an eight-hundred-pound gorilla sleep?" The answer, "Anywhere he wants." Same for the Jaguar.

The disquieting rumble of the Jag engine, together with the audacity of blocking the stable entrance, brought a hopping Mr. Dowd through the door ready to have someone's head.

"What in the bloody hell do you think you're—?"

By the time his eyes adjusted to the sunlight and he recognized the Jaguar, I was out of the car with my arm around his shoulder leading him back into the stable with a running monologue.

"Mr. Dowd, the pleasure of seeing you again is all mine. I'm here to talk to you about just one thing. Money, Mr. Dowd. I'm here to make you a wealthy man, and not do so badly by myself as well. Are you ready to stop babbling about parking spaces and listen to me?"

He caught enough of that to clam up. He just looked at me with his mouth agape and a totally confused look on his face.

"I told you last time, Mr. Dowd. You've got talent. And it's being wasted on chicken feed. I've got contacts that can turn your talent with horses into more euros than you can count in a week. Are you listening, Mr. Dowd? Don't waste my time."

I gave him a second to close his mouth and swallow before he could get his tongue in gear.

"I don't understand a word you say, fella. You didn't make any sense the last time, and you don't make any sense now. Who the hell are ya?"

"Damn, you are obsessed with names, aren't you? I'm Arnold Schwarzenegger. I'm Mickey Mouse. What the hell difference does it make? I can't waste time with this. I want to hear just one word. Say yes or no. I have no time for anything else. Say yes, and we'll do business that will put you on top of the world. Say no, and I'll drive out of here and you'll have your damned parking space back. What'll it be?"

He took two paces backward and looked at me. He started to laugh.

"You are the most confusing son of a bitch, whoever the hell you are. You blow in here like a damn tornado. I don't know what you want. Yes. No. What the hell is all that?"

I smiled back at him. "That's excitement, Mr. Dowd. You look like the big shot around here. That's why I'm talking to you. How about giving yourself half an hour off? There's a pub ten minutes down the road. Let me buy you a pint. Fifteen minutes later I'll bring you back and drive off. It'll be as if I've never been here. But I'm betting the price of a pint or two that we'll be in business together. What's to lose?"

I held open the passenger door to the Jaguar. Whether it was curiosity at the audacity of this Yankee, the offer of a windfall of money, or just a ride in a Jaguar that did it, inside of a minute we were on the road to the Horse and Hares Pub.

Within ten minutes we were at a back table behind two creamy pints of Guinness's finest, absorbing the warmth of a peat fire in the back-wall fireplace.

"Now, Yank, for lack of the name you won't give me, what are we doing here?"

"We're getting to know each other. I need to know I can trust you. I'll tell you what I know already. You're a hell of a horseman. And at the same time you're a hell of a scam artist."

He stiffened. It was a gamble. I could have lost him then and there. I put a friendly hand on his shoulder to prevent any rapid retreat.

"Don't take me wrong, Mr. Dowd. To me, it's a term of admiration. I like to think of myself the same way."

He studied me for a few seconds before taking a sip of the Guinness.

"Now, Kieran, may I call you that?" It seemed the moment to slip into his first name. He showed no response.

"You and the group you work for have gone to extremes to conceal the talent of a horse called Black Diamond. Total fraud. You took him to the States to make a real killing. The first try didn't come off, but he's ready to go again. Are we in synch here, Kieran?"

He simply took a long draught of the Guinness and set it down deliberately. "You have a way of demanding a lot and giving nothing, Yank. What part do you play in all of this?"

"None. Yet. But I have the ability to multiply the profits from Black Diamond's next race into a figure that neither you nor the bunch you work for have ever dreamed of."

We just looked at each other for several seconds. "I'm just askin'. How does it work?"

"Ah, that's for me to know, and for you and your boys to induce me to tell you."

"And how do we do that?"

"For you it's simple. I need you to set up a meeting."

"With whom?"

I took a long draw on the Guinness to fake a nonchalance that covered nerves pulsing all over my body.

"Martin Sweeney."

He leaned back and just laughed. "Oh, Yank. No one could accuse you of faint heart."

"Meaning what?"

"Meaning why don't you ask something simple? Maybe I could set you up with Queen Elizabeth."

"I don't think so. The queen's not into horse scams. Martin Sweeney is. I once told you I worked with Seamus McGuiness. He's no longer among the living. That puts Sweeney in his spot. I can do him more good in fifteen minutes than all of his bank robberies put together. When you talk to him, you can put it just that way."

Dowd was looking at me now with seriousness mixed with curiosity.

"And tell him this. He can put me to the test. I'll make him twenty thousand euros in twenty-four hours just to prove I can do it. But I need fifteen minutes of his time first."

I let him chew on that while I finished the Guinness. I stood up while he just looked at his glass.

"And if he did want to talk to you?"

"Tell him to leave a message with the desk clerk at the Keadeen Hotel. Just say where and when. It has to be in the next twenty-four hours. Preferably in Dublin."

"And what name might he leave it for?"

I threw a ten-euro note on the table in front of him for the pints.

"Arnold Schwarzenegger."

I checked out of the Keadeen Hotel within half an hour. I was less than comfortable staying at an address known to the gang of thugs I'd be dealing with.

The desk clerk who helped me check out was tall, polished, and perfectly tailored—the ideal specimen of Irish hospitality. I told him that I was expecting a message, and that I'd call later if he would do me the kindness to read it to me over the phone.

"Certainly, sir."

"The message will be for me in the name of Arnold Schwarzenegger."

"Excellent, sir. And when you call, shall we address you as Mr. Universe or simply governor?"

"Just Arnie will do. I don't want to flood you with autograph seekers."

"Most considerate, sir. Must be such a bother."

"Happens all the time. Very embarrassing."

I slipped him a twenty euro note. "It'll be our little secret, sir."

I returned the car to the rental agency and caught a cab back to the Gresham. I called the desk clerk at the Keadeen from my room phone. Sure enough, Kieran Dowd had hopped to it. The message was to the point.

"Eight o'clock tonight. McShannon's Pub."

I rode down to the lobby for a brief chat with Tommy, the older concierge who treated me like a returning son when I checked in. We slipped around the corner from his station for a quiet word.

"Tommy, I need a bit of wisdom from a man who knows the city. I have an appointment at McShannon's Pub this evening. I'm not sure I'd trust the man I'm meeting as far as I could throw the Gresham—with you in it. What am I getting myself into here?"

"Absolutely nothin' to fear, if you take a bit of advice."

"Good."

"You haven't heard the advice."

"Which is?"

"Take the first cab in the line in front of the hotel to the Dublin Airport, and get as far the hell away from McShannon's Pub as you can get."

"Ah, Tommy. My mother, my partner, and a very pretty girl would probably all second your advice. I can't do it. Tell me about Mc-Shannon's. Forewarned is forearmed."

"That's a sweet little phrase. It'll probably get you killed if you walk into McShannon's for anything but a pint."

"Let's go at it this way. I have a meeting with a man whose name you're better off not knowing. I can't avoid it. What am I looking at?"

He took my arm and led me around another corner to heighten the isolation.

"If you're a tourist, you'll walk in, have a pint, enjoy the *craic*, and breeze out again. If you ask any pointed questions, you'll as likely as not be carried out the back door. Do you hear what I'm saying."

"What is this place?"

"It's the headquarters of a bunch you don't want to get crosswise with." We were alone, but he looked both ways anyway. "They're the remnants of the meanest of the lot that're left from the times we'd like to forget. Do I have to say more?"

A number of thoughts were vying for first place in my mind. Topmost was Tommy's idea of catching the first thing rolling to Dublin Airport. Attractive, but not in the cards. The second thought was that I'd been blessed—if that's the word—with an entrée into the dragon's den that neither Billy Coyne nor Superintendent Phelan could even dream of. Lucky me.

With some urging, Tommy gave me a good notion of the physical layout of McShannon's Pub. Now I needed a ticket that might buy my way both in and out with no scars.

I rode back up to my room to make a couple of calls. It would be coming up on eleven-thirty a.m. in Cambridge—the one in Massachusetts. That would put my old Harvard classmate, Harry Wong, in his office at MIT, contemplating a bowl of Schezuan noodles for lunch at the Quing Dao Restaurant on Mass. Ave. Harry is a creature of habit.

Harry and I met ten years previously when we formed a mutual defense alliance on our house wrestling team at Harvard College during our freshman year. We were the oddballs, and therefore the targets of the rest of the team. Harry came over as a boy from a city in northern China. He had some early connections with the tong in Boston's Chinatown. He had managed to put that part of his life behind him when he decided to focus fulltime on gaining admission to Harvard.

My background with a dicey little Puerto Rican gang in Jamaica Plain made us a matched pair of misfits on the house wrestling team from the outset. Our popularity with our straight, white, preppy teammates was not exactly fostered by the fact that in those days, I still carried enough street smarts and attitude to pin anyone on the team—with one exception. Harry.

After graduation, our paths diverged. Harry collected an alphabet full of graduate degrees and became part of a brain trust at MIT. I went to law school. The thing that held us together was a standing invitation for Thanksgiving dinner at my mother's home. Again setting our own traditions, we feasted annually on *pollo guisado con pasteles,* so tasty it would have given the Pilgrims a Puerto Rican accent. Harry always supplied Schezuan fried rice, spicy hot enough to cook your tongue on the way down. Fortunately, the three of us had inherited asbestos mouths.

Harry was surprised at the call off-season, but there was precedent. On two earlier occasions, when only Harry could play a role that would enable me to pull off a maneuver that was leagues over my head, he had come through like the Lone Ranger.

I cut quickly to the chase. "Harry, we're a natural team. I need my old partner one more time."

"Oh crap, Michael. What is it this time?"

"I'd be less than honest if I didn't say there's a modicum of danger involved. Just enough to make it interesting."

"Why me? Don't you have other friends dumb enough to put their asses in a bear trap for you?"

"I did. They've all been killed. I'm down to you. Besides, you're the Chinese Lone Ranger, remember?"

I could hear the barest grin in his voice in spite of himself. "So what is it? How bad is this one going to be?"

"Piece of cake, Harry."

"I've heard that before. Who am I going to be this time?"

"You'll like this. You Asians are supposed to be big on gambling. You're going to be the head of a wagering syndicate that has a network of contacts with every bookie operation in the United States. Italian Mafia. The Russians. Anyone that operates a book. You're going to agree to place just one bet with all of them. That's it."

"You do come up with some intriguing crap. On just what you said, I can think of six ways of getting killed."

"Not to worry. Here's the good news. I only need you to fly into Dublin. You play one scene before a very select audience. I'll have you back at your little mouse maze at MIT in two days tops."

"What audience?"

"You can catch the nine o'clock plane for Dublin tonight. You'll do your act tomorrow night. I'll drop you at the airport for the flight home the next morning. What could be easier?"

"I must have missed your answer. What audience?"

"A nice crowd of Irish gentlemen. I'll introduce you tomorrow afternoon. When your plane gets in, catch a cab to the Gresham Hotel. You'll have a reservation under the name—I don't know. You pick it."

I could hear sighs and groans and pages flipping in what I assumed was an appointments calendar.

"Why couldn't you call me for a Ping-Pong tournament or something."

"I don't play Ping-Pong."

"Neither do I. But all I could lose is a game. All right. I could stall for an hour and I'd wind up saying yes anyway. I'll be Qian An-Yong. I survived with that name last time."

That was the easy one. The next call was to Colin Fitzpatrick. His appointments secretary, Ms. Paxton, must have been stunned out of her gourd that Mr. Fitzpatrick actually joined me for a sandwich in the Public Garden. With that track record, she buzzed his line with no chatter. Within fifteen seconds, he was on the line, taking down my phone number for a callback on a more secure phone.

I caught it on the first ring.

"Mr. Fitzpatrick?"

"Mr. Knight."

"It's showtime, Mr. Fitzpatrick. I have very little to say. Later today I'm meeting the head of that gang of thugs that's been draining you and your buddies. I'm going to do my best to solve both of our problems. Within the next hour, I've got to know that you're willing to deposit twenty-six thousand dollars in my personal bank account. That's the equivalent today of twenty thousand euros. With it, we've got an outside chance. Without it, I probably won't live to see tomorrow's sunrise. That probably sounds dramatic. It happens to be true. And right at this moment, I've got nothing to offer you for the money but the truth."

I could hear him dropping the level of his voice.

"Actually, you do have something else. I've done a good bit of cautious checking on you and your senior partner. Mr. Devlin is apparently an icon of integrity in this city. You should have told me he was your partner at the outset."

"I didn't know it would—"

"Allow me to finish. Apparently you also have something of a reputation for backing your word to the hilt. You're an interesting pair."

"Does that mean—?"

"It means I'm not going to jeopardize your life for an amount of money I pay these people every month."

The last duck just found his place in the row.

CHAPTER TWENTY-SEVEN

I made one last call to complete the stacking of the deck. It was a bit after noon in Massachusetts. Alberto Ibanez would be doing his loosening up exercises in the jockeys' room at Suffolk Downs before the first race.

I got him on his cell phone and kept it in Spanish for added security.

"*Hola,* Alberto."

He went into hush mode and mumbled, "*Hola. Que pasa?*"

I could hear him hustle to a vacant corner of the room. What I said then could be loosely translated as follows:

"Alberto, I'm in Ireland. I'm doing some shopping. I want to bring you back a nice wool scarf. Like I promised. What color would you like?"

There was silence. I gave it five seconds.

"Alberto, this is the third store I've tried. This salesman has very little patience. I need an answer. What color will go with the rest of your outfit?"

His voice came down another ten decibels.

"I like Irish wool. How about a green one?"

"Excellent. You're sure it'll go with what you'll be wearing?"

"*Sí, Amigo.* Perfect match."

I had an hour before meeting Sweeney. It was just time to catch a bowl of Irish lamb stew at O'Brien's by Trinity College to feed the mice that were gnawing holes in my stomach lining. My last stop was at Arnott's on Henry Street for a pair of Docker pants, a flannel shirt, and a huge Irish wool sweater, all of which I donned before leaving the store. With a hearty lamb stew inside, and a typical pub crawler's outfit outside, I was as ready to face the head of the worst thugs Ireland ever produced as I'd ever be in this life.

McShannon's Pub in the heart of the Temple Bar section was rocking on its foundation. Four singers with guitars were belting out Thomas Moore's rebel song, "The Minstrel Boy," at the top of their lungs, but you couldn't hear a sound out of their mouths. At least fifty well-lubricated patrons were belting it out with them with a fervor that would make you wonder how English rule lasted as long as it did.

I wedged my way to the bar and finally caught the eye of one of the bartenders who was singing along with the best of them. When the final note was sung, and the sound level dropped from deafening to merely thunderous, I mouthed two words to the bartender. "Martin Sweeney."

I saw him shoot a look at a table of five hefty men at the rear of the pub. Their bulky sweaters seemed to cover some serious muscles and Heaven knows what other weapons. The bartender caught the eye of one of them and pointed to me.

They talked with each other for a few seconds before one of the five got up and worked his way through the crowd. He cupped a hand beside his mouth and shouted in my left ear.

"Who are ya?"

I lied at the top of my lungs. "Friend of Kieran Dowd."

My guide looked back at the table and gave a nod. The other four men left the table and climbed a flight of stairs behind them. My host and escort cocked his head toward the stairs. I followed close behind, as he ran interference through the crowd.

The bend in the stairs cut the noise level to a point at which I could feel myself recovering the sense of hearing. I followed him up the last half of the flight of stairs and through the door at the top.

Four steps inside the dimly lit room, I realized that I was ringed by the five men, each of whom had at least three inches and fifty pounds on me. There was one chair in the center of the room and another against the wall straight ahead. The man who sat in the chair by the wall took command.

"So who the hell are ya, Yank. What do ya want with me? Make it quick."

I said nothing. I simply made deliberate, slow moves in slipping the bulky sweater over my head and dropped it on the floor. I unbuttoned the flannel shirt, peeled it off, and dropped it on the floor over the sweater. I was down to bare skin from the waist up. When I unfastened the belt buckle on my Docker pants, four of the men broke out in an amused grin. The one standing to my left kept a frosty, uncommitted poker face.

The one in the chair in front of me broke the silence.

"I don't know who you think you're playin' to, Yank, but I think you're in the wrong part of town."

I still said nothing. I shook off my loafers and slipped off my Docker pants. I felt like a peeled shrimp on a buffet table. By this time, four of them had broken into open laughter. Even the fifth to my left cracked a smile.

I stood as straight as my embarrassing circumstance would allow, happy to be wearing clean underwear and praying that it would stay that way.

I steadied my voice in a low octave and addressed the group.

"Gentlemen, there's a point to all this. Do I have your attention?"

That was a rhetorical question. I had every eye in the room, and now every ear.

"I invite you to look closely only for the purpose of seeing that I have no hidden weapons. No guns, no knives. I have no wires, no recording devices. Nothing. You'll also notice that I don't have enough muscle structure to give any of you a run for your money. Agreed?"

They just looked.

"Then, gentlemen, this is the point. I'll assume that I have your trust that I pose you absolutely no threat."

That brought hearty laughs from all of them.

I spoke above the laughter. "Good. Then let me also assure you I'm not here to entertain you. I'm here to do business with Martin Sweeney. And no one else. So if four of you would be gracious enough to leave Mr. Sweeney and me alone, we'll get down to business. Mr. Sweeney, I think you'll find it well worth your time."

That silenced the laughter and wiped away the smiles. I let the silence hang while I slowly redressed. The man in the chair in front of me continued as spokesman.

"What you say to me, you can say to my comrades. And you can start with your name."

I finished fastening the last button on my shirt and buckling my belt before responding. I looked the speaker in front of me straight in the eye.

"No disrespect, friend, but I'm not speaking to you. I'm speaking to Mr. Sweeney. I thought I made that clear."

The man in the chair stood up in a flash of temper. "You're lookin' at Martin Sweeney, and I'll have your name or there'll be blood spilt in this room."

I slipped the sweater back over my head, partly to hide the ripple of nerves that was coursing through every inch of my body. I kept my voice low and as free of quivering as possible.

"Very frightening, my friend, but you need to unblock your ears. I'll speak to Mr. Sweeney and no one else. This is not a debate."

I turned to the man standing to my left. I knew I was on the thinnest possible ice, but when the bartender first looked at the five men at the back table downstairs, he looked straight at him and none of the others. He was also the only one who took my little strip act seriously.

The face of the man in front of me flushed beet red. He took a step toward me with his fists clenched. I braced for wherever his punches would land. My eyes were closed when the voice of the man to my left froze him in his tracks.

"Back off, Mugsy! He's entertained us so far. Let's see what else he has in mind."

He looked back at me. "So, Yank without a name. What do you have to say for yourself, before Mr. McGuire here finishes what he had in mind?"

My body came unclenched enough to speak in a steady voice. I knew I had to make the sale of my life.

"I have just one purpose here, Mr. Sweeney. I'm going to make you and me richer than you ever dreamed. I'm the only one you'll ever meet that can do it. And I'll do it on your own scheme with Black Diamond."

I prayed to God that I'd roused his curiosity, because his curiosity was the only defense I had against the beating of my life. Sweeney was eyeing me like a bug under a microscope.

"And just how might you do that?"

I played my last card. "That's between you and me. You let this thug loose on me, and you'll kill the only goose that can fill your pockets with golden eggs."

A fractured metaphor, but Sweeney remained silent in thought. Possibly a good sign. At least I was still in one piece.

"It's a simple matter of trust, Mr. Sweeney. I came into this hornet's nest alone and unarmed to show that you can trust me. Now I need a little trust on your part. When you and I are alone, we'll do business like you never imagined. It's your decision."

I went back to the busy work of straightening my sweater and pulling the flannel collar over the neck of the sweater. I could feel every eye scanning me, particularly those of Martin Sweeney. The superintendent was right. He was clearly the brains of the outfit.

Ten years passed in the next ten seconds. Sweeney's eyes never left me. I had no clue as to which way he'd go. Finally, after every nerve in my body was strained to exhaustion, he gave a nod of his head toward the door. The three behind me moved slowly back through the door and down the stairs.

McGuire was still standing three steps ahead of me looking daggers into my eyes. I saw Sweeney give him a slight nod of the head. McGuire moved close beside me toward the door. His eyes were riveted on mine when he approached to pass. There was a flame of rage in those eyes that burned into my soul.

As he passed close by my side, I looked over at Sweeney to break the heat. I was about to speak, when a paralyzing pain shot through my back and buckled my knees. My legs dropped out beneath me, and I crumbled to the floor. It was only the ravaging pain radiating through all my limbs that kept me from losing consciousness.

In a second and a half, I passed from shock and pain, through confusion, to stark terror that I'd been paralyzed. I couldn't move a muscle to ward off whatever was coming next. I finally realized that McGuire had caught me with a blow of his fist that came from the ground up. He scored a direct hit on my kidney and laid me low.

He stood there looking down at me and grinning. He enjoyed the triumph for a full ten seconds before turning and moving slowly toward the door. That's when it came over me like an avalanche. The pain and even terror could not hold back the torrent of exploding fury. There was no conscious thought in my head. Pure instinct took control.

I grabbed the leg of the chair next to me. I used it to pull myself up into the highest crouching position I could manage. With every mite of strength left in me, I lifted the chair and hurled it at the back of McGuire. It hit the wall beside him with a force that shattered the chair.

McGuire turned, stunned. When he realized what had happened, he came for me in a fit of rage.

Sweeney caught him in his tracks with a word. "Mugsy!"

McGuire froze like a dog at the command, "Stay!"

I was teetering on rubber legs. If McGuire came at me again, I was defenseless. I looked at Sweeney. He gave the command like a drill sergeant. "Mugsy! Back off! Get out of here!"

Rage was still trumping my pain. I shouted at the top of my lungs, "Leave him! Let him hear this, Sweeney. If one of those apes, or you, Sweeney, ever so much as breathe on me again, you'd better kill me. If you let me live, I'll take down every one of you."

I was shaking like a leaf from pain and rage. It was the only way those words would ever have left my mouth. I was suddenly seized with enough consciousness of reality to be absolutely certain that they'd be the last words I'd say on this earth. My next words were for God alone while I had seconds for one last prayer.

Strangely enough, I felt a quietness pass through my body and mind. It left me in a state of calm. My only determination was to remain on my feet. Whatever came, I'd face the two of them standing up.

Sweeney waved McGuire out of the room. McGuire was slow to do it, but he obeyed the command. When we were alone, Sweeney walked to the chair McGuire had been sitting in and brought it over to me.

"Sit down, Yank. You're a skinny runt by Irish standards, but I'll give you this. You've got some steel about you. I could use ten like you. I'll hear what you have to say."

I grabbed the back of the chair, but I refused to sit. I wanted to speak to him eye to eye.

I took a number of deep breaths to get control of my slowly returning bodily functions. When I could stand on my legs without support, I looked at Sweeney.

"I've come with an offer, Mr. Sweeney. I'm told you're the big shot around here. If that's true, let's talk."

"Let's talk indeed. Follow me."

He led me to the room next door. He opened it with a key and turned the lights on in an oak-paneled office that would have done any American law firm proud.

"Sit down, Yank."

He pointed to a burgundy leather chair facing a walnut desk with a chair behind it not unlike Mr. Devlin's. He leaned back in the chair in a pose that reminded me of Mr. Devlin listening to one of my outlandish plans.

"There are not many have seen the inside of this office. Tell me something that deserves my interest."

"I've said I have the means of using what you've set up with Black Diamond to make more money than you could ever imagine. Does that interest you?"

"Not yet. So far, it's a lot of Yankee braggin'. What's behind it?"

"Contacts. I have them, and you don't. You've set up Black Diamond with a dismal workout record that'll make him a long shot the next time he runs. He showed some speed in his first race, but that won't be noticed by the majority of bettors since he never finished the race under a jockey. Next time out, in the right race, he'll go off as a long shot. You and I'll know he's fast enough to outrun every other horse on the track. He can win in a walk. That's the part you control."

"And you, Yank. What can you add?"

"Contacts to place bets at long odds with every gambling syndicate in America and Canada. They all go by the track odds. They don't communicate with each other. I can bet all the money you can get your hands on and collect from all of them at a long-shot price."

The chair squeaked and groaned under his weight as he rocked back in thought. He looked at me sideways.

"It's big talk. I don't even know your name."

"My name wouldn't mean anything to you anyway. I'll tell you what will mean something. Let me give you a demonstration. This is not my first time around the block. You put a thousand euros in my pocket before I leave here today. I'll be back here tomorrow with twenty thousand. That'll be yours. Call it an affirmation of trust."

He rocked back laughing.

"Oh shite, Yank. You've got steel nuggets. Do you know who

you're trying to scam for a thousand euros?"

"I do, Mr. Sweeney. And it's no scam. Not on you anyway. The horse I bet it on will win. He should go away at twenty-to-one at the least. I'll be back in this office tomorrow at one o'clock with your twenty thousand. Plus something else. What can you lose? You're going to have me tailed from the time I leave here anyway, right? I'll make it easy. I'm staying at the Gresham. I'll be there tonight right through tomorrow morning."

The laugh was gone. He was searching my eyes for any hint of deception.

"Give me one more thing, Yank. What's the horse?"

"All right, I'll tell you. No harm. Eighth race today at Suffolk Downs in Boston. Number five's going to win the race. Check it out yourself. It's five hours earlier there. The race should go off around four thirty Boston time—nine thirty here. Number five will win the race."

"How do you know?"

"I'll say it one more time. I have contacts."

He eyed me with a tentative look I couldn't analyze.

"You said you were bringing something else tomorrow. What else are you bringing?"

"I'm bringing the man who makes it all happen. I didn't say I could do it alone. I said I had contacts. You'll meet him tomorrow. He has to be in on it from the beginning or he's not interested. So far, you and I've been talking about chicken feed. The next time we play this game, it'll be for the kind of money that makes it worth the playing."

"How much?"

"If we're not talking in the millions, I'll be on the next plane home, and we'll forget we met each other. I don't have time to waste."

He grinned at me. I could sense that he was swaying toward the attraction of a windfall sizeable enough to make the plans Billy Coyne feared the most seem feasible.

"You're a piece of work, Yank. A thousand euros for twenty thousand at one tomorrow. Do I need to tell you that if it doesn't happen that way, we won't just forget we ever met each other? You'll find yourself planted in Irish soil. In a number of different locations. Are we clear on that?"

"Do I look worried?" The look of nonworry I managed could have pulled in an Academy Award.

"How do you know what horse'll win the race?"

"I said it before. This is not my first time around the block."

It was a nonanswer, but he read enough into it to get me off the hook. Actually, Alberto had signaled me the last time I saw him at the track that the next fixed race was on Friday, the eighth race. My phone conversation with him earlier that afternoon told me that number five was fixed to win.

When I called Alberto that afternoon, he knew I wasn't buying him an Irish wool scarf. He picked it up as a coded excuse to mention a color. At every track, the saddlecloths worn under the saddles are color coded to make the post position numbers of the horses easier to spot. The saddlecloth of horse number one is always red, number two is white, number three is blue, number four is yellow, and, to the point, number five is green. When Alberto told me he wanted a green scarf, he was telling me that Paddy Boyle had the fix in for number five to win the eighth race. I saw no point in sharing that with Sweeney.

For another ten seconds, Sweeney just studied my face before something clicked and he came to a decision. He bent down and used a key to open a lower drawer on his desk. He straightened up with a bulk of bills bound together with a band that read 1,000 euros. He flipped it across the desk to me.

"Remember, Yank. I don't make idle threats."

I pocketed the bundle of bills. I had one last word before going out the door.

"Neither do I, Mr. Sweeney."

CHAPTER TWENTY-EIGHT

I walked slowly from McShannon's Pub through the Temple Bar section, along the Ashton Quay beside the Liffey River, across the O'Connell Bridge, and straight down O'Connell Street to the Gresham Hotel—all open public streets. I made it as easy as possible for whoever Sweeney had following me. My grandmother could have tailed me with no difficulty.

I spotted the two mugs Sweeney had put on the assignment every time I turned a corner. In passing through the crowds of revelers in the Temple Bar section, I slowed to a crawl so they wouldn't lose me. I wanted Sweeney to know exactly where I was every minute I was out of his sight—at least for the time being.

When I got back to my room, I made two calls. First I reached Colin Fitzpatrick in his office. His secretary, Ms. Paxton, was beginning to warm to the belief that I had some function in Mr. Fitzpatrick's life other than to annoy her. She put me through directly.

"Mr. Fitzpatrick, it's time. You wouldn't believe where I spent the afternoon, and I don't have time to tell you. In brief, I need to have the dollar equivalent of twenty thousand euros electronically transferred to an account I'll set up in the morning. I'll use the Ulster Bank down the street from the Hotel Gresham. I'll have them contact you with the numbers. I need to draw it out in cash tomorrow morning, ten o'clock Dublin time. Not to be dramatic, but what I said before about life or death could not possibly be more on the nose."

He must have caught the sincerity in my voice. He agreed immediately. No questions. That was one down—a big one.

My second call was to Rick McDonough, Black Diamond's trainer. I could have called others for the same information, but I wanted to break the newly frozen ice with Rick.

The exchange of hello's left no doubt that there'd been no thaw since our last encounter.

"Listen, Rick, I'm going to ask you two favors—a small one and a rather large one."

No answer.

"Let's take the large one first. There's much more than you know going on around Black Diamond. I wouldn't know where to begin to explain it. I'm so far over my head in it, I may never see daylight. But if I do come through this, I might get some answers to Danny's death. I'm going to try to make it up to you for the bind I put you in. I'm only asking for right now that you not come to any conclusions until I talk to you. For Miles and Danny's sakes if not for mine."

There was no commitment, but there was a noticeable softening when he asked, "So what's the second?"

"That's the easy one, Rick. Who won the eighth race today?"

I knew he'd know off the top of his head. "Fancy Gal. She won it in a walk."

"What number was she?"

I could feel my stomach muscles clench while he dug out the day's program. Even with a fixed race, nothing in this life is certain. I felt everything relax when he said the word, "Five."

"Thanks, Rick. Take care of yourself."

I was about to hang up, when I heard him say, "Hold on there, Mike."

"I'm here."

There was a pause, and I could visualize that old cowboy roughing up his hair as I'd seen a hundred times.

"Listen, Mike. You go easy, son. You got no worries with me."

I felt a golf ball in my throat that stopped the words. I had literally no idea what the next day might bring, and I didn't want to check out with a roughness between Rick and myself. For one thing, I'd have no idea how I'd explain it to Miles O'Connor.

My first move the next morning was to check with the front desk to see if a Mr. Qian An-Yong had checked in. Sure enough, good old Harry Wong. I hardly needed to ask. I had the desk buzz his room. The sleepiness in his voice told me that he couldn't sleep on a plane any more than I could.

"Harry, welcome to the Emerald Isle."

"Mr. Qian, if you please. Let's not blow my cover before I have one."

"To be sure. And may I invite Mr. Qian to a sumptuous Irish breakfast downstairs? Good chance to talk over the game plan."

"Done. Give me fifteen minutes. By the way, do I know you or do we play it like strangers?"

"Excellent question. You were cut out for this work."

"God forbid. I already miss my maze mice. So?"

"We're old business associates. Two crooked, big-time rollers actually. We'll be under surveillance by a couple of clumsy thugs so don't be subtle. I want them to see that we're old acquaintances."

I was at a table for two in the Gallery Restaurant off the Gresham lobby when Harry showed up at the door. The maître d' led him halfway to my table when he spotted me. Never one to do anything halfway, Harry threw up his arms and approached me at quick time for what was shaping up as a hug. I was on my feet in a flash with my right hand out to shake hands.

Being a quick study, Harry toned it down to a reserved handshake and a polite Chinese bow.

I whispered, "Relax, Harry. Mr. Qian. We're not strangers, but we're not lovers. Just a couple of old friends."

With that, he gave me a stage grin and a good-old-boy slap on the

back. If that didn't have the two thugs watching from a corner table
totally confused, we were home free—for the moment.

We ordered coffee without getting into anything more touchy
than the Irish weather. After going through the breakfast buffet line,
I laid out the plan for our one o'clock meeting with Sweeney in a
tone only Harry could hear. I figured that if the two in the corner
were the sharpest tacks in their box, we had no worries about sophisticated listening devices.

When I outlined the cover story we were going to take into the
meeting with Sweeney, I thought Harry was going to lose the part of
the breakfast he'd eaten.

"Oh, shit, Michael!"

"Harry. Keep a low profile. Did you have a question?"

"Damn straight! That's all of it? That's the little act we're going
to put on for this bunch of killers?"

"No problem. I can ad lib if necessary. Besides, I've already set
the scene with them. This is pretty much what they're expecting.
Your function is to lend an authenticating air."

"Terrific. And how do I do that?"

"Just by being your natural Chinese self. Forgive the ethnicity,
but you people are supposed to be into high-stakes gambling. It'll go
a long way to sell the cover story."

"That's a myth."

"So what, as long as they believe it."

He nervously wiped his brow with his napkin.

"Easy, easy. You're a sophisticated, cool, big roller."

"I'm going to get my high-stakes Chinese ass sliced up for Irish
stew. This is not my idea of a super, can't-miss plan."

"Not to worry, Harry. My low-stakes ass will be right up there
on the block with yours."

"Oh, that's comforting. Could you at least stop calling me
'Harry'?"

"Not a problem in the world, Harry. Mr. Qian. We have two

things on our side. Number one is I'll do all the talking. You tend to ham it up. Second, we'll be going in with a gift of twenty thousand euros. Sort of a test I set up to pass. It'll be duck soup. Eat your breakfast, Harry."

He flinched.

"I mean, Mr. Qian."

I left Harry to rest up for our matinee performance while I walked down O'Connell Street to the Ulster Bank. I asked for the manager and was escorted to an upstairs office. Mr. Dwyer welcomed me as if there was no need for an explanation. In fact, there wasn't. Apparently Colin Fitzpatrick had set everything up for me in advance. From the tone in which Mr. Dwyer spoke of him, Colin Fitzpatrick was a heavier hitter than even I had assumed. Mr. Dwyer seemed tickled to start his day doing business with him.

In any event, I walked out of the bank with an envelope containing exactly twenty thousand euros in cash. Strangely enough, seeing Sweeney's thug tail me gave me an unexpected sense of security carrying that amount of cash.

At one o'clock sharp, Mr. Qian An-Yong and I stepped out of a cab in front of McShannon's Pub. At that hour, it looked like a funeral parlor compared to the rocking boom box it had been the night before.

One of the men who had been in the upstairs room during my last visit met us at the door. He led us through the pub and up the stairs to Sweeney's office. On the way to the staircase, I could see McGuire hunched over a Guinness at the far end of the bar. He gave me a sideways look with a sneering grin that knocked the crap out of the euphoria I had built up in selling the plan to Harry at breakfast. I was back to full-blown reality.

Sweeney was in the chair behind his desk. He was in a well-tailored suit with an open-collared shirt. He stood and extended his hand to me for a handshake with a pleasant "Good afternoon, gentlemen." I introduced Harry as Mr. Qian. Sweeney offered a gracious hand to Harry and they exchanged salutations.

I was slightly rattled by the entire opening scene. First, seeing Sweeney in his current attire and manner dispelled any comforting notion that he was a beer-besotted thug with the IQ of a bar brawler. The idea that that mistaken impression might have been deliberately planted by Sweeney the previous day gave me a double jolt.

The second cause for unease was that good old Harry had responded to Sweeney's extended hand with a low bow and worse yet, he'd slipped into a Chinese accent. I gave him a hopefully unnoticed jab in the back to tone down his performance. He jumped just enough to make me wish I hadn't.

I played my best opening card. I placed the envelope holding twenty thousand euros on the desk in front of Sweeney. He eyed it, and looked back at me with either hesitancy or suspicion.

"Please count it, Mr. Sweeney. It's yours."

Sweeney leaned forward in his seat and simply lifted the flap on the envelope. With one momentary look, he closed the flap and let the envelope sit there between us. The air of suspicion still hung heavy. It had me off balance.

"You seem unhappy, Mr. Sweeney. I believe I've passed the test. I'm sure you know who won the eighth race yesterday. You know I had the winner before the race was run. Unless I misread you, you're still suspicious. I told you three times yesterday, this can only work on mutual trust. If you're not capable of trust, we'll call it a day. I've enjoyed seeing Dublin, and you're up twenty thousand euros. Shall we leave it at that?"

I stood up and gave every indication of walking out the door. Poor Harry was totally confused, but he took his cue from me and stood. The only obstacle to a grand exit was the two-hundred-and-fifty-pound thug standing in the doorway. I thanked God he was there, because if Sweeney had not stopped us from leaving, we were back at ground zero or below.

I turned back to Sweeney and raised my hands in a what's-with-the-goon-in-the-doorway gesture. Sweeney responded, but the businesslike tone had an unsettling edge to it.

"Please, gentlemen. Sit. Allow me to be curious."

"About what? I promised you I could get a twenty-to-one return on your bet before the horses even went to the post. I did that. Every dime of it is in that envelope. I assumed that you'd understand that if I could do that with peanuts, I could do it with interesting money. Apparently I was wrong. Is there anything more to say?"

Sweeney smiled from one to the other of us.

"You're a hell of a puzzle to me. Either you're a man I could do business with, or you're—something else."

I raised my hands again in innocence. "What else?"

"That's what I'm trying to figure. You lay twenty thousand euros on my desk like it's subway change. Then you're going to walk away. No one does that."

I sat down, and poor befuddled Harry followed suit.

"I do, Mr. Sweeney."

"Why?"

"Because I said I would. I keep my word. I'm entitled to your trust. I hoped this would prove it."

He looked at me again with those piercing, questioning eyes. He seemed to be on the verge of something, but just couldn't cross the line to a decision. He looked straight at me.

"I'll tell you what I can't figure out, Yank. If you could make twenty thousand overnight, why do you need me?"

I leaned back in the chair and forced a knowing grin.

"You've finally asked an interesting question. We spread the bets so thinly with betting syndicates across the United States, we can pluck out twenty thousand on a routine fixed race at Suffolk, and no one notices."

I came forward with the fire of enthusiasm in my eyes and my elbows on his desk.

"What I have in mind is a real killing. High millions. It can only be done once. The kind of fix that was in on yesterday's race would be suspect to the people who'd have to pay off large sums of money. They wouldn't suffer it gladly. They'd work over the jockeys till they got the truth about the fix. We'd all be dead within a week. Or wish we were."

"So how is this different?"

He was looking at me like a trout eyeing a piece of bait just before he decides to strike. I had to make the trout want to believe.

"You set it up perfectly with Black Diamond. You just don't know how to use it."

"Tell me."

"It's perfect. We don't need to fix the race. There's nothing for the syndicates to detect. Nothing the jockeys can tell them. It's a normal race. It's not uncommon for a horse to run routine races and then break out with a convincing win in one race. Horses are animals. They're not machines. Even the syndicates understand that."

"But he could still lose the race."

I sat back and took a breath as if I were looking for the words to simplify it.

"You've got a good grip on the obvious. He could break a leg coming out of the starting gate. He could be hit by a flying meteor at the eighth pole. A sinkhole could swallow him up."

Sweeney was not taking my last comment kindly. I couldn't let the trout back off the bait.

"Life's full of crappy accidents. But I've seen that horse run. We pick the right race, and I'm willing to bet more of my own money than you've seen in a lifetime that he'll break on top and waltz home. Mr. Qian is willing to put his entire network of contacts and a good bit of his own money on the line. We need you because you control Black Diamond. It's a one-time thing, Mr. Sweeney. You're in or you're out."

I sat back and made a point of looking at my watch. Sweeney was getting the itches like a man at a major fork in the road. He stood up and swung his chair around. Then he swung it back and sat down again.

"How much are you looking for?"

I scratched my temple and looked at Harry, who, thank God, was keeping his mouth shut. I spoke in a hushed tone to Harry, but just loud enough for Sweeney to hear.

"How much can you handle? I'm in for six million. You? Probably double that."

Good old Harry refrained from favoring us with his phony Chinese accent. He just nodded in assent.

"So we can let Mr. Sweeney in for what? Remember, it's his horse."

Harry had no clue as to what number I was looking for. He just squinted as if he was thinking.

I turned to Sweeney. "You name it, Mr. Sweeney. Give us a number."

Sweeney looked as perplexed as Harry. He may have been the top dog in the Irish Mafia with his bank robberies and extortion and whatever, but he was on the spot and totally out of his element in this game. Thank God. He finally mumbled a number.

"A hundred thousand."

He looked like he was going to choke just to say it. I just sat there with my mouth open like I couldn't believe what I was hearing. I looked at Harry who was looking equally shocked. I nearly fell over when Harry stood up and started berating me.

"What you get me over here for? You play some kind of joke?"

I tried to calm him. "Please, Mr. Qian. Let's give him a chance."

Harry had the bit in his teeth. There was no turning him off. He was sputtering staccato syllables in fractured English as fast as he could get them out.

"Chance to what? Chance to humiliate me? My people not take this well. Not well at all. I lose face."

He was wiping his face with a large red silk handkerchief that he probably bought for the occasion. I had totally lost control. The words kept pouring out.

"I tell you this. I don't know what they do about this man. I try to explain, but I don't know. They not like this."

I took Harry by the shoulders and placed him back in the chair. I gave him a look that finally put a cork in it. I turned back to Sweeney, who, for the moment, seemed not to know who was on first.

"Mr. Sweeney, let's think this thing through. Some serious arrangements have been made by Mr. Qian on the strength of what I assumed you'd commit to. I was told you were a major figure over here. You never denied it. Representations have been made to people who deal on a commission basis. I don't know how to express this other than directly. We all have a great deal to lose if we pansy out now. I obviously mean more than money. I don't think I have to explain that to you. Let's start again. How much can you put into this, remembering that we're looking for at least a ten-to-one profit?"

He looked no more comfortable than he did a minute ago, but at least he was thinking. He was steering clear of the Chinese firecracker. He looked straight at me.

"How much did you expect?"

I looked back at Harry. It was the right gesture, but I prayed it wouldn't set him off again. Having my right shoe on his left foot helped. He left the ball in my court.

"I think five million minimum. I'm talking dollars. You'll walk away with at least fifty million at ten-to-one. I'm hoping for more."

Sweeney's Irish complexion had ranged between blanched white and tomato red in the previous ten minutes. It was currently on the blanched side.

"I don't have five million right now."

"That's not the question. Can you raise it?"

He rubbed his face with his hands. The whole thing must have seemed surreal. Drops of sweat were oozing out of every pore.

"I don't know. It'll take time."

I looked at Harry. "When do you have to leave?"

Another unanswerable question. I think Harry went with his most earnest desire. "As soon as possible. Tonight."

It was a good answer. I nodded in assent, and addressed poor Harry. "I'll stay one more day for Mr. Sweeney's answer. You can leave this evening, Mr. Qian."

I turned back to Sweeney. "I'll be at the Gresham until tomorrow noon. We'll need to hear by then. Do what you can. I'll take your note for as much as you can put together now. You can commit to the rest when you've raised the credit. Bear in mind, you don't give us cash. Not a dime. We don't deal in cash for obvious reasons. It's all strictly debt owed to Mr. Qian's syndicate. You'll owe nothing until after the race. At that point we simply transfer your winnings electronically to any bank account you name. I'd set up a numbered account in the meantime to receive your winnings. Perhaps in Switzerland."

I stood and held out my hand to Sweeney. He still looked a bit blank, but he took my hand. Harry rose and bowed at the waist before I could stop him. Sweeney gave him a slight bow in return.

I took Harry's arm and guided him through the door. I turned for one last word to Sweeney.

"I'll look for your message by tomorrow noon. I'm at the Gresham, as you know. You can use the name, 'Alexander Hamilton.' Just remember that serious commitments have been made. I would not want to disappoint these people for the well-being of all of us."

Given the business he was in, I was sure he could fill in the implications of that statement.

CHAPTER TWENTY-NINE

Harry and I caught a quick lunch at the Sports bar in the Gresham before he caught a cab to the Dublin Airport for the flight back to Boston and his safe, comfortable laboratory. Bizarre as his performance had been, it might have been exactly the touch that was needed to edge Sweeney into a decision. At the very least, he left the suggestion that the people he represented could make pot stickers of Sweeney and his army.

In looking around the bar and lobby, I was surprised that my finely tuned antenna for someone on my tail was turning up no signals. If I was right, it left me free to use the afternoon to tend to what Rick McDonough would call a "burr under my saddle."

I was never comfortable with the official record of Black Diamond's unimpressive sire and dam. It's true that occasionally a horse with blazing speed pops out of a line of sluggards. But it's rare. If I were going to all the deceptive effort it would take to distort the time of every public workout of a two-year-old colt, beginning with the very first, I'd want some high-test blood flowing through that colt's veins to bank on.

I called Kieran Dowd at the Dubh Crann Stables. He was in his office, planning the morning's workouts for the fifty or so horses he trained. I got him alone, so I was able to test a theory.

"Kieran, I'm with Martin Sweeney. We have a question for you." I figured that would imply that Sweeney was right there approving of anything I asked.

"Mr. Schwarzenegger. Or is it your excellency, the governor?"

Thank God he mentioned it. I'd forgotten what name I'd left with him.

"'Mister' will do. A question for you. This has both of us curious. There was another horse in the stable that was foaled about the same time as Black Diamond. What's his name?"

That was a guess.

"What makes you ask that?"

"Curiosity. We have a bet. He told me you'd know."

There was a hesitation that led me to believe that my shot-in-the-dark suspicions might be on track.

"I think I'd better be speakin' with Mr. Sweeney himself."

"Suit yourself. We're having lunch. He's gone to the men's room. He told me to get an answer by the time he gets back. I could call him out of the men's room, but I don't know how that would go over."

Another hesitation.

"Your call, Kieran. Hold the phone. I'll go get him."

"Wait a minute. Damn it, you're always in a hurry. What do ya want to know again?"

"The other two-year-old colt in the Dubh Crann Stables that was born the same time as Black Diamond? It's a simple question. Mr. Sweeney says he just can't think of the name."

"Shannon Moon. Born the same night in March."

"I'll tell him. He'll be pleased. He thought it was the name of a river. Thank you Kieran."

"Hold the line. I'll be speaking with him when he comes back if ya please."

"Here he comes now. I'll put him on. Oh, wait a minute. He stopped to talk to someone the other side of the room. We'll have to call you back."

That was interesting. I went to the guests' computer room of the Gresham, put in a couple of euros, and got on line. I used Bing.com to get into the registry of Thoroughbred breeding. I typed in the name Shannon Moon and got another interesting bit. The sire of

Shannon Moon was listed as an Irish stallion named Knight Thief. His dam was Blue Rose.

I used Bing.com again to find that Knight Thief had won the Irish Derby in his day. He had gone on to sire a number of Grade One stakes winners. Blue Rose was also descended from a line of champions. They were a powerful combination, and each of them had a record for passing their best genes on to their offspring. Another strange coincidence was that both Knight Thief and Blue Rose were owned by and stabled at the Dubh Crann Stables. As Kieran Dowd had mentioned, both Black Diamond and Shannon Moon were foaled the same night in the Dubh Crann foaling barn.

I checked out the track record of Shannon Moon and found that he had run two races in Ireland, coming in at the back of the pack in both.

One last curious bit of information was that every registered son of Knight Thief had the word "Thief" in his name—except Shannon Moon.

I brought up a picture of Shannon Moon and found, to no great surprise at this point, that his markings were not exactly identical, but very similar to those of Black Diamond. They could have passed as brothers.

I recalled the words of Mick, my guide at the National Stud Farm, that a representative of the Irish National Registry was required to be present at the birth of every registered Thoroughbred born in Ireland. The official would insert a chip under the skin behind the foal's ear. A simple scan of the chip would reveal the sire and dam of the foal from then on.

Mick also said that the system cannot be beaten. Well, I wondered. What's that old expression about a chain being only as strong as its weakest link?

Now it was more than a burr under the saddle. It seemed more likely than not that these thugs had gone the full distance. They not only fudged Black Diamond's track times, they might have messed with his recorded lineage. I was sure enough to put it to the test.

A bit more research indicated that a board called Horse Sport Ireland keeps the register of Thoroughbreds, as well as other pure-bred horses foaled in Ireland. The offices are in the town of Naas, the county seat of Kildare County, and just a short hop from the Dubh Crann Stables.

When I showed up at the car rental agency on South Circular Street, the agent grinned and automatically reached for the key to the Jaguar. This time I was going for a low profile. When I asked for a Honda Civic, the grin dropped from his lips like dying rose petals.

I was at the Horse Sport Ireland registry offices in an hour. I put on a happy, innocent face and used my "novelist" cover story. I asked the young clerk at the desk which agent attended the foaling of Black Diamond and Shannon Moon. Since it was hardly classified information, and since there was the distinct hint of a mention of her name in "the novel," she checked the records and came up with the name, Thomas Casey. She was, in fact, a fountain of information. I could find our Mr. Casey at the Shamrock Stables about five kilometers away.

Our Mr. Casey was a tidy little white-haired gentleman in a perfectly pressed suit and a bow tie. I found him in the office of the head trainer. He appeared to be about to leave. I introduced myself and suggested that we walk together to his car.

"What is this in relation to, young man?"

I loved it. He exuded the kind of "officialness" that infects some older minor officials. His choice of "young man," instead of the perfectly good name I had given—Chevy Chase—was the clincher. He was ripe for the picking.

We were approaching his car when I gently tucked him under my right armpit and guided him to the shade of a gorgeous weeping willow, whose hanging branches gave both shade and privacy.

"Mr. Casey, you've probably guessed that I'm American."

He snapped off, "Yes." He seemed somewhat antsy under my armpit, but I wanted him close.

"There would appear to be a problem with some paperwork. Your paperwork."

He stiffened and popped out from under. He rose an inch or two in indignation. He was still snapping his words. "What paperwork?"

"We're talking about Black Diamond."

That put his head on a swivel, but there was no one in sight. "Young man, I have no idea what you're talking about."

I looked up the path and saw one of the grooms coming in the distance.

"Very well, Mr. Casey. We can do this slowly and chance being overheard. Or we can cut to the chase. I have just one simple question. How shall we do it?"

He caught sight of the groom approaching from about a hundred yards.

"What is it? What do you want?"

I smiled benignly.

"Please relax, Mr. Casey. I'm on your side. I do business with Dubh Crann. I'm reaping the benefit of your handiwork. We'll want to do it again someday. I have no interest in exposing anything, shall we say, out of the ordinary."

He eyed the groom. "Quickly, young man. What?"

"To recall the occasion. Black Diamond and Shannon Moon, born the same night. You observed for the registry."

I paused. He just fidgeted. I went for the kill.

"There was an arrangement. A switch of identity between the two. Do I have to be more specific?"

His breath was getting shallower and his pink Irish complexion was becoming rosy. But he was not leaping in to deny it.

"When you did the paperwork, there was apparently a spelling error. There was an *e* on the end of Moon. It could cause registration problems in the States. We wouldn't want that would we? Especially in this case."

He was edging close enough to tuck him back under my armpit again. I resisted.

"That can't be, young man. I saw to that paperwork myself."

"For which you were well paid, Mr. Casey. We'd simply like you to pull the records in the registry here and be sure the spelling is correct. If it is, there's no problem. I can handle it in the States. Can you do that?"

"Certainly. But—"

"That's all. If it's correct, don't contact us. We'll be in touch when we can use your services again. Now, see there, Mr. Casey, that was harmless, wasn't it?"

I shook his hand before he had a chance to answer.

"Incidentally, Mr. Sweeney sends his very best wishes."

He was looking me straight in the eye when he said without the slightest apparent purpose of deception, "Who?"

I'd said it clearly. There was no point in repeating. It was not exactly like a blow to the kidneys from Mugsy McGuire, but I have to say it was close. Only someone at the top of Sweeney's organization would have the clout to pull a switch with the national registry. I'd had it from Rick McDonough and Billy Coyne, and confirmed by Superintendent Phelan that the top man was Sweeney. That one word from Casey set everything spinning. I was virtually sure now that all of them were wrong. There was someone higher than Sweeney.

That was a personal rocker for me because now I had no idea where the heavy fire might be coming from.

I was back at the Gresham by noon. I left word with the switchboard that I was taking calls for Arnold Schwarzenegger. When Sweeney called at nine the next morning, I was seeing him in a different light. I wondered what kind of commitment he'd make if he were not the top dog.

The answer came quickly. Apparently his slightly subordinate position was no deterrent. A night's sleep seemed to have fortified his determination to go for broke. That raised the interesting question of whether our Mr. Sweeney had consulted his higher-up or was striking out on his own.

I had set a figure of five million as the minimum table stakes, but that was just to get him thinking in terms of serious money. He came on ready to take no guff over a commitment of three million euros—about three million, nine hundred thousand dollars at the then-exchange rate.

"And that's it. That's my last word. Take it leave it. And you can tell that to your damn syndicate."

"I don't tell my damn syndicate anything. In case you didn't get the picture, they tell me. I'll take it to them. Maybe if I kick in a few more dollars, they'll go for it."

"And you can tell them for me, I pull the strings on the horse. Without me, they have nothing."

"I hope you don't mind if I soften that a little before I pass it on. You really don't want to know what's happened to people who gave them attitude."

He seemed to go into neutral. Perfect.

"Mr. Sweeney, there are documents. I'll need your signature. I'll come by at one this afternoon. Your office?"

"Yeah."

This time there was no escort to the upper office. McGuire was not in sight, and the pub was virtually sleeping. I made my own way up the now familiar stairs and knocked on Sweeney's door. He was his gracious self.

"What?"

It sounded more like a command than a question. I took it as an invitation. I came in and stood across from him at his desk. I set a small sheaf of stapled papers in front of him. I had used the Gresham Hotel computer to print out a debt instrument with every relevant legal term I could think of. Stripped of legal crap, it said that in exchange for adequate consideration, Mr. Sweeney assumed a legally binding debt to Mr. Qian's imaginary syndicate—to which I gave an impressive title—in the amount of three million euros.

"And the top of the morning to you too, Mr. Sweeney. By the way, do the Irish really say that?"

He looked at the paper and then up at me. "No. Only in American movies. What the hell is this?"

"That's your commitment to pay three million euros to Mr. Qian's syndicate—see right there—in the unlikely event that the horse in question loses the race."

"What the hell good is this? I thought gambling contracts were illegal. How are you going to collect?"

"This is not a gambling contract. Did you see one word in there about a bet? This is a simple loan agreement, binding on both parties. The syndicate is advancing you credit for three million euros. How you use them is your business. The debt is to be repaid, by coincidence immediately after the race. You'll repay it out of your winnings on Black Diamond. The rest of the winnings, less commission, are, of course, yours. That said, Mr. Sweeney, I can assure you that collecting on this debt is not causing them sleepless nights. If you should welsh on this little obligation, you'll be paying it off in body parts."

I gave that a second to sink in. "But why are we talking about that? The chances are overwhelming that you'll be on the receiving end of more money than you've seen in a lifetime."

He pulled a pair of reading specs out of a desk drawer and began perusing the legal gobbledegook I'd crammed into it. It was a bit like fiction writing to draft a fictitious debt instrument for an imaginary obligation owed to a nonexistent syndicate. No problem. I doubt that he understood six words of the mishmash he was reading.

When the glasses came off, he pulled out a pen. I'd printed the signature line in bold to make it easy to find. It all apparently passed his careful scrutiny. He scribbled a blotch of hen-scratchings in the right place, and I picked up the "legal document."

Binding or not, and the operative word was "not," I wanted the leverage I'd have over Sweeney if he thought he owed three million euros to an organization more conscienceless and bloody than his own.

I knew this was probably the last time I'd have Sweeney in a face-to-face chat. The so-called paperwork was all smoke and mirrors to produce the desired leverage. My second purpose in being there was to squeeze out one last bit of serious information. I went for nonchalance.

"I'm curious, Mr. Sweeney. Since we're now officially partners in all this, maybe you can clear something up for me. Our people have asked the same thing. I'll take it back to them."

"What?"

"Black Diamond ran once before. It seemed like a perfect setup. And yet, you didn't let him win? Why not?"

The suspicion I was trying to avoid was creeping back into his slightly squinting eyes. I couldn't just back off and leave it that way. I had to go full into it.

"I'm asking because the people I represent can't afford any slipups this time. It's a matter of some concern. You understand. Why didn't you let him win, Mr. Sweeney?"

"I had my reasons. What the hell's that got to do with anything?"

"As you've mentioned a couple of times, you pull the strings on Black Diamond. A double cross this time could be a major concern to these people. I need some answers to take back to them."

He just played with the pen on the desk.

"Let me assure you, we're now partners, Mr. Sweeney. As far as the authorities are concerned, we're all in the same boat. We sink or swim together. That being said, I can't go back without an answer. It affects future plans. Was the jockey a problem?"

He opened a drawer, threw the pen into it, and slammed it shut.

"The little bastard wouldn't play ball. He wouldn't take orders."

"And I assume that it was important enough to have him lose on Black Diamond to apply some pressure. I remember reading about the kidnapping."

He looked up at me with steel back in his eyes. I tried to keep a dispassionate attitude while my blood was reaching the boiling point.

"You can take this back to your syndicate. They're not playing with some slum street gang here either. No one steps out of line on us."

"That kidnapping was a neat ploy. We could take some lessons from you too."

"We had to show that little punk who he was dealing with."

"But it didn't work. He was still going for the win at the eighth pole. He was taking the lead. You had to knock him out of the saddle to get the Diamond to lose."

"The little bastard didn't know the price he'd pay. You don't mess with us. Tell that to your syndicate."

"I'm impressed. I certainly will. They'll be asking this. How did you people manage to knock him out of the saddle?"

He just clammed up. I could see a wall go up. Before I went too far and invited a backlash, it was time to pull out.

"Someday when we know each other better, maybe you'll let me in on that one, Mr. Sweeney."

I pocketed the paper Sweeney had signed, forced myself to shake hands with him, and left.

I walked the long way back to the hotel to get a grip on emotions that were seething just under the surface. I had just left that smug wart on the face of an otherwise decent society without telling him straight out what pain he had caused to a family that had deserved a life free of his despicable greed and self-serving violence.

I had to put out of my mind the faces of my forever friend Danny, of sweet Colleen, and of that little angel Danny would never see blossom into a lady. It was the only way I could get some equilibrium.

Back in my hotel room, I actually enjoyed the pain I felt pulling the tape off my skin that held the recorder. I was fairly sure they wouldn't search me for it this time.

I played back the conversation I had just had with Sweeney. It was mildly satisfying to have on record by his own admission the fact that Erin's kidnapping was in fact committed by Sweeney's gang to force Danny to lose the race on Black Diamond.

The questions still hanging were why they wanted the Diamond to lose, and how they managed to knock my friend Danny off his back and over the rail to his death.

CHAPTER THIRTY

There was one last thing to do before packing for the flight home the next morning. As promised, I needed to fill Superintendent Phelan in on my adventures of the last few days. I knew he'd be more than interested, since I'd been able to go places off-limits for him in his official capacity. I also knew that he'd save me time when I got back to Boston by sharing the information with Billy Coyne.

I made a call to the number the superintendent had given me. Within ten minutes there was an unmarked car from the Dublin office at the side door of the Gresham to take me to his country office. Neither of us trusted the phones.

I reported my discussion with "our Mr. Casey" of the registry. I also played the tape of my last conversation with Sweeney. It gave the superintendent a double whammy, as it had me. He was as shocked as I was to get the notion that there was someone in the organization above Sweeney. Perhaps more shocked, since it suggested a flaw in his intelligence gathering. The real leader had managed to remain totally under his radar.

The second disquieting revelation was that this gang of thugs was as close as they appeared to be in attempting to raise the funds that would let them make their move across the ocean. He understood that they had nothing to gain from my imaginary scheme to wager on Black Diamond. Nevertheless, the fact that they were willing to put up three million euros of borrowed money right now to rake in the necessary winnings to launch their Boston operation meant to him that they were much further along in their plans than he had been led to believe.

When I got back to the Gresham, I called our office in Boston. Just the sound of Julie's voice conjured images of a normal lawyer's practice. I could visualize weeks on end in which the most dangerous element of my day would be crossing Franklin Street during rush hour. I made a silent promise to myself that if this thing ever ended, I'd limit my practice to appealing parking tickets.

I arranged to have Julie book me onto the first flight out of Dublin Airport in the morning. Then I asked her to transfer me to himself, Mr. Devlin.

Mr. D. nearly came through the phone. I hadn't realized how long it had been since I'd assured him that I was still among the living. His relief at hearing that I'd be in the office the following afternoon defused the burst of pent-up frustration at my lack of communication.

I had nothing on my agenda until the flight the following morning. That meant I could go into great detail in filling him in. He reacted to most of my disclosures pretty much as I had. We both reached the conclusion that a sit-down with Billy Coyne was definitely in order. We planned it for the following evening over dinner in a private room at Locke-Ober's.

I was packed and into a cab at seven the next morning, bound for the Dublin Airport and home. There are some moments that are so etched into your memory bank that you know they'll be crisp and fresh and startling right through senility. One of those moments occurred when I stepped out of the cab onto the sidewalk at the departure terminal. Another passenger was heading in the same direction with a copy of the morning's *Irish Times*. I caught just enough of the headline to impel me to catch him by the arm and ask with some urgency to see the front page of his newspaper.

Thoughts began flooding my consciousness faster than I could process them when I read the headline. "Reputed gangland figure found dead of multiple gunshot wounds. Martin Sweeney's body was discovered by the Gardai early this morning in an alleyway behind McShannon's Pub. The Garda Siochana reports that no immediate suspects have been identified, but that they have every intention—"

I got Superintendent Phelan on his cell phone. I figured to hell with security. There were other official-sounding voices in the background. He sounded frazzled, as if he were dealing with a number of people and issues at the same time.

"I'm sure you've seen it, Superintendent."

"I've been dealing with it all night. Apparently it happened just before midnight."

"Where does this leave us?"

He muted his voice.

"Perhaps there's a positive side. Thank God you turned up that information. This might give us a lead to who was above Sweeney in the chain of command. Where are you now?"

"Airport. I'm flying home. I assume you'll be in contact with Billy Coyne. We can stay in touch through him."

"Fine. Have a safe trip, Michael. I really have to ring off. It's a bit hectic here."

I was still processing information when I went through security. I bought an *Irish Times* to read the full report while I sat by the boarding gate. The details were vivid, but they added little to my understanding about the significance of Sweeney's murder. I'm sure that most of the citizens of Dublin took it in with their omelettes and blood sausage and chalked it up to thugs murdering thugs. I just let it ruminate.

Just about the same moment they called my flight for boarding, a flash of thought jolted me out of my seat. I grabbed my carry-on and bolted back through security to flag down a cab. I was back at the Gresham, to the surprise of my favorite concierge, forty minutes later. I took him aside and spilled out every fact I could recall about the country church I'd been taken to in the middle of the night a week previously, the church where an elderly priest and nun had put little Erin back in my arms for safe keeping.

Thank God he knew the countryside of Ireland like I know Boston's Back Bay. He made an educated guess and called me a private driver. The concierge gave the directions, and I gave the driver a tip sizeable enough to add serious weight to his foot on the gas pedal.

Half an hour later, we pulled into the gravel courtyard outside of what looked like a church that must have been built in ancient times. I recognized nothing, since my last visit was in the middle of the night.

I remembered hearing with shock from my driver of that night, Paedar Kearney, that the elderly priest had been tortured and murdered. I used the knocker on the stone cottage beside the church in the hopes that the nun might have escaped the same fate and might still be there.

Five knocks, and I was about to give up hope, when I heard slow, uneven footsteps on the other side of the door. The old nun, who still wore the habit, opened the door and stood speechless to see me. She had been through a great deal, beginning with the harboring of a kidnapped child, followed by the vicious murder of the priest.

She looked around behind me cautiously before asking me in. Her first words were regarding little Erin. I began by pouring out the news of Erin's emotional reuniting with her mother and the fact that they were both alive and well. That raised her comfort level in talking to me. Being Irish, she insisted that we talk over tea and scones.

She was in tears when she recounted the treatment that the priest had suffered at the hands of the thugs who tortured him. I noticed that she moved around the kitchen with a limp that I didn't remember being there before. When I mentioned it, she waved it off, saying it could have been much worse for her but for the fact that the priest convinced them that she knew nothing about the child.

I gave her time to dry the tears and suppress the thoughts that still terrorized her. I wanted to give her more time, but now I was under serious pressure. I had to ask the question, even though it would surely open raw wounds.

"Sister, I'm so sorry. I have to ask it. So much depends on this. Did either you or Father tell them where I was taking little Erin?"

That brought another flow of tears, but through it she spoke with emphatic certainty.

"No. I can assure you of that. I was right here every minute. God love him, the good Father died at their hands without telling them a thing."

"Forgive me. I have to ask this, Sister. How about yourself?"

"Not a word. I swear to God Almighty."

My driver took me back to the Dublin Airport. I was able to get onto the last Aer Lingus flight for Boston. I used the duration of the flight to fit some disconnected thoughts into a pattern that was making more sense to me every minute.

I replayed a dozen times in my mind my last conversation with Sweeney. I searched every line of his face that I could conjure in my mind's eye. I finally reached a conclusion that I was ready to act on. When Sweeney refused to answer my question about how Danny had been knocked out of the saddle, he wasn't being evasive. He just flat-out didn't know. And he didn't know because he had had no part in Danny's fall. He'd been relying on the kidnapping of Danny's daughter to keep Black Diamond from winning the race.

When we landed at Logan Airport, I hopped in a cab. I passed a sizeable tip to the driver before she put it in first gear. I could have sworn I'd ridden with her before—Carlotta something. I remembered that she had a knowledge of shortcuts and a willingness to treat speed limits as suggestions. She had me in the bowels of South

Boston at the door of the Failte Pub in the time it would take most drivers to reach the tunnel.

There was still a hole in my reasoning that needed to be plugged before I could make a move. It was five in the evening. The pub was doing a modest business by Irish standards. Being early in the week, the Irish music was recorded, which kept the sound level at a comfortable pitch.

Among the handful of men at the bar, I recognized Sean Flannery. I remembered him as the one who relieved Vince Scully in keeping watch over Colleen's home the night after Erin had been taken. He was the only one I knew for sure to be double-dealing on Boyle with the Irish mob.

I sauntered casually to the door to Boyle's office with a prayer that Flannery would keep his attention on the Bruins-Canadiens game on the bar television. The score was tied in the third period and the Bruins were on a power play. Thank God. He was glued.

I finessed knocking. I startled Boyle at his desk with a direct entry. I closed the door behind me immediately. Boyle made a grab for his telephone, probably to buzz the bartender. If I had Boyle sized up right, it was probably the first time he had ever been alone in his office with another human being and no muscle to watch over him.

I leaned over his desk and put a finger on the telephone disconnect button. I snapped off, "Sit there, Boyle!"

He sat frozen like a figure in a wax museum, still holding the dead phone. I reached over and grabbed it out of his hand and hung up.

I looked down on him from an advantage of height. He could have made one cry, and I'd be dealing with the entire row of thugs at the bar. But he didn't. I think he knew that I could do him serious bodily harm before anyone could come through the door. I was probably more fear stricken than he was, because whatever I could do to him in a few seconds would be doubly repaid at their leisure when his thugs arrived. The trick was not to show it.

More than a physical advantage, which never seemed to work out for me, I had a theory that I was ready to go to bat with. I laid it on him with more self-assurance than I actually had in the tank.

"Sit quiet and listen to me, Boyle, and you just might find yourself in one piece when I leave here. I have a little test for you. Are you ready for the first part?"

He was just staring. I don't think he even heard me. At least there was no response. I slapped the desk with my open hand directly in front of him. He jumped about three inches, but he had his mouth closed when he landed.

"Once more, Boyle, open your ears. Do you read me?"

He nodded. That was better than nothing. I backed off a couple of steps to improve his concentration. He seemed to loosen up a bit, but he knew I could be within arm's reach in an instant.

"Here's the way it stacks up. There's a mob of former IRA thugs that are squeezing a number of people who used to donate to their cause. Right now, it's pure extortion. They send a man over here periodically to pick up the take and bring it back to Ireland. You know about that?"

He was slow to respond, but when he did, he shook his head.

"No. No. This won't do. Bad start. I don't have all night. I know the answers to these questions. It would be in your interest to get the answers right the first time. Let's try again. You know about that, right?"

I had moved closer and his eyes were widening. He slowly nodded.

"A little louder, Boyle."

His voice was hoarse, but he got it out. "Yeah. I know. All right? Ya through now?"

"Next part. You and your boys are the collectors over here. You hold the money for the Irishman. He picks it up from you. You listening?"

I was becoming more emphatic as I reached the end of that last sentence. He nodded.

"Good. Then understand this. I don't give a rat's ass about your shenanigans with those Irish goons. That said, are we in agreement on the facts?"

I leaned slightly over the desk. He nodded in agreement.

"Say it, Boyle. We're communicating here."

"Yeah. Yeah."

"Good. Next point. Periodically, you have your own goons put the muscle on the jockeys at Suffolk to fix a race. I can prove that too, so you might as well agree to it."

He mumbled something I couldn't hear.

"Louder, Boyle. We're still not where I give a crap about your business. Are we in agreement about fixed races?"

"Yeah, yeah. So what?"

"Don't get cute. I'm still within reach."

He straightened up in the chair. I had his full attention. He could see the deep water ahead.

"Now to the heart of the matter. You've been playing a little game that might interest the boys in Ireland. You collect the extortion money the day before the Irish thug comes over to pick it up. You bet it all on a race at Suffolk that you've fixed. You skim off the winnings before the Irishman collects the extortion money the next day. Very clever. I finally matched up the timing of the Irish collections and the fixed races. It took me two weeks to catch on to that one."

Boyle's eyes were as round as a couple of fried eggs.

"Now hear this. I'm not shooting blind here. I can prove all of it. The only question is who do I give it to. The police? No, not yet. The thugs from the old IRA? Quite possibly. They might just want a share of your winnings. Like one hundred percent. They may even want to take the past winnings out in broken bones. Do I have your attention?"

He nodded with more vigor.

"Good. Then let's do business. Suppose you show some good faith by admitting that everything I've said is true."

Silence.

"Okay by me, Boyle. You've heard that old expression, 'It's your funeral.' In your case, there'll be a good old Irish wake to go with it."

I leaned across the desk and yanked the cord out of the telephone. I turned as if to leave, which was the furthest thing from my intention with the bar full of knee breakers just outside. He caught me on the second step.

"Wait. What the hell are you doing?"

I came back the two steps. "I'm waiting to hear you say that everything I said is the truth. But not for long."

"All right. Yeah."

"Yeah what?"

"It's the truth. So what?"

I pulled my cell phone out of my pocket in the open position.

"Congratulations, Boyle. You just made your first recorded broadcast. Copies are being made by my associate as we speak."

That was not exactly true, but it had the desired effect. He was almost bouncing on the chair. "What the hell you gonna do?"

"I'm going to give you some new rules of life, you miserable excuse for an Irishman. Here's the first. You've made your last collection for those extortionists. It ends now."

"They'll kill me. I can't just stop."

"Ah, but you will. If that raises the risk of personal danger, I'd suggest you get your pampered ass out of town. Here's the second. If you or any of that scum at the bar make one more threat to a jockey or try to fix one more race, the tape of this conversation goes directly to Martin Sweeney and his gang. Do you read that?"

His expression said he heard me loud and clear. Fortunately, I was sure he was still thoroughly uninformed of the recent demise of Mr. Sweeney. When and if he did hear, I was sure he'd be equally terrified of Sweeney's replacement.

That left just one last point. I left it until last to be sure Boyle was softened up enough to insure the truth. I said it slowly.

"Last question. Here's the test. Did you or anyone you're connected with have anything to do with knocking Danny Ryan out of the saddle?"

I was scanning his features like a human lie detector. I believe to my core that he was totally truthful in whining that he had nothing to do with it.

That closed that door. It left just one possibility.

CHAPTER THIRTY-ONE

The "recorded broadcast" to an "associate" of my conversation with Boyle was a complete fraud, but it accomplished my purposes, including getting my entire body, quivering knees and all, out the door of the Failte Pub unbent, broken, or spindled.

The next morning, I called Mr. Devlin from my apartment. He told me the dinner was set with Billy Coyne for six that evening. I asked him to call Billy back and set up an interview for me with our client, Hector Vasquez. Things were beginning to move at the speed of light, and I couldn't leave any pieces of the puzzle unchecked.

Vasquez looked drawn and maybe a shade lighter for being out of the daily sun at the track. He was, needless to say, seriously worried and eager for any updates. I filled him in on what I'd been doing on his behalf, leaving out only the final theory I was about to test. For him, the whole story was an eye-opener. As far as he'd known, it began and ended with fixed races. Then I got down to business.

"Hector, we've got new ground rules. I'm dealing with some ugly people in this. My neck's been on the block more times than I'd like in the past week. From now on, I need to be playing with a full deck. That means you tell me the truth, the whole truth, and nothing but the truth. Both of our lives may depend on it. *Comprende?*"

He nodded.

"No, Hector. I want to hear it from the heart. I can't do this on a nod."

"I understand, Mr. Knight."

"Good. Then let's jump right into the deep end. Did you know before the race that Danny's daughter had been kidnapped?"

"Like I said, Danny was acting jumpy in the jockey's room."

"That's bullshit, Hector. I heard that version before. It does neither of us any good. This time I want an answer. Did you know about the kidnapping before the race?"

He looked down. I reached over with my hand and lifted up his face until we were eye to eye. "Did you?"

He said it in Spanish as if it would soften it. "Sí."

"Did Danny tell you?"

"Yes. I told him that the fix was in for my horse to win. I thought he should know. They didn't approach him with the fix because they thought his horse had no chance to challenge anyway. That's when he told me about his daughter."

I sat back. It was just what I hoped to hear. I asked another question just to nail it shut.

"Why did you deny it before?"

"I was afraid you'd think I was part of the kidnapping. I thought it'd look worse for me."

"Damn, Hector. I'll tell you what does look worse for you. If you lie to me in the smallest detail, it makes me wonder about everything else you say. Is that finally clear?"

"Yes, sir."

"Good. Then on that basis, I'm going to ask you just one more time. Did you have anything to do with physically knocking Danny out of the saddle?"

This time he said it so the entire cellblock could hear him.

"No, Mr. Knight. No."

By my figuring, the next extortion payment from Fitzpatrick and the others would be due to be picked up from Boyle by the Irish gang's emissary in four days. That meant that Boyle had probably already arranged in advance for the fixing of a race at Suffolk in three days. I checked with Alberto Ibanez and found that my calendar estimates were right on. The fix had been set in place for the sixth race in just three days. Number four was to be the winner.

At this point, timing was everything. I drove to the track and found Rick McDonough at the backside finishing up the workouts for the day. I was emotionally relieved to find that the freeze between us had thawed. It was essential that I have his complete trust for what I was about to ask.

I spent twenty minutes giving Rick every detail of what had gone on since I came into this case after Danny's death. I could see that he was stunned and angered by what was really going on around Danny and Black Diamond. I needed his anger to ask him to do something that could be personally risky.

"Rick, I need you to enter Black Diamond in the sixth race three days from now. I know you've been acting on instructions from Ireland, but that's over. Your contact, Martin Sweeney, is dead. If no one else has contacted you, it's your call. You're the trainer. I have to know now. Will you do it?"

Even I may have underestimated the depth of Rick's anger at the people who had manipulated him and possibly even caused Danny's death. He was on his feet almost before I finished asking.

"Where you going, Rick?"

"I'm going to enter the damn race. Let me know if you need anything else."

I thought I'd better put in a call to Superintendent Phelan in Ireland. Now that I had positive information, I filled him in on Boyle's game of betting the Irish gang's money before handing it over to the Irish collector. I also told him that Black Diamond was entered in a race in three days.

"I know you're a busy man, Superintendent. Especially with Sweeney's murder. But I suggest that the action is going to be over here the day of the race. I suspect that Sweeney's replacement will get word that Black Diamond is running. He'll probably be over here to collect the extortion money personally the way Sweeney did. If he does, he'll probably be betting it on Black Diamond. This is the pay-off for them for all the deception about his speed and lineage. "

"That makes sense, Michael."

"There may be fireworks. Boyle's no longer doing the pickups for them. He's out of the game. They'll have to do it themselves. That may not sit well. Boyle knows the names of too many of their play-ers. If he's off their team, he could be a liability they'll have to elim-inate."

"This is getting more interesting all the time."

"Here's something else to think about. You know the cast of char-acters better than I do, but if I had to guess who'll move up to Sweeney's spot, my money'd be on Mugsy McGuire. He was clearly the first string backup when I met with Sweeney."

"That would be my guess from what we know here. The absolute top man is still invisible, but Sweeney and McGuire seem to be the action level."

"Then you know what you have to do better than I do, Superin-tendent. I'm thinking this whole thing could come to a head the day of that race. If you and Billy Coyne were working together as a team on this side of the ocean, the whole business might be blown wide open once and for all."

I knew this was a late shift in his plans when he already had a plateful in Ireland. Nevertheless, what I said made sense. I added the thought that he could see a great Irish horse trounce a field of American horses.

He needed time to think about it, but suggested that he might make preliminary reservations just in case it all worked out.

The dinner at Locke-Ober's that evening was clearly up to par for that classic Boston eatery. It also provided a setting for something akin, on a decidedly minor scale, to the planning of the invasion of Normandy. I waited until coffee was served after dessert to unleash the beast. I laid out a plan that appeared so preposterous at the out-set, that Billy didn't know whether to laugh out loud or have me committed.

Then I laid out each of the pieces of the jigsaw puzzle I'd been collecting and slowly pieced them together. By the time I finished, Billy just sat there staring at me. He gave Mr. Devlin a look that asked, *How do you live with this kid?*

Mr. Devlin, God love him, leaned in and said quietly, "Billy, think about it. And then tell me where there's a flaw in Michael's think-ing."

Billy sat staring into his coffee. He finally broke into a scratch-ing of the back of his head with a look of either frustration or resig-nation. Probably both.

"Damn it, kid. You do make life interesting. So what am I sup-posed to do in all this?"

I laid it out in all the detail I'd been able to work out on the long plane ride home. For better or worse, to paraphrase Julius Caesar, the die was about to be cast.

I was in my office two days later when I got the call I'd hoped for. Superintendent Phelan told me that he had arrived in Boston and was staying at the Parker House on School Street. I welcomed him to our sunny shores, remembering Irish weather.

It was about ten a.m. I arranged to meet him in the Parker House dining room for dinner at six that evening. I called Billy Coyne and suggested that he join us to meet his Irish counterpart. Billy never turned down a dinner at defense counsel's expense in my memory, and he was not about to start now. Mr. Devlin made the perfect fourth.

I made the reservation, and then called my now phone pal, Ms. Paxton, and asked her to convey my invitation to Mr. Fitzpatrick for another Zaftig's corned beef sandwich on the Public Garden bench by the swan boats at noon.

He was there right on time. He accepted the proffered sand-wich immediately after we sat down with a readiness that made me think he was developing a taste for Zaftig's fine fare. He ate while I mostly talked. I'd briefed so many people at this point that I was be-ginning to fall into set speech patterns.

He chewed in silence, shaking his head occasionally when I cov-ered the more risky parts.

"It comes down to this, Mr. Fitzpatrick. There'll probably be a demand to pay the extortion money one more time. Probably in the next twenty-four hours. The procedure will be different. It won't be Boyle's man. I've neutralized Boyle. He's out of this business. My guess is that one of the Irish thugs from over there will be over here to collect the extortion money from you directly. When it happens, it's important that you let me know immediately. I'll give you my cell phone number."

"And you'd like me to do what about the demand?"

"Pay it. I don't want to rock the boat now. But I can tell you this. If things work out the way I hope, it'll be the last cent you'll ever pay those thugs."

That brought a cautious smile. But he appeared troubled at the same time.

"I don't like this, Michael. You've gone through too much already. If this goes wrong—"

"Not to worry. My strength is as the strength of ten men, for my heart is pure."

He looked at me sideways. "Michael, when Tennyson said that, he was talking about a fictional character."

I was hardly back in the office ten minutes when I got a call on my cell phone from Mr. Fitzpatrick.

"Your prediction came true. I got a phone call from one of them. And you're right. The procedure is different."

"In what way?"

"I'm supposed to have the money in cash in a plain brown bag. I'm to leave it on a particular shelf behind a certain set of books at the Barnes & Noble on Washington Street."

"Where specifically?"

"In the Harvard Classics section behind the letters of Cicero."

"Good choice. You won't be fighting a crowd to get into that section. When?"

"This afternoon. One o'clock."

"Good. Please do it to the letter. Did he give a name?"

"No. No name. One more thing, Michael. I'm especially glad this may be the last time."

"I can imagine. But why especially?"

"He doubled the amount of the demand. We're getting into serious money."

I no sooner hung up than I dialed my trusty confidant/private eye, Tom Burns.

"Mikey, haven't heard from you in a while. Have you been keeping your ass out of those bear traps you get into?"

"I don't think I'd say that. The bear traps have just been out of the country. Out of your bailiwick, so to speak. Obviously I'm back and in need of your exclusive services. I mean you personally, Tom. Good as they are, no subordinates. I need the best."

"I assume that's why you called me."

"It most certainly is. Don't ever get infected with humility."

"Why would I, Mikey?"

"To be sure. Here's what I need."

I told him about the cash drop at Barnes & Noble. I needed him to be invisible and see who made the collection, and then tail him to wherever he went from there.

"And give me a call on my cell as soon as you have something. Agreed?"

"Piece of cake."

"The hell it is, Tom! This is no damn piece of cake. These are professionals the same as you. You go into this with your head up your ass and people will die. Namely me. Pay attention!"

Actually, that's not what I said. I thought it, but I knew it would only light Tom's short fuse. He might just tell me to get another boy. Besides, he was right. He was the best there is.

I just said, "Thank you, Tom. You have my cell phone number."

CHAPTER THIRTY-TWO

The dinner at the elegant, historical Parker House was a jovial affair, in spite of the ominous cloud hanging over us. Even Billy Coyne exuded charm. He and the superintendent seemed to share a personal pleasure in meeting face-to-face the one with whom they had had so many clandestine telephone conversations.

We discussed plans to meet before the first race the next day in the Suffolk Downs clubhouse box that I'd reserved. The four of us could watch the races together.

I saved one dark element that I had to introduce until after we had enjoyed a magnificent repast at the hands of the Parker House chef. Over coffee, I huddled the four of us together to speak in the quietest possible tone.

"There's been one change. I spoke to the jockeys who are going to ride in the sixth race tomorrow. Boyle had already gotten to them. The race is fixed for a win by the horse ridden by Vinnie Hernandez. Post position four. He'll be the longest shot on the board. Probably twenty-to-one. Boyle even got to Black Diamond's rider this time. It'll be Alberto Ibanez. He won't dare let him win. Boyle has them all scared to death. They won't cross him."

I could see consternation on the three faces around me.

"Listen. This could work to our advantage. If the Irish mob plans to make a killing by betting the house on Black Diamond, they'll lose it all. That could cripple their plans for a Boston takeover. It could even weaken their hold in Dublin. That works in our favor. Right?"

On their reconsideration, I got thoughtful agreement around the table. Even the superintendent seemed to get over the fact that the Irish horse would lose to an American horse.

Before we disbanded, Billy asked the question that had plagued me too until I had enough information to match up the timings.

"If that gang in Ireland put so much effort into setting up Black Diamond for a big win the first time, why did they pull off a kidnapping to make him lose?"

"Because they had more to lose if Black Diamond won, Mr. Coyne. By that time, Vince Scully had come over to their side. He must have told them that Boyle had bet the entire extortion collection on Hector Vasquez's horse—the one he had it fixed for. If Black Diamond won that race, Boyle would have lost their entire extortion collection—which was considerably more than they would have won if Black Diamond had won the race. That's why they had to make Diamond lose, even if it took a kidnapping to make Danny disappoint his trainer, Rick."

It was nine o'clock by the time we went our separate ways. The superintendent went up to his room, Billy went home, and Mr. Devlin offered me a ride to my apartment. Before we left the lobby, I got a call from Tom Burns on my cell phone.

"Give it to me, Tom."

He did. And for a full five seconds I basked in the vibrant glow of a rare moment when all of the schemes and plans and prayers of the past two weeks fit gloriously together. Thank you, Lord. I shared the glow with Mr. Devlin on the walk to the car.

My last act for the day before settling into a short, fitful sleep was a call to check on Terry, Colleen, Erin, and Kelty. Whatever else was spinning beyond my control, my little band of refugees was holding up like troopers.

The next morning, I was up at six with a serious case of the jumping jitters. I dropped by my favorite Starbucks out of habit. My usual sixteen ounces of Bucky's strongest did nothing to anaesthetise the butterflies.

It was the longest morning of my life. The only business I could concentrate on was a call to Rick McDonough to have him get me credentials so I could come into the paddock with him at race time when he saddled Black Diamond.

I met the other three of our foursome from the previous night's dinner in the clubhouse box I'd reserved at one p.m. It was just before post time for the first race.

We settled in for a day at the races, and actually enjoyed the first three races. By the fourth, the butterflies were back and had invited relatives.

I excused myself when the winner of the fifth race was unsaddled and left the winner's circle. I made my way down to the paddock. Rick was just fastening the last girth strap that goes around the jockey's saddle. We shook hands, and I pulled him over to the back of the stall.

"Rick, I have no time to explain. I want you to get out your checkbook, your credit cards, and all the nickels and dimes you have in your pockets. Here's what I want you to do before post time."

Even that old cowboy's eyes showed surprise, then doubt, then wonder, and finally an exuberance that could only come from a bursting feeling of hope and faith. I don't think I'd ever actually seen him smile before.

When the jockeys came out in the silks for the sixth race, I caught Alberto Ibanez for a short quiet word. I laid it out for him as directly and briefly as I could. He looked me straight in the eyes. I knew he was searching his soul to decide if he could actually trust what this lawyer was saying to him.

I heard Rick give Alberto his final instructions, which pretty much followed Rick's philosophy of the communication between a jockey and horse.

"Try to settle him in the backstretch. When it's time, let him go. He'll take care of business from there."

Rick gave Alberto a leg up, and he rode out in the post parade. When he passed me, there was no expression whatever on his face. I really had no clue to what was going on in his mind.

I was back in the clubhouse box as the horses approached the starting gate across the track for a run of six furlongs—three-quarters of a mile. I just nodded to each of the three with me. I was not up to conversation.

I used binoculars to watch Black Diamond being led by the pony boy up to the starting gate. It gave my heart an extra boost to see him prance more than walk. He was saying with every step, "This one is mine. Let's do it."

The assistant starter took the lead line and led him up to the third post position in the gate. He went in quickly and smoothly, as if he were anxious to get started. By the time all nine were loaded by the starters, and the track announcer roared, "They're in the gate," I was jumping out of my skin.

"They're off!"

A storm of dirt hit the starting gate as nine horses dug in from the hips to hit top speed in three jumps. Five leaders went full out for an early advantage. They pressed in on each other to get a position on the rail.

When the leading cluster fanned out, there were three abreast across at the front. The horse that Boyle had fixed it for, Tailgunner, was on the rail and edging his head into the lead. I picked up Black Diamond's colors. He was settling into fourth position on the rail.

With the binoculars, I could detect the other jockeys beside Tailgunner working the reins to seesaw the bits in their horses' mouths to give Boyle's horse, number four, the undisputed lead. It was subtle, but I knew what I was looking for.

They came into the turn in that order after a blazing fast two furlongs. The Diamond was hanging onto fourth position, nearly a length behind the leader and saving ground on the rail.

Halfway around the turn, Tailgunner opened up a length lead. The announcer picked it up and blared, "It's Tailgunner driving into the stretch! He's heading home!"

I was dying more and more as the gap widened. I had to grab the railing in front of me to keep from screaming, "Open him up, Alberto!"

It was as if he heard my thoughts. I saw Alberto crouch lower across Black Diamond's neck. I could see his lips working close to Diamond's ear.

In a flash, the Diamond burst into a new dimension of speed. He veered off the rail to the right. In three strides, he was on the heels of the horse running third. The jockey ahead of him seemed startled to have the Diamond at his back and driving. Before their hooves clicked on each other, the jockey ahead pulled slightly to the outside. Alberto saw daylight. He seemed almost possessed. He was on Diamond's neck, thrusting forward with every stride.

The Diamond caught the fever and turned the heat up another notch. He blew through on the inside, past the third and then the second horse. He had a clear track. He went for the leader.

The announcer was screaming into the mic. "Here comes Black Diamond! The Diamond is flying."

The Diamond lengthened his stride and dug in with every powerful thrust of his back legs. He cut the lead to three lengths, then two. By the time they passed the eighth pole, it was half a length.

The jockey on Tailgunner turned back for a fleeting glance. He went to the whip. Tailgunner responded with everything he had left, but he was nearly spent.

Alberto never let up. His legs drove against the stirrups in perfect rhythm with the Diamond's strides. They were twenty yards from the wire when the nose of the Diamond burst into the lead. At the wire, he had the lead by a full head.

I saw Alberto rise straight up in the irons with both arms lifted to Heaven. His fists were clenched. He was pumping them skyward as if he were finally beating off the beast.

The race was over, but Black Diamond never slackened his pace for another half mile. And Alberto just let him run. It was a victory lap for both of them.

I could have fallen back into the seat in exhaustion, or I could have leaped in the air and hugged anyone close by, but there was business to do.

I looked over at the superintendent. For the first time I clearly saw an emotion in his eyes. He was looking at me, and the emotion was stark hatred. He just glared with no words.

I heard a rustle of activity behind me. Seven uniformed officers lined up against the back rail of the box. The superintendent started to rise, and then just sank back down in his seat.

There was no fuss. Two of the officers lifted the superintendent out of his seat and told him he was under arrest. A third put handcuffs on him, while one of the arresting officers began the rote, "You have the right to remain silent, anything you say can and will be used against you—"

Whether because of the Miranda warnings or just because there was nothing to say, the superintendent was taken out of the box and up the steps without a word.

The business of preferring charges would be taken care of by Billy when he got back to his office. For the time being, the familiar threesome—Mr. Devlin, Billy Coyne, and I took a table in a far corner of the clubhouse bar. I don't know what they ordered, but a soothing three fingers of Famous Grouse went a long way to settling my raw nerves.

"All right, kid, now lay it out. All of it. What tipped you to the superintendent? You blew my mind last night when you told me. I've been working with him for a year and never got a clue."

"A bunch of things that didn't come together until the last few days. You, for one, Mr. Coyne."

He just held up his hands in a question.

"When I picked up little Erin from the priest and the nun in Ireland and brought her home, I left her and her mother with Terry O'Brien in a house on the shore on a dead-end street in Winthrop. Nobody knew where. Not even the priest and nun. I checked that. Except you, Mr. Coyne. When I filled you in, I told you that they were with Terry. You told me later you briefed the superintendent on everything in confidence. It was the only way the Irish mob could have found out. When I went to Terry's a couple of days later, one of their thugs was there to finish the job on them."

I saw a look of almost repentance mixed with anger on Billy's face.

"Damn it, kid. I never thought. It was a secure line. I remember now. He asked me. I must have spilled it."

"It's all right, Mr. Coyne. I probably would too if he'd asked me. It was only when I started piecing it together that I knew he had to be with the Irish gang. I'll give you another shocker. I recently found out that there's a top guy in that Irish outfit who remains invisible. I'd bet my Corvette that our superintendent's the head of it all. No wonder you and he never got anywhere in shutting down that gang."

Billy just shook his head. I think he was replaying confidential conversations with the superintendent over the past year.

"There's another piece to it. Before I left Ireland, I briefed him on what I learned about Martin Sweeney. Harry Wong and I played a wagering scam on Sweeney when I thought he was the top man. We arranged a phony loan of three million that he was going to bet on Black Diamond with Harry's imaginary syndicate. He was going to make twenty or thirty million on it. I did it to get information. When I told the superintendent about it, that was the first he'd heard of it. Sweeney was apparently doing this on his own. It must have smacked of a move by Sweeney to take over the top spot. That midnight, Sweeney was gunned down in an alley behind his office. That was too much of a coincidence. But even that wasn't the final clincher."

I paused for a long, slow sip of the Grouse. It wasn't thirst. I'll admit it. I was playing the scene for all it was worth. And it felt good.

Mr. Devlin leaned in for privacy.

"Now you've got both of us, Michael. What final clincher?"

I leaned back in the chair. Privacy be damned. I was enjoying this business for the first time since Hector Vasquez walked into my office.

"Well, it's this way. The last time I saw the superintendent in Ireland I tried to convince him to come over here for the race. Once I figured who he was, we needed to have him over here so Mr. Coyne could arrest him, at least for extortion. The problem was how to convince him. I suggested he could work closely with Mr. Coyne and see the race and a bunch of other stuff that I see now didn't really matter. He had to come over. He knew he had Sweeney murdered, and it was time to collect the extortion money from all the Americans they had on the hook. He had no one else he knew he could trust. Certainly not Boyle, who, by the way, has probably packed up and left town before the Irish boys could get to him. That meant the superintendant had to make the collection himself. I had Tom Burns tail whoever picked up the money, which, by the way, was doubled this time. I heard back from Tom. Guess who made the pickup from a dead-drop at Barnes & Noble in person?"

"Our very own superintendent."

"Right on, Mr. Devlin. That tags him with an extortion charge at the least. I should tell you this, Mr. Coyne. Before the race, I made a strong point of telling the superintendent that Boyle had the race fixed for number four. I told him even Black Diamond's jockey was too scared to cross Boyle. I figured that with that kind of assurance, he'd put the whole extorted collection on four to win instead of Black Diamond. From the look I got when Black Diamond won, that's exactly what he did. That was a major loss of funds. It might have hammered that outfit financially. They just lost their leadership and their financing in two days. I don't think they'll be a threat to us over here for a while, Mr. Coyne."

Mr. Devlin fairly exploded. "Damn well done, Michael! Damn well done!" He turned with a flourish to the dour Billy Coyne. "And wouldn't you like to join in the kudos to my junior partner, Billy Coyne, for pulling your chestnuts out of the fire?"

Billy Coyne dug deep and forced what appeared to be a genuine smile. He held his hand out to shake hands.

"Kid, I've got to admit—"

"Uh, uh, uh, Billy." Mr. D. was scowling at him.

"All right, Michael. You done good."

I settled for that. Just the "Michael" instead of "kid" felt like a victory of gargantuan proportions.

Billy stood up first. "I've got work to do. There are indictments to draft."

His last words as he left the table were, "I'll be in touch, kid."

Sic transit gloria.

CHAPTER THIRTY-THREE

It was three days later that our little troop gathered in Judge Peragallo's courtroom. After our last visit with Hector, and the events that led to the arrest of the superintendent, I had the time to pull together all of the information we'd turned up and finally focus single-mindedly on every possible cause of Danny's fall. After eliminating all of the impossible and extremely unlikely explanations, I was stunned to be left with just one.

I went back over the video of Danny's last race one more time. This time I knew what to look for. And there it was. The only remaining question was how I could have missed it the first hundred times through that video.

We filed a motion with Judge Peragallo for dismissal of the indictment against Hector. Angela Lamb raised a cloud of dust over the abruptness of the motion and hearing, but she subsided when the judge reminded her that she was the one pushing for a trial immediately, if not sooner.

The three days between the last race and the hearing day on our motion had been the best I could remember in the past three weeks. I deliberately slowed the pace and spent time doing practically nothing other than preparing for the hearing.

There were two other things I did enjoy doing during those days. I paid a visit to the backstretch the morning after the race. I gathered the jockeys together between exercise rides. There was no need to be furtive about it. In fact, I was delighted to say it in both Spanish and English for the world to hear. There would be no more fixed races at Suffolk Downs at the hands of Mr. Boyle. His day was done, and their day was just dawning. The grins and jokes and backslaps and even cheers convinced me that maybe it had all been worthwhile. In fact, maybe I'd go on doing more than appeals of parking tickets.

I got a special handshake that turned into a mutual hug from Alberto Ibanez.

"You rode one hell of a race, Alberto."

He seemd a bit emotional when he just nodded a thank you. I started to leave when he held my arm.

"I just want to say it. When you said those words to me just before I went up on Black Diamond. You said, 'Ride like the wind, 'Berto. Bring him in. It's going to be all right." He put his hand on his heart and couldn't seem to say anything further.

I simply pressed his shoulder, which said, "I know."

Before I left, I dropped down to Rick's barn. I could see him looking at me while I was with the jockeys.

He held out that twisted, knuckley hand, and I took it. He had a grin like I hadn't seen. "We did okay on that race, Michael. Like you said, I bet the ranch on Diamond."

"Way to go, Rick. What're you going to do with all that money? Retire?"

He came up sharp.

"Hell no! I'm just gettin' started. I'll be at the yearlin' sales in Florida next month. You won't recognize this place when I bring in some new blood."

"I'll be here at the backstretch the day they come in, Rick."

"You'd better. I'm thinkin' of namin' one after Miles O'Connor. What do you think?"

"I think he'll be up there cheering every time he runs. I wonder if they have pari-mutuel betting in Heaven."

"Hell, if they don't, Miles'll start it."

On the morning of the hearing, Judge Peragallo rapped the court to order at nine thirty sharp. I was at defense table with Hector waiting for Mr. Devlin. Hector was jumpy as a cat, which had the odd effect of settling my nerves down.

Just as the judge took the bench and gave the "be seated" signal, I saw Mr. D. coming in the back door. He took a seat in the back of the courtroom. I caught his attention and signaled him to come up to defense table, but he waved it off. I could read his lips, mouthing the words, "It's your case, son. You finish it."

It would be hard not to notice that the two center rows of spectators' seats were filled with Hector's fellow jockeys. I didn't recognize the two women in the front row. Hector whispered to me that his mother had flown in from the Dominican Republic, and the young woman beside her was his wife. I had no idea how much English they spoke, but the lines of intense worry on their faces spoke clearly how much depended on the outcome of that hearing. Now Hector's case of nerves became contagious.

Judge Peragallo looked down at me. "I have a full docket, Mr. Knight. What have you got for us?"

I called Hector to the stand and had him sworn in. I had had a giant television screen brought into the courtroom and positioned so that the judge and counsel at the prosecutor's table could get the full view. There was no jury at this hearing.

"Judge, I'd like the permission of the court to play a video recording of the running of the race in question. This is the race in which Danny Ryan met his death."

"Any objection from the prosecution?"

Both Billy Coyne and Angela Lamb had seen the video scores of times, as had we all. There was no objection.

Before hitting the remote to play the video, I said to the court, "Your Honor, we've seen this tape more than most golfers have seen *Caddy Shack*. So what's new? Just this. We've always focused on what we could see of Hector Vasquez's hands and his whip. I'm going to show you a close up of Hector during the stretch run. This time I want you to focus on his face. His lips."

I rolled the video. It showed two horses and two jockeys locked in a wide-open, full-bore drive for the lead down the homestretch. Even without sound, the intensity was riveting.

Just at the point at which Black Diamond began to gain the edge over Hector's horse, I had had my tech focus a close-up in the video on Hector's face. It showed clearly that Hector was yelling something directly at Danny.

I played it for the court twice. Then I addressed Hector.

"I want the complete truth here, Hector. Was that race fixed?"

Hector was fidgeting in discomfort, but he answered clearly. "Yes, sir."

"And how was it fixed."

"Mr. Boyle, he let us jockeys know we'd be killed. Our families would be killed, if we didn't make the race come out his way."

"And what was the outcome he wanted on this race?"

"My horse was supposed to win."

"Was Danny Ryan also threatened if he didn't lose?"

"Yes, but a different way."

"How?"

"His little daughter was kidnapped. They said they'd kill her if he didn't lose the race."

"All right, Hector. Now listen to me. We've just seen from the video that in spite of that, Danny's horse came up alongside of you and even passed you. Why did Danny do that?"

"He didn't, Mr. Knight. That horse, Black Diamond, he has a will to win. Danny couldn't hold him. The horse was running away with him. Danny couldn't stop him."

I walked to the other side of the bench so Hector would be speaking directly to the judge.

"Tell us please, Hector, what did you yell to Danny when he was passing you?"

Hector looked straight at the judge.

"I yelled, 'They'll kill her if you win, Danny.'"

He hit every syllable for emphasis.

"And what did Danny do?"

Hector rubbed his face with his hands. I could see tears forming.

"He jumped off the back of the horse. He jumped."

"Why did he do that, Hector?"

"So his horse would be disqualified. So my horse would win the race. He did it for his daughter."

The rumble of voices among the jockeys in the spectators' section had to be quieted by an order of the judge. It gave Hector a chance to gather in his emotions.

"And why didn't you tell me this before, Hector?"

"I was afraid that would mean I had a part in killing Danny."

I took a slow walk back to counsel table to let it sink in. I finally turned back to the bench and addressed the judge.

"Judge Peragallo, that's not murder. In fact, it's not any kind of homicide. That's the action of a man who's been a victim of the greed of a vicious syndicate for more years than I want to think about."

I gave it a couple of seconds. "Your Honor, I'd like to move that this parade of horrors that's been inflicted on these brave jockeys be ended. It can start with a dismissal of this indictment."

I sat down.

Judge Peragallo looked over at the prosecution table. Angela Lamb started to rise to make an argument, but Billy Coyne caught her by the arm. She sat down without a whimper.

The judge rapped his gavel.

"This indictment is dismissed. The defendant will be released from custody immediately."

The burst of cheering and shouting, mostly in Spanish, that erupted drowned out the rapping of the judge's gavel. I think Judge Peragallo concluded that the celebration was in order, if not overdue. He simply left the bench without the usual "All rise."

The rows of jockeys who had come to support one of their own emptied to the front of the courtroom. They would have surrounded him immediately and probably carried him out of the courtroom on their shoulders. But two others were first in line. Hector's wife was in one of his arms and his mother was in the other. There was a closed circle so tight that I thought I'd never get a chance to congratulate Hector. I was wrong. When I went to walk by, two arms reached out and pulled me into the circle. There were now four of us hugging each other with such a grip that I could hardly breathe. No words were being spoken, but enough tears were flowing to float an ark.

When our circle finally opened, Hector was totally mobbed by the jockeys. They must have heard the cheers at the State House on Beacon Hill.

I looked to the back of the courtroom and saw my mentor, my friend, and my practically adoptive father, Lex Devlin. He had a grin that lit up his whole face, and his hands clasped above his head in a victory sign. I could even see moisture in those eyes that had seen everything in a courtroom.

When I left the court, I went straight to a rental agency and rented a van big enough to move three people back to their homes. I drove to Milton, New Hampshire, at a speed I don't want to record in this writing. And I brought three of my favorite people and one Shetland sheepdog home, and the celebration began in style.

Funny thing. The next time I went into the office, my secretary, Julie, asked if I could help her with a legal problem before I did anything else. She asked me to appeal a parking ticket.